S.B. CAVES

WHEN WE WERE EVIL

DATURA

DATURA BOOKS
An imprint of Watkins Media Ltd

Unit 11, Shepperton House
89-93 Shepperton Road
London N1 3DF
UK

daturabooks.com
The Mirror Has Two Faces

A Datura Books paperback original, 2026

Edited by April Northall
Cover by Sarah O'Flaherty
Set in Meridien

ISBN 978 1 91741 516 3
Ebook ISBN 978 1 91741 517 0

Printed and bound in the United Kingdom by CPI Group (UK) Ltd, Croydon CR0 4YY

The manufacturer's authorised representative in the EU for product safety is eucomply OÜ – Pärnu mnt 139b-14, 11317 Tallinn, Estonia, hello@eucompliancepartner.com; www.eucompliancepartner.com

9 8 7 6 5 4 3 2 1

FSC
www.fsc.org
MIX
Paper | Supporting responsible forestry
FSC® C013604

For B. Ronin, R. Akira, and S. Leticia

"Folie imposée is where a dominant person (known as the 'primary', 'inducer', or 'principal') initially forms a delusional belief during a psychotic episode and imposes it on another person or persons (known as the 'secondary', 'acceptor', or 'associate') with the assumption that the secondary person might not have become deluded if left to his or her own devices."

– Collins Dictionary Definition

"Maybe there is a beast… maybe it's only us."

– William Golding, *Lord of the Flies*

CHAPTER 1

My appearance now is completely different from my Year 10 school photo and my infamous mugshot, taken just over a year apart. Those are the two images most people connect with the name Ruby Wilcox. If you lived in the UK at the time the story broke, you couldn't get away from them; the photos were blown up on the front page of every newspaper and used as stills on the TV. Both photos show a scrawny, unremarkable-looking girl with bright red hair, thin lips, and a pointy nose. Today, my hair is bottle-blond and cropped short, which gives me a more pixyish look that would probably be cute if not for the lines carving across my forehead and scraping from the corners of my eyes. I'm about fifteen years too old for the style I'm trying to pull off, but my ever-changing looks were never for the sake of vanity. I have two piercings in my left eyebrow, a small hoop in my nostril, and a ring in the centre of my bottom lip, as well as a stud in my tongue. Occupying one side of my neck is a smudged-looking tattoo of a butterfly that, from a distance, resembles the faded bruising of a throttling.

Unless you were actively searching for me, you wouldn't recognise that haunted teenager in the weathered husk of my forty-year-old body. The High Court rejected my appeal for anonymity under the Mary Bell Order, so hair dye and an alias are the only things protecting my identity. To track me down, all you'd have to do is know your way around the restaurants and pubs in London that pay cash-in-hand, ask a few questions, and drop a general description. The butterfly tattoo that I got shortly after my release seemed like such a necessity at the time (I was still only twenty-six), but like most things in my life, it's something I sorely regret. I wanted a visual metaphor to remind me that I was a new person, but all I did was brand myself with a homing beacon to help any True Crime fanatic or media bloodhound spot me. Usually, after a few months at a new place, the paranoia will creep up on me and I'll start to wear high-collared shirts, or even go so far as to smear my neck with foundation.

Age and gravity have had their way with me, and I am considerably heavier now, which all keep the masquerade moving. But sometimes, through no fault of my own, the mask slips.

The moment I saw the man approaching the bar, I knew *he* knew. I had spotted him about ten minutes before, lingering by the fruit machines, checking his phone as though awaiting some urgently important message. It was a Thursday morning, and the Ship and Bottle was empty except for the red-faced regulars dotted around the tables at the back, stretching out their pints with calculated sips.

With his flannel shirt and tight jeans, the man was about as out of place in this pub as I would have been on a catwalk. When he had summoned enough courage to cross the empty dancefloor, my stomach rolled over. With each step he took, I could see sparks of nervous excitement dancing in his eyes through his horn-rimmed glasses. He reminded me of a wary gazelle nearing a watering hole. With his slight, almost childish build, and his smooth unblemished face, he could almost pass for a student, but I guessed he was probably closer to thirty.

"Hello," he said, fidgeting a fiver out of his wallet. "Could I have a glass of Coke, please?"

I didn't move. I waited for him to make eye contact again before saying, "Is that *all* you want?"

His Adam's apple bobbed sharply in his slender throat. "Well, perhaps a moment of your time." A smile twitched on his lips. The butterfly felt like sunburn on my neck.

"A moment of my time?" I sprayed Coke into a pint glass and plonked a slice of lemon into it but held the drink hostage. "What do you want my time for?"

An airy laugh slipped from his mouth. His fingers wriggled back into his wallet, feeling for a business card. "My name is Peter Fidditch," he began, relieved to have made his introduction. He cleared his throat and said, "I work for um... well, it's my company, actually, Z-uh, Zelda Lane, um..."

My mouth was full of cotton balls. I took a large gulp of his Coke.

His eyes flicked to my name badge. *Luanne*. "I'm not here to cause trouble."

"Then listen to me." I leaned on the bar, my forearms soaking in a puddle of Foster's I'd spilt earlier and neglected to sop up. "I don't know what Zelda Lane is. I don't care to know, either. Whatever you're here for, I'm not interested. Do we understand each other?"

He nodded thoughtfully, fanning his business card against the palm of his other hand. The aura of nervousness began to recede, and I could see his body language changing; he pinned back his shoulders, stood taller. Perhaps he realised that the demon he had been psyching himself up for was nothing more than a cranky, middle-aged woman; a thing to be pitied.

"They're making a film about Vincent Street. A dramatization, I mean. I don't suppose you knew that. Or maybe you did?"

I took another gulp of his Coke. There had been rumours of films and a TV series about Vincent Street since the trial, but to date, the only thing to come close was a BBC documentary that was so factually inaccurate, it received almost six hundred complaints from the public.

I always knew they would find a way to glamourise Vincent Street, and had carried that particular dread like a tumour growing in my stomach, but always hoped that the subject matter was too grisly to redeem for the screen. A naïve part of me believed that nobody would go near the case for fear of public outcry, condemning anyone who tried to profit from our crime.

"Netflix are going to announce on Monday. They're still in pre-production, haven't mentioned any cast members or anything yet, but it's slated for next summer. There's an embargo on that information, but I'm in the business. I'm a documentary maker."

I concentrated on my breathing, watching the bubbles fizz and pop in the pint glass. Moisture beading my forehead, tendrils of hair sticking to my face. An image flittered through the confetti of my memory: *Mia sitting on the stairs, her face painted red with blood.* I felt a weight lodge in the centre of my chest. I tried to swallow it down.

"I'm not here to interfere with your work," Fidditch told me. "My being here is completely confidential."

"I have nothing to say to you," my voice cracked. "Please, look, I'm sorry I was rude to you. I don't..." The grovelling was making me breathless. I wiped my clammy palms on my thighs and shuffled off down the bar. There were empty glasses streaked with suds sitting on a tray. I picked it up, the glasses clinking together, and began toward the dishwasher. Fidditch watched me pass, saying something about him not judging me, about me finally having my say. A glass rattled off the tray and smashed on the floor to a scattered, sarcastic applause from the regulars.

"Look what you made me do," I hissed at him, bending to pluck the shards from the sticky floor.

His shadow loomed over me as he leaned across the bar. "I'd love to just sit and have a ten-minute chat with you. And I promise, if you don't like what I have to say then I'll just leave you alone. You won't hear another thing from me or anyone at Zelda Lane again."

"I have nothing to say," I almost shrieked, my hands curled into claws.

"Alright, then, that's fine," he soothed like a dad trying to calm a screaming new-born. "But let me just say this–"

A piece of glass bit into the webbing between my thumb and index finger. I brought the wound to my mouth, tasted blood.

"They're going to cash in on your life story and use their artistic license to paint you however they want."

Light glinted off the glass. Black spots bloomed in my vision. Madonna singing *Into the Groove* funnelled in and out of earshot over the bleating fruit machines.

"They're basing the series on Simon Ward's book, *Dead Behind the Eyes,* and you and I both know that it is riddled with inaccuracies. It's... it's a lot of assumptions, conjecture... They'll sensationalise it."

I reached under the sink for the dustpan and brush and swept up the remaining chips of glass. Air worked its way up my gullet. I wanted to burp or be sick, but neither happened. A tide broke against the walls of my stomach. Grabbing the counter, I pulled myself to my feet.

"Zelda Lane is my production company," Peter said. "I've won awards for my work, and I can assure you, I would never take liberties with your story." He pulled in a breath, assessed my expression, and continued. "I want to tell *your* story, in *your* words. I want people to know the truth about The Vincent Street Incident, and I want to get it out ahead of Netflix."

My eyes rolled across the room, scouting for Louise. I saw her by the toilets, wiping down a table with a J-Cloth. "Louise," I yelled, and waved my bloody hand in the air. She looked up from her idling with a frown. "Louise, can you come and relieve me for a second, please?"

Peter's head snapped toward Louise, then back to me. When he spoke again, it was frenzied, a sprint to the finish line. "I can offer you a substantial fee. *Substantial.* With residuals, of course. And that's before we even discuss the redemptive aspects of the documentary, what it will do for your profile." He ran a hand through his hair, on his way to becoming flustered. "Don't you want people to know the truth, Ruby?"

"Don't use that name in here," I spat in an angry whisper. "I just want to be left alone."

"I'm sorry, I'm sorry, okay? But do you think they're going to leave you alone when the film premieres? When it's trending, when the Netflix press machine gets all the cogs moving and this thing picks up steam? It's going to blow all that dust off the case and open Vincent Street up to a whole new generation. You're going to have every internet detective hounding you, and that's before we get to the social justice warriors who weren't even alive when Vincent Street happened. And the only way to combat that is to hit them with the truth first, take the wind out of their sails."

Louise padded across the pub in no hurry at all, tying her blue-and-green hair into a ponytail with a scrunchy. Peter gave her a quick glance to gauge her proximity and became antsy, rolling his shoulders, shifting his weight from foot to foot.

"Why do you want to keep punishing yourself, Ru– sorry, *Luanne*? Because let me tell you something: I know that things didn't go down in Vincent Street the way they were portrayed to the public. They were looking for a scapegoat and they found it. But I believe *you*; otherwise, I wouldn't even be here speaking with you now. I believe *you*, and so does my partner at Zelda Lane. I mean, Jesus Christ, there's far more evidence to suggest that you were telling the truth than anything else. And you'll have our full support. We even have an investigative journalist at *The Guardian* ready to do a big piece on your story to help promote the documentary. They're going to go in-depth and finally give people the truth. It's going to completely blow everyone away. We'll stand behind you all the..."

"What's up?" Louise asked me around a wad of bubble gum, the sickly strawberry smell wafting from her glossy lips.

"Don't feel well," I managed. "Might be sick."

"Okay, go then." Her face became alarmed. "Don't take ages. I mean it, Luanne."

"Yep." I brushed past her and made a beeline for the ladies. I became aware of Fidditch following my stride. "You're harassing me. This is harassment, what you're doing," I snarled. A kickdrum began beating a dull rhythm in my skull. The room was starting to gently pull away from me.

"Please, just take this." He extended his business card; black calligraphy splashed on eggshell. "All my details are on there. I'd really love for you to just hear me out on this properly. My mobile number is there too; that's my personal number and you can call me any–"

I snatched the card, blotting it with blood, and charged for the toilet, feeling more drunk than any of the patrons.

Then he grabbed me, his hand catching my bicep. I whirled, fists clenched so tightly that my forearms throbbed up to the elbows. His grip loosened and he stepped back, jaw slack with anticipation.

"I didn't mean to touch you," he blurted, his hands flying up in surrender. "Sorry, it was reflex. I shouldn't have touched you, I just..." His expression softened. In any other situation, his handsome features might've been disarming, but just then, he was a child pulling a tried-and-tested puppy dog routine. "You've done your time. Don't take the blame for Mia anymore. Let us help you." He brushed a single curl from his forehead and added, "I know you want to stay hidden. But that's not going to be an option for much longer."

CHAPTER 2

The flat stank of bleach by the time I heard Henry scratching his key in the front door lock. I'd scrubbed the place top to bottom, which, given the size of the shoebox we lived in, didn't take very long. He called out for me as he trundled into the hallway, then, seeing the gleam in the parquet, swore and apologised. "Didn't notice you'd done the floor. Gosh, just got a footprint on it. That's my fault. Sorry, hun. Hun?"

He found me at the kitchen table with a cigarette between my fingers, burning to the filter. I'd ordered in Domino's and picked up a bottle of Jack Daniel's on the way home. I couldn't stomach any food but had killed about half of the whiskey.

Henry faltered at the kitchen threshold, loosening his tie. The wheels were turning but nothing was clicking into place just yet. "It's not our anniversary," he said, unsure whether it was a question or a statement.

"No." I shook my head, squinting through a ribbon of smoke.

He paused, eyes going to the ceiling. After a few seconds, he stabbed a finger at me. "And your birthday is in July."

"It is," I said, and stubbed the cigarette into the ashtray. "Same day every year."

"Oh, phew." He mock-wiped sweat away from his brow and pulled up a chair opposite me. "Thought I'd walked into an ambush." He went to lift the pizza box lid and stopped abruptly. "Can I have a slice or was this all for you?"

"No, I bought it for you." I rose from the table, legs wobbly from the whiskey, and grabbed a glass from the draining board and filled it with Jack.

"Yikes," he said, pulling a string of cheese free from a slice of pizza. "Didn't know you served spirits by the gallon at the pub. What is that, a quadruple shot?" He laughed nasally, and with his mouth full, muffled. "What's the celebration?"

I sucked from the neck of the bottle and felt the booze kick me in the head. Drinking on an empty stomach had provoked the first tremors of a migraine. A sharpened pencil was slowly turning in the centre of my skull. "I wanted to talk," I said, my lips and tongue dancing out of time to the beat of the sentence. I wasn't quite slurring just yet but was dangerously close to tripping over my words. Telling him sober was never an option.

"Oh, is everything alright? You got one of your headaches?" he asked, picking at a shred of onion that had fallen onto the table.

"No, head's fine." I offered him a reassuring smile, but the muscles in my face were taut.

"I'm glad. Tell you what, though, you want to talk about headaches? That Marianne has been driving me bonkers. Imagine this: she came in about twenty minutes late this morning, huffing and puffing like she usually does to try and make it look like she's been rushing, and she knows we have our client reports due on Monday mornings and–"

"Henry, wait a second please, love." I patted his hand.

He licked the film of oil from his lips, set the slice back in the box and asked, "Are you alright?"

"No." I shook my head. The sudden look of concern in his eyes, magnified by the thick lenses of his glasses, made me want to cry. We'd been together almost two years now. He had come into the pub one evening and ordered three pints of beer, then sat and drank them alone at a booth.

"Celebrating?" I'd asked, collecting the glasses.

"No," he'd said, coughing, blinking tears from his glassy eyes. "I need the courage."

"For?"

"To er... to ask if you might like to get something to eat one day. With me. Because I..." He cleared his throat, combed his fingers through his thinning hair. "I happen to think you're lovely."

Last Valentine's Day, he bought me half a dozen red roses and sheepishly announced that he had written me a poem. He said it was the first time he had tried to write a poem – had tried to write *anything* that wasn't an invoice or order form – and fished a folded sheet of paper from his trouser pocket. I watched the paper tremble in his fingers as he stuttered out the first line: *You are sunshine on my coldest day, my cool breeze on a summer's day.* It didn't matter to me that he had rhymed the word *day* twice, because before he could finish the first stanza, my eyes were brimming with tears. I wrapped my arms around him and sobbed into his neck. He kept asking me if he had done something wrong, apologising profusely for the poem, saying that it was a stupid idea and that we could still go to dinner. He had no way of knowing just how much his poem meant to me. After years of hateful column inches, entire books packed with lies to portray me as some kind of evil maniac, websites dedicated to decimating me as a human being, to finally have someone on my side was… the best feeling I'd ever had. And with that was an undercurrent of cold and catastrophic panic that I carried every second we spent together. What would happen if he were to one day unearth my secret? Would that break us entirely, or would there be enough for me to salvage?

"I have something I need to tell you, and I'm not sure how you're going to react," I said, and just starting the conversation made me feel wobbly.

The chair creaked as he shifted his weight. His hand reached up to loosen his tie further until it hung around his neck like a noose.

"I haven't been entirely truthful with you about… some things."

Except for the slightest flicker of worry creasing his brow, his reaction was unreadable. When things got heavy – the looming threat of redundancies at his workplace, the landlord fleecing us for rent we could barely afford – he used silliness to stifle seriousness. He was an expert in changing the subject to avoid anything that might crack open the cabinet to his true feelings. I had never seen him upset, and I think it was because he didn't want to inconvenience me with his problems, that he thought it would be selfish or rude somehow.

"Well, what is it?" he exhaled, his hand touching the glass of whiskey for the first time. "Whatever it is, you can tell me. You know you can."

I'm fairly certain that he was gearing up for news of an affair; preparing himself for the possibility that I was leaving the damp confines of the Rickson Way estate for a fancy new build with another man. His low self-esteem had always skewed his estimation of me.

"Do you remember a thing called The Vincent Street Incident?" I felt a slight twist on the pressure valve, a whisper of steam released.

"Vincent Street?" A fingernail tapped the glass. He was chewing the inside of his cheek. "I don't think so, but I'm not very good with names and things. Have we been there or something? I mean, *should* I know it?"

Yes, you should, I thought. Vincent Street was one of the larger stains in the annals of British crime, a nefarious buzzword in the popular consciousness. The term should have been as recognisable to Henry as The Yorkshire Ripper, or Fred and Rosemary West. Or was that my paranoia again, assuming that everyone would have extensive knowledge of my past?

"Do you remember," I began, my knee trembling against the table so rapidly that the whiskey in his glass jumped. "Do you remember... George McDermott?"

"McDermott..." he said absently, eyes misting over as he rifled through his memory cabinet.

"Jesus, Henry, is that name not ringing a bell at all?"

"I'm sorry." He shrugged. "I don't know. I told you, I'm bad with names. You know that."

"He did that show *Magic Moments*? You're looking at me like I'm speaking Arabic. The guy from TV who was murdered."

"Oh." Henry nodded and clicked his fingers. "*Wake Up, UK.*"

"That's it," I said. "He hosted *Wake Up, UK* for a little bit."

"I was backpacking in Thailand when that all happened," Henry said, scratching his head, the kitchen light bouncing off his balding pate. "That was right before I did that teaching job in Japan. I didn't know a lot about it until later but...

yeah, sad, I guess." He shrugged and then squinted at me, eyebrows coming together in confusion. "What about it?"

"Give me your phone a sec," I said.

His hand dipped into his trouser pocket, then he passed me the iPhone. My thumb tap-danced across the screen to enter the passcode – 090724, the day we met – and then I misspelled the words "Vincent Street" in Safari. The highest search result was the Wikipedia entry. I slid the phone back to him, could see my clammy fingerprints smeared across the screen and case. The only thing that stopped me from chugging the rest of the Jack while he read the entry was the throbbing ache in the base of my skull. The hangover had arrived early, filling my head with ball bearings.

"Yeah, I sort of remember a bit better now," he said, pushing his glasses up the bridge of his nose as he skimmed the details. Then, he cast a perplexed glance in my direction. "What's it all about?"

"We," I began, my mouth dry enough to produce sparks. "Me and my friend... my best friend. Well, we did something... terrible." My stomach clenched and I clawed anxiously at my jeans, tensing for that expression of horror. But it didn't come. "Henry? I was one of the girls from The Vincent Street Incident."

He ran a palm down the side of his face, studying me to see whether it was a joke or not. Then, noticing the tears plinking from my lashes, he picked up the glass and sipped. He was about to set the glass down when he reconsidered and took a long gulp, swallowing with a hiss. Then he massaged his cheeks as the alcohol began to anesthetise him.

"I'm not sure I understand," he said finally. His mouth fell open to say more, but instead, he rose from the table, tore off a piece of kitchen towel and handed it to me. "Please don't cry. Whatever you think you've done, I'm uh… I'm sure it's alright now."

"Henry, did you hear what I just told you?"

"I heard." He nodded.

"And that's it? That's all you're going to say?" I dragged the kitchen towel across my eyes and worked at blotting the snot as it leaked from my nose.

"I'm really not sure what I'm supposed to say."

"Henry, this isn't about you. It's about me, and who I am, who I've been running away from."

He was thoughtful for a long time, and there were several false starts as he opened his mouth and closed it again, before eventually saying, "What does that mean, Luanne? *Who* you've been running away from? You're not making much sense. I don't know what it means."

My stomach churned painfully. There was no easy way to do it, but I'd pushed us to the edge of the cliff now. Nowhere else to go. I covered my face with my hands, sure that I was about to hyperventilate. After a few seconds, the words came.

"My name isn't Luanne; it's Ruby Wilcox. Look at the photo on Wikipedia again. That's me when I was sixteen. I spent six years in Coldham, and ever since then I've been trying to get away from it, trying to outrun this fucking nightmare that my life has turned into."

The silence thrummed between us. I collected my tears on the damp ball of kitchen towel, and eventually he picked up his congealed slice of pizza and resumed the machinations of eating. As if I hadn't told him I was a convicted murderer. As if The Vincent Street Incident hadn't been the biggest story in the entire country.

"What're you doing? Why're you just eating like that?" My breathing sped up. "This isn't a joke. Why aren't you freaking out, Henry?"

Then it occurred to me.

"Oh, my God, Henry. Did you know already?" I asked. "Henry, look at me. Have you known who I am all this time?"

His cheeks bloomed. He swallowed; it sounded like the food got stuck somewhere on the way down. "I don't know anything." He drank and then tossed the remainder of the slice back in the box. "And I don't want to talk about this anymore. This is... very upsetting to me, the way you're talking."

"You've known all along, haven't you?"

His eyes flashed at me behind his glasses. "What are *you* talking about? No, I don't know anything. All I know is what you're throwing at me now." He was panting, unaccustomed to raising his voice. "You can't just hit me with this and then turn it on me like *I've* done something wrong. I don't even know what's going on." He held his head and released a low, pained whimper. "You just shove a phone at me and say, 'I'm a killer', and expect me to act a certain way? I don't know what you want, Luanne. I really don't. I think I'm going to take a shower."

He stood up, knocked back the rest of the whiskey, and started for the bathroom, not quite slamming the door behind him. I followed, my shoulder brushing the hallway wall as the flat jerked out of focus around me, and tried for the doorknob. It was locked. The crash of water from the shower would drown out any further conversation.

I stood outside the door for a few minutes, the pounding headache making it almost impossible to still my rioting thoughts. Had Henry really known about me all along? Was that the attraction? Was I nothing more than a morbid fetish to him? Did he think about murder every time we made love?

No, this was my Henry. If he said he didn't know, then I had to take him at his word. My sweet, naïve Henry who chased flies out the window rather than swat them, who came and rescued spiders from the bathtub whenever I yelled for him to drown them. He had no idea that I was mad Ruby Wilcox. That was just the snakes hissing in my head, trying to make an enemy out of him.

"Henry, I'm sorry I flew at you like that. Please, love." My blunt fingernails scratched at the door. "I'm all over the place at the minute. I'm paranoid, I know I'm paranoid. Please forgive me. This is the most difficult thing I've ever had to do, believe me. Henry, honey. Can you come out, please?" When he didn't answer, I sank to the floor. "They're making a film. A big-budget thing, and they're going to have every journalist around hunting me down…" *Digging up the past,* I almost added, before mentally amending. "They'll write stories. That's what I'm trying to tell you. Henry, please…" My forehead bumped the door and rested there. "Please open up. We need to talk about what we're going to do."

The water stopped. A moment later, I heard the scrape and click as he unlocked the door. He was still fully clothed with steam curling around him, his red, watery eyes like marbles against his waxy skin.

"What do you mean, *what we're going to do*? We don't need to do anything."

"Yes, we do. They'll make our lives unbearable. They'll follow us around taking photos. Believe me, I'm not just thinking about myself, here. They can make things extremely difficult for you, too."

"Oh, yeah? How?" Of all the reactions I'd shuffled through in my mind ahead of this transaction, anger was the one I least expected.

"They'll put your picture in the papers, have nasty headlines about you, make things up."

"Sticks and stones." He shrugged. "I've got nothing to hide."

"That's what you think now. But you have no idea how terrible this could be."

"They might not do anything at all." He shrugged. "It's old news, ancient history. The film will probably be a flop. Look how many bloody films they throw on TV every week. I mean, I seriously doubt anybody is going to bother seeking you out."

"They already have," I said. "There's a guy… a uh, documentary guy." I scuttled into the bathroom, fished out the blood-smudged business card and handed it over. "They want me to tell my story ahead of the film coming out. They believe that I'm innocent, and I've never… I've never spoken to anyone about it, other than my solicitors back then. I've had offers before – magazines, a publisher – but" – I shook my head – "now my back's to the wall and… I feel so old, Henry. I feel so tired. I don't know how much longer I can go on running and pretending." A weak sob sailed from my mouth, ending the pitiful soliloquy. "I've often thought about trying to come out and set everything straight. But it just seems so… so fucking scary."

He took a seat on the edge of the bathtub, one pale, limp hand pressed thoughtfully against his lips. "This is… a lot to unpack, Luanne. It's a lot of information to take in. A documentary?"

The bathroom floor felt as though it were tilting. When I tried to make eye contact, he looked away.

I could have died right there on the spot.

"Henry, I know what you must be thinking about me right now. And believe me, the last thing I want to do is embarrass you or put you through any stress. I *love* you. If I didn't love you, I wouldn't have even told you about any of this, I would have just taken off. And… will you look at me a second, Henry? *Please.*" When he turned down to face me, his eyes were wet with tears behind his misted glasses. "If you say the word, I'll pack my things and leave tonight. Nobody ever has to know that you lived with Ruby Wilcox. You can deny it. But I will say this" – I paused, swallowing a lump that had slowly been working its way up my throat – "whatever they call me, it isn't true, not completely true anyway. I'm not… I'm not *evil.* And it didn't happen the way they say it did."

It wasn't just me, I wanted to add, but couldn't gather the strength. I couldn't bring myself to think of her again. Not yet. Not after working so hard to block her out.

"I know you're not evil," he whispered, lifting his glasses and wiping his eyes on the sleeve of his shirt.

"I tried to help him," I said. "You have to understand, Henry. I tried to help him."

"You have a good heart, Luanne. I've known that all along. Whatever you did before was… well, we all make mistakes, don't we?" He sat down on the floor next to me, his back against the bathtub. When he spoke again, his voice sounded small and far away. "And I don't want you to leave. Whatever's coming, well, I guess we'll face it together, won't we?"

A shudder rippled through me. Warm tears trickled into my mouth. "Don't make it sound so fucking normal, Henry. It was more than a mistake… It was… it…" The words became a wheeze, my stomach muscles tightening as I battled for breath.

"Calm down," he soothed. "Easy, come on. Breathe. Breathe. That's it."

Clumsily, he looped his arms around me and held me close, our warm, clammy cheeks pressing together. I could feel his heartbeat slamming against his chest.

"I'm scared," I said. "I'm so scared. I just want this to stop."

Brushing hair away from my mouth, he said, "Do you think you can stop it? With the documentary, I mean."

Slowly, I shook my head. "I can't stop whatever's coming from the film they're bringing out. People made their minds up about me twenty-five years ago, and nothing I do or say can change it. But I can do it for me. I can tell the truth, and whatever happens after that, however the film portrays me, well, it's out of my hands. But at the very least, I mean, assuming this documentary thing is legitimate, I can have a fighting chance. That's what I think anyway."

His thumb stroked my cheek. "Then tell the truth. It's the only armour you have. Otherwise, your past is just going to chase you forever."

"I don't... know how." The sentence fragmented between gasps. "I don't know how to begin. I... don't even know if I can. I've pushed so much of it away, buried it... convinced myself that maybe I *was* to blame, that maybe it was my fault."

"I'll help you," Henry said. "Why don't you start with me, hmm? Tell me what happened. You know you can tell me anything. I'll never judge you, Luanne. Never. And you don't have to be alone with this. I'm here with you."

It took me a very long time to calm down before I could answer him.

"Alright. I'll tell you. But you're not going to like what you hear."

"In many ways it is easy to diminish the scale and severity of the crime, to suggest that the depravity that unfolded in the house on Vincent Street could have been orchestrated by any teenager in the country given the circumstances. Likewise, one might argue that such a tragedy could easily have been avoided, were the warning signs – of which there were many – professionally addressed when they first appeared."

– Simon Ward, Dead Behind the Eyes

"Yes, it's important to remember the victims. But Ruby Wilcox was just as much a victim as anyone else."

– Floyd Wilkinson, Mayhem in Mind:
The Untold Truth of The Vincent Street Incident

CHAPTER 3

It took almost four hours to tell Henry everything, in as much detail as I could stand. Every so often, my mind would malfunction and I'd begin to stutter, unable to process my thoughts. This inability to articulate certain details wound me up in knots of frustration, and I found myself almost screaming, desperate to spew everything out in one great stream of bile. If I tried to skim past the horrific parts, or skip over them completely, the stammering would return, and I'd be forced to stop.

"Slow down," he'd say, and that was of no help to me at all. The third time he said it, I snapped back at him, told him that I would go as fast or as slow as I needed, and after a few breaths to compose myself, I apologised profusely.

Saying everything aloud for the first time in over twenty-five years was a bizarre and uncomfortable experience. I found myself bursting into tears, as though the story had opened floodgates that allowed all that bottled bitterness to come pouring out. Then, in the next moment, the venom would seep into my system, and I'd become a spitting cobra, adamantly defending my position.

About forty-five minutes in, we took a break. Henry made strong coffee in the cafetière, and we relocated to the living room. Although I'd put a huge dent in the bottle of Jack, I only felt the alcohol when I stood up; it had done nothing to diminish the pain, anguish, and overwhelming shame that accompanied the confession. I drank two cups of black coffee, which quickly became a poisonous concoction when added to the whiskey already swishing around my stomach. We had toilet breaks. I threw up, wiped my eyes and mouth, and continued.

For his part, Henry was the perfect listener. I'd expected nothing less. The only other time he stopped the staccato flow of my story was to seek clarification on certain points. He did not try to soothe me in any way, perhaps instinctively knowing that coddling would curtail the progress. I just had to tell it straight and endure everything that came with it, riding the waves of emotion whilst trying not to drown in the whirlpool of self-pity.

My head thumped, and thumped, and thumped.

When I was through with it all, my brain felt like a sponge being wrung dry. The stress congregated behind my eyes, throbbing in my sinuses. I rushed to the bathroom to be sick again but had nothing left to expel, the dry heaves twisting my stomach into knots.

"That's it?" Henry asked softly as I flushed the toilet and splashed my face and neck. "I mean, is that all of it?"

I nodded, staring at my ghoulish reflection in the bathroom mirror. He lingered in the doorway behind me, thoughtfully chewing his thumb, his forehead crinkling as he struggled to process the information. He glanced up, blinking rapidly, and said, "Are you okay?"

"Are *you*?" I replied.

"Yes. I'm fine. Well, actually..." He drifted off, rubbing the stubble that had seemingly sprouted throughout the course of my little therapy session, and said, "I'm caught between sadness and anger for you. It's not fair."

"It sort of is." I shrugged.

"No." He shook his head. "It isn't. At all. You took the blame for it."

I gave a weak laugh. "Nobody believed me."

"But how could they not... not..." He broke off, the mental exhaustion robbing his concentration. "I can't understand how this was allowed to happen to a fifteen-year-old girl."

"I'm not the victim," I reminded him, my voice croaky from the coffee and whiskey. "I'm still alive today. George McDermott isn't."

"You *are* a victim," he said, with a tone of indisputable finality. "You were..." He rubbed the tiredness from his eyes and continued. "You were *groomed*." To this, I gave no reply, which only seemed to flummox him further. "Groomed," he muttered again. "The way you've just described that, well, it has to be the biggest miscarriage of justice in the country's history, surely?"

"I wouldn't go that far," I muttered.

"You don't go far enough, Luanne. And maybe that's the problem. You've had all the fight beaten out of you. It's... diabolical what they put you through."

I felt an enormous swell of gratitude. Even if he was biased, even if he was exaggerating to take the weight off me, I appreciated it with all my heart. "Why don't you go to bed, Henry. You're out on your feet."

"Come with me," he said. "Let's both go."

There was no way I'd be able to sleep now, and I wasn't sure I wanted to lie down and be trapped beneath a duvet with my thoughts. What I wanted to do was slip out and go for a long walk, maybe catch a bus, ride it until the sun came up. But now that I'd unleashed my nightmares onto Henry, I owed him some semblance of solace. After everything I'd told him, I was sure that he'd need comforting, reassuring.

We shambled to our damp, draughty bedroom, stripped, and slipped beneath the covers. Our nightly routine mainly consisted of lying in bed and falling asleep with the TV flashing frenetically in the dark; but this time, the TV remained off. We held hands and I listened as our breathing synced.

"What do you want to do?" he whispered, his voice like brittle leaves.

"What do you think I should do?"

He exhaled through his nose and took his time to answer. "I think you should let everyone know. They've only got one side of the story, and it's not the truth. That only hurts you, Luanne. And it's going to keep hurting."

"Yeah, maybe."

"There's no maybe." He rolled onto his side to face me in the dark. "If I were you, I'd want to set everyone straight. Why carry all their hate forever? You didn't earn that baggage, Luanne. It's not yours. Offload it."

In a small, almost inaudible whisper, I said, "What if I'm not strong enough."

"You are, though." His hand cupped my cheek. "You're stronger than you know. And you've got me. I'll help you with it. I'll be your emotional support. You can't..." There was a hiss of frustration as he stopped to consider his words. "You can't just keep going into hiding. It's not fair on you. And how long would you be able to do that for until they found you again? A few months? Probably not even that." He propped up on one elbow. "You have a window of opportunity here with the documentary. That's what I think."

"What about your work?"

"Who fucking cares about work? I'm an underpaid accountant for a shitty furniture outlet. I'm never sick and I must have about six years' worth of annual leave that I've accrued. This is more important. The *truth* is more important, Luanne… for you, and for George McDermott."

"Yeah," I said, feeling far away now, my head like a cinderblock sinking through the pillow. "Yeah, I think you might be right."

He stroked my cheek, and we didn't say anything more about it that night.

CHAPTER 4

Henry stirred awake as I stepped out of the bed, quietly rummaging around in the dark for some clothes to wear.

"What is it?" he croaked.

"Nothing, love. Go back to sleep." I slipped into the jeans I'd been wearing the day before and groped for my socks.

He squinted against the glow of his phone screen as he checked the time. "It's not even seven yet."

"I know. I'm just going out for a few minutes."

"Oh, alright. Well, hold on a sec, I'll get my clothes on–"

"No, Henry. Relax. Go back to sleep. I just want to go for a walk. By myself. Please."

"If you're sure."

"I am." I sat on the edge of the mattress and patted his thigh before pulling my socks on. The rims of my eyes felt dry and sore. "You get some rest. I'll be back in before breakfast. I'll bring those bagels that you like."

He was still a moment, and then he sighed deeply, almost snoring. "That'd be nice. Just call me if you get stuck, alright?"

I told him that I would, unsure of what he meant exactly about getting stuck, and headed out the flat. Did he think I was going to have a mental breakdown in the street? Or maybe that a panic attack would seize me into submission and render me a blubbering mess. *Stuck,* I thought. *I've been stuck for a little while now, Henry. Stuck in a nightmare that I can't outrun. Stuck on a treadmill of guilt and shame and fear and loathing. And I want to get off. I want to get off so badly.*

It was dark and the streetlights were still on, the aubergine sky spitting a fine misty rain that wasn't altogether unpleasant. Cats hunkered down beneath the shelter of parked cars while foxes scurried through gardens searching for scraps. Aside from a couple of commuters on their way to work, the neighbourhood was still and silent. I wove a random path through the streets, walking with no destination in mind, thinking about everything I'd told Henry. He had taken it all so well, and I tried to wonder how I might have reacted had our scenarios been reversed. If Henry had admitted his part in killing someone years ago when he was just a boy, would I have been horrified? It was impossible for me to know. I'd spent so many years being horrified by my inclusion in the Vincent Street Incident that I just didn't have the bandwidth to think outside of my own trauma. I'd like to believe that I would have comforted Henry, that I would have been as caring and sympathetic to him as he had been to me. He had taken it too well, perhaps? Did that say something about his character? The fact that I had unspooled my story in all its grizzly detail and he had remained staunchly on my side had made me wonder about him. Did he have some perverse fetish that I didn't know about, or was he somewhere on the sociopathic scale and I just hadn't realized? Or could it really be that he truly loved me, and had wanted to do everything in his power to shield me from any further criticism? Yes, I thought maybe it was the latter. And maybe Henry was just as terrified of losing me as I was of him. That tracked, didn't it? He'd reluctantly admitted to me that he'd never had much luck with relationships, though he had been engaged once when in his early thirties. His fiancée had cheated on him with a co-worker whom she later went on to marry, and Henry had never really reclaimed the self-esteem needed to get on a dating app.

"Meeting you was a bit like fate for me," he'd once told me shyly, during one of those rare occasions when we both ended up drinking a bit too much at dinner. He'd been looking away from me, embarrassed because his eyes were sparkling. I know he probably regretted the confession, disliking the uneasy way it had slipped from his lips, but I immediately concurred. Meeting a kind, loving man like Henry was the best thing to ever happen to me, and now, after how he'd handled the news of my past, that feeling was reinforced tenfold.

I was almost sure that I wanted to go through with the documentary. The idea of ripping open these old wounds and incurring the country's wrath brought on a wave of fear that threatened to drown me. Yet, if I kept my head above that tidal wave long enough to think beyond the fear, I could almost envision what redemption might be like. It would surely be the most shocking news of the past few decades, and maybe the biggest comeback story the country has ever known. And how would it feel seeing those journalists who had torn me to shreds now all humiliated by the truth? That would be the sweetest revenge, wouldn't it? A new generation of blogs and social media accounts getting behind me, an army of voices rewriting my history.

Like the fear that rose and crashed through me, so too did the doubt. No sooner had I envisioned how happy I would be to shrug free of these weighty chains around my neck than I thought about the opposite scenario. What if I went ahead and relayed the truth on camera and it changed nothing? What if… God, I had to swallow down the rising acid… What if it made things worse?

Was that even possible at this stage?

CHAPTER 5

Later that morning, Henry asked me how I was feeling. I'd slipped in and out of sleep throughout the night, jerking awake every time I was on the verge of dreaming. I think it was my mind protecting me against what might await me in my nightmares.

In the frosty morning light, with the hiss of the wind and the gentle patter of rain against our flimsy windows, the past no longer seemed sinister and inescapable. It seemed conquerable, a once-fierce beast that had lost its bite and was ready to be slain. I was willing to forget, and the only way to do that, was to remember.

I set about making breakfast despite the absence of an appetite. I brewed a pot of tea and toasted the bagels for Henry, and when he was done with it all, his attention circled back to the business card that he held between his fingers.

"So what do you think? Would you like me to call them today?"

"What today? As in, now?"

"Yes. I don't think there's any reason to wait." He dabbed his mouth dry with a piece of kitchen towel and said, "Did he mention what your fee might be?" And before I could draw a breath to reply, Henry added, "Not that I care about that. That's not the important thing in all this, I just wondered."

"It is important. If he wants to strip me bare before the world, he's going to have to cough up for the privilege. God knows we could use the money."

"Right. You're right," he grumbled, smoothing his forehead with his palm. "We'll probably need a solicitor, but… I'm getting ahead of myself. Let me call him first. What time is it?" He checked his watch. "Hmm. Still early."

"He said to call him at any time," I assured Henry, running a finger over a chip in the rim of my mug. My stomach began to feel loose and watery. "I didn't get the impression that we would be bothering him. I think he's waiting for this call like a kid on Christmas morning."

"Okie-dokie, then." He tossed the balled-up kitchen towel onto his empty plate, retrieved his mobile and said, "No time like the present."

"Wait." I rose from the table, suddenly hot inside my dressing gown. "Don't do it while I'm here."

"What if he has questions? Like if he wants to arrange a meeting to go over terms and stuff?"

"You handle it. You're better at logistics and things. I don't mean to be a bitch, but I can't start… talking shop about it. Does that make sense?"

"It's okay." He got up and approached me the way a wary stranger might approach a stray dog they intended to pet. In a way, that's what he did. He patted my upper arm and said, "Go in the living room and wait. I'll hash it out with him. That alright?"

"Yes," I said, liking the idea very much. "Thanks."

"It's fine. I do expect an agent's cut of fifteen percent upon you signing the contract, though," he said dryly, barely cracking a smile. "And then of course, there's my accounting fee."

"You can have it all," I said, and hurried off to the living room, where less than eight hours ago I'd told a tale of insanity and murder so depraved that it'd had the country in a stir for almost a full year. I plopped down into our threadbare armchair and watched the cigarette-smoke sky through a window misted with condensation.

When I heard Henry talking, I plugged my fingers in my ears, and tightly closed my eyes.

It all sounded simple enough, Henry assured me in the cab ride to Soho, before furnishing me with the other details about the project. Henry said he'd got a vague idea of fees and a baseline starting point for payment but was confident there was room to negotiate something higher – providing, of course, I felt comfortable enough to go ahead with it all. Beyond that, there were still things like royalties and percentages to discuss, all of which seemed about as important as the type of air freshener dangling from the cab's rear-view mirror. Ideally, if everything sounded agreeable after we'd met, Peter Fidditch would get a contract across to Henry later today, with a mind to begin filming as early as next week.

"So soon?" I'd asked, now unnerved by the speed at which this was all unfolding. This thing we had talked about, giving my confession on camera, was turning from a mercurial idea into a solid reality with every inch of road the cab covered. I felt as though I couldn't take a proper deep breath.

"They need to move fast if they're going to beat Netflix," he said, watching the journey progress through the driver's windscreen. "I know it's not any indication of how this endeavour might play out," he began, "but he sounded like a nice enough fellow. Very enthusiastic, polite."

Polite to the point of pestering, I thought, but didn't voice this opinion, nor did I relay how he'd grabbed my arm back in the pub. Henry might think I was trying to back out if I started airing grievances now, and I'm sure it would only serve to get me more worked up than I already was. So, I kept quiet until the cab pulled up and let us back out into the rain. Sharing an umbrella, we huddled through the streets, following Google Maps on Henry's phone until we came to an inconspicuous doorway next to a jewellery shop. There were no plaques or signs to describe what type of establishment we were about to enter. The anonymity of the red door and intercom stirred my unease.

Henry buzzed and was let in, and we ascended the dingy, narrow stairwell for two flights before being greeted on the landing by Peter Fidditch. He wore a white shirt rolled up to the elbows, almost comical round glasses that I suppose were fashionable but couldn't understand why, and jeans so tight they looked as if they'd been painted on. If Mia had been there, she might have said something like those jeans were so tight she could tell what religion he was. And as soon as that popped into my head, I had to work very hard to push the image of her giggling face away again.

CONFESS YOUR SINS, YOU FUCKING PIG!

Go away.

"Henry," Fidditch said with a delighted smile, extending his hand. A series of woven leather bracelets dangled from his thin wrist. When he turned to me, he adjusted his expression. The smile didn't fade, but it did recede, becoming gentler. "And Luanne. We meet again. I'm so very delighted that you could make it. Please, come right through."

In complete contrast to the almost decrepit stairwell, the office was bright, spacious, and inviting. Framed movie posters decorated the bare brick walls. Plants were plentiful, their lavish green leaves clashing pleasantly against the solid-white décor.

"I've just brewed a pot of coffee, if you'd like some," he said, leading us through to a kitchenette area. "Or tea? Water? Juice?"

"Water," I croaked, cleared my throat. "Water's fine for me."

"Sure." He went into the obligatory small talk about the weather and the journey over as he prepared coffee and water before taking us into another meeting room a few feet away. We sat down at a large round table, walled in by glass. Fidditch poured water for us, and then removed what looked like a black leather notepad and a fancy ballpoint pen. He began with his spiel about himself; he was an award-winning independent filmmaker and co-owned Zelda Lane, along with a producer called Adelpha Jones.

"Actually, this story – *your* story, Luanne – will be Zelda Lane's maiden voyage," Fidditch said, setting his pen down and running both hands through his hair. "We've received considerable financial backing based on our previous works, and from the very first day we sat around this table to discuss ideas, your name was all we fixed on. And that's way before we ever heard rumblings about the Netflix film. We believe that this could potentially be earth shattering. A true crime documentary unlike nothing before it."

"How do I know you're not going to take liberties," I asked. "What guarantee do I have that you won't just film what I say and then fuck me over in the editing?"

He shrugged it off. "What would the point of that be? If someone wanted to see a documentary about how evil Ruby

Wilcox is, all they need to do is run your name through YouTube. There's dozens of those."

Next to me, Henry tensed and then turned to check how I'd taken the blow. My face was aflame, and I began to feel slightly giddy, as though the seat of the chair were pulling to one side and I the other. Still, I kept my attention locked on Fidditch and said nothing.

"The point I'm trying to make is that we know you didn't kill George McDermott. And I'll tell you something else: there are a lot of others who subscribe to this way of thinking. I mentioned typing your name in YouTube just now. Have you ever done it?"

"Of course not. I don't look at anything to do with it." *I can barely look in the mirror, let alone the internet,* I thought but didn't say aloud.

"Right, right. But if you did a quick search of your name on YouTube, you'd find several videos debating the legitimacy of your incarceration. The only thing you won't find" – he paused, picked up his pen and tapped the nib against the blank page – "is anything directly from the horse's mouth. And that is the selling point here. You, telling your story, in its entirety. Not some snooty BBC mishmash thrown together by some hack with an agenda. Not some glossy big budget production with pampered actors and a script that's so removed from the truth it might as well be *The Lord of the Rings*. This is Ruby Wilcox, giving the first-hand account of The Vincent Street Incident, and the damaging impact this wrongful conviction has had on your life. This is you telling everyone the truth about what Mia did, what she put you through."

He held me with his unwavering gaze and allowed the silence to swell through the room. This was not the same nervous man who had accosted me at work yesterday. This was a professional, well-educated person who had made a success of himself. If this whole pitch were the setup to some elaborate scam, then it was a masterful one, because right then and there, I believed him. I believed that he was on my side.

Under the table, Henry's hand found mine and squeezed gently. "I think you can understand Luanne's reluctance," Henry said, with the same tone of voice I imagined him using when explaining financial reports to his managing director. "She has gone through extreme lengths to conceal her real identity. Even I had no idea," he said, and gave me a comforting smile that almost brought me to tears. "What you're proposing completely goes against her nature. She wants to be left alone. She doesn't want to be hounded. The only reason she wants to do this at all is so that everyone knows the truth. The whole truth."

"Completely understandable," Fidditch reaffirmed. "In fact, given the circumstances around Luanne's arrest, her age at the time and the scandal surrounding the case, the way it was so botched from the beginning, it's incredible – *incredible* – that she wasn't granted a Mary Bell Order. By all rights, she should have been given lifetime anonymity. That's just one of the places where they dropped the ball. The way they apprehended Luanne was criminal in itself. How could she remain anonymous when the whole street saw what was going on? That blew everything up. She didn't get a fair shake at a trial. Then you have all the circus surrounding the psychologists and all the rest of it. It's scandalous; it really is."

"How *did* you find me?" I asked.

Fidditch cleared his throat and stared off through the glass wall behind me as he began. "I have a contact who finds people. It's nothing shady. They have a subscription to a database that isn't available to the general public, and it's usually used as a means of tracking relatives through genealogy to settle inheritances, things like that. You've done a good job of hiding, Luanne, but you did leave a trail of breadcrumbs for us to follow. You changed your name by deed poll a few times, and once we uncovered your most recent alias" – he gestured toward me – "it was a case of following the trail. You're legally employed by the Ship and Bottle, and they're paying your national insurance tax. Given the gaps in your employment record, I'm guessing you couldn't find anything that paid cash over the counter anymore. Anyway, it was easy – or as difficult – as that. Some ten-a-penny podcaster or freelance journalist wouldn't have gone through those lengths because, frankly, the service is expensive and it's time consuming. But" – he raised an index finger – "if a big newspaper decided they wanted to do a lengthy piece on The Vincent Street Incident, I could see them carving out a budget for that. Thankfully, though, as I've already told you, we have the press on our side. *The Guardian* are raring to go."

A slow tide of nausea lapped against my stomach lining. I turned to Henry, massaged my neck, and wondered what was going through his mind. I'd lied to his face for two years. And while his expression remained gentle and understanding, I couldn't help but wonder why he was being so cool about all of this.

"I know that all sounds slimy and treacherous," Fidditch said, interrupting my thoughts, "but I can assure you, we did it with the best intentions. If you want to turn us down, then of course, I think that would be a mistake, but we're not going to sell you out, Luanne. You can go back to the life you've built and enjoy that for however long it lasts. But changing your name again, dyeing your hair again, it's not going to be enough. But" – he opened a drawer and removed two sets of documents; I was unable to read the writing on the front page without my glasses – "if you do decide to tell your story, then we can control the narrative. We have a huge, global PR machine on our side, and great relationships with most of the mainstream media. Luanne" – he leaned forward, angling his head to catch my eye – "we're going to look after you. We believe you. The rest of the world will too, once they know the facts. But they won't if you go on the run again and stay silent."

I thought about this for a long time. Then, hesitantly, I reached out and claimed a copy of the contract.

Next to me, Henry smiled and, almost whispering, said, "We can do it together, Luanne. I'll be with you every step of the way. Right by your side."

If I didn't have Henry, I wouldn't even be in that office, let alone seriously considering the offer. I brought his hand to my lips and kissed it, almost physically moved by his unshakable positivity.

"Don't suppose I have anything to lose at this point, do I," I said, licked my thumb, and turned the first page.

CHAPTER 6

On the first blustery day of shooting, a chauffeured Prius picked up Henry and I from outside our hotel. I had given Louise the courtesy of a text message to end my tenure at The Ship and Bottle. I did not receive a text back. Henry took some emergency leave, which his boss signed off without any pushback. Apparently, they hadn't even asked why he had to call in two weeks of annual leave at such short notice. They just told him to make sure he put his out-of-office on.

My bag was packed full of emergency supplies; peppermints to crunch on if my acid reflux began playing up and co-codamol to crunch on in case I got one of my headaches. There was also a spare change of clothes, a hairbrush, aerosol, milk of magnesia, and most importantly, a small bottle of cooking brandy; cheap, nasty stuff, but quick.

It took just over an hour to reach our destination. The Prius pulled off a main road, continued down a long industrial lane. We rolled around to a large concrete lot, in the middle of which was a vast building with a domed roof.

"Looks like an old airport hangar," Henry said, as the driver slid the Prius into a bay across from a bank of blue portacabins lining the far side of the lot. "So this is the sound stage, huh?"

Through the yawning maw of the sound stage entrance, I could see Fidditch talking intently to a gangly woman in her early thirties, who paid close attention to everything that was being said, concentrating as though her life depended on the information.

"Where is everyone? Probably inside, I imagine," Henry said, asking and answering his own question. Fidditch spotted the Prius and came marching toward it, battling against the wind to keep his waxed and styled hair from tousling.

When I stepped out of the car, Henry immediately relieved me of my bag and rubbed my lower back.

"Luanne," Fidditch called, rolling his sleeves up his arms. He was wearing a baggy pea-green cardigan, offset against a pair of purple trousers. The clash of colours was nauseating. I sucked in the cool, damp air as the breeze blew through my coat, biting at my skin. "Have you already eaten?"

"No." I shook my head. "No appetite."

"Right." His eyes scrolled over my outfit, mentally making alterations. "Well, you'll find that appetite by the end of today, I promise you. Come on inside; it's warmer."

He wasted no time on Henry. Now that we had signed the contract, Henry was a redundant entity to them. Fidditch led us inside the cavernous soundstage, which felt more like an old warehouse. A rig of immensely dazzling lights beamed down onto the stage area in the centre of the room. A large greenscreen served as the backdrop. That was about as elaborate as the setup got.

"We've been working with a journalist at *The Scribe* who was the first reporter on the scene," Fidditch was saying, his hair bouncing as he strode. "He actually broke the story. He's since gone on to do an eight-part podcast about the

VSI. The reporter interviewed your form tutor back in 2002 – Mr Springer? – and was able to sneak a few snaps of your old classroom. Want to see something cool?" He smiled, then reconsidered. "Well, 'cool' is probably not the most appropriate word to use, but…" He placed an index finger to his lips and amended, "would you like to see your old classroom? We'll make it look like you're sitting here for part of the segment."

A camera was pointed in front of the green screen, but just next to it was a table with an open laptop.

"Here, look, check this out." He tapped on a key and a slideshow began on the laptop screen.

The sight of the whiteboard, tables, chairs, even classwork tacked on the plasterboard walls, stole the breath in my lungs.

"We have this really clever AI program that's going to reconstruct your old classroom right down to the dust motes." Fidditch looked from the screen to my face to read my reaction. "It'll all be painstakingly recreated from these photos. Even the proportions of the space and objects should be almost correct. Luanne?"

"Luanne?" Henry's voice this time, distant.

Fragrances washed through my memory; a puff of dusty plastic covering the textbooks, a suggestion of body spray aerosol applied after PE, spearmint on breath, the high, chemical stink of marker pens.

The classroom photos had almost successfully jumpstarted my brain. The initial shock of seeing everything laid out in a way that I could confidently recognise had the same effect as slamming back a large glass of vodka. The nostalgia hit me straight in the head.

"Very good," I managed, not wanting to imbed myself any deeper than I had to.

"Now, Luanne," Fidditch began, snagging my attention. "I'd like you to sit here at this chair with your back to the greenscreen."

"You want me to sit down now?"

"In a moment. First, if I may, I'd like a quick word. Away from everyone else, if that's alright?"

I looked at Henry, who gave me a subtle half-shrug. Had I been expecting him to intervene, to insist that anything Fidditch had to say to me, he could say in front of Henry, too? The gangly woman, who I hadn't been introduced to, watched me through large glasses, a smile pulling at her lips. She'd had some cosmetic work done, cheekbones, fillers, maybe a nose job, and the combination made her appear almost like a caricature.

"Sure," I said, shadowing Fidditch to a dark corner away from the garish, hot glow of the set.

"Luanne, before we get rolling today, I just want to commend you for your bravery. I know this hasn't been an easy decision to make, and I can see that your defences are still up. That is completely understandable. But we're here to tell the truth. That's all I want."

"I didn't come here to lie," I snipped. "I have nothing to lie about. My story's always been the same and it's always been the truth."

"I am with you one hundred percent," he said. "Now, I wanted you to see those old photos because I was hoping it would stir something up in your memory, but to be sure – do you think you can recall it all, faithfully?"

I snorted, my head whipping to the side in search of Henry, but he had his back turned to us and was observing the soundstage. Knowing him, he'd be fascinated at this little glimpse behind the curtain, seeing how documentaries are made. "Of course, I remember it all. It's not something I can ever forget. It's been burned into me."

"I understand. Now, I'm going to let you tell it how you want to tell it, but I may prod you here and there, ask for clarification, like if something doesn't make sense or if I'm not following. I'll try not to derail you too much, but this is a very strange story and it's important that the viewer understands everything. Do you agree?"

"Yeah, sure, fine." I shrugged, feeling the first gentle squeeze of pressure.

"Marvellous. And one last thing." He was very expressive with his hands. It was distracting. "I want you to know that I'm going to look after you throughout this whole shoot. I'm going to give you space, give you time – as much time as you need – to get everything out because I know how painful this is. Okay, Luanne?" He lightly tapped my elbow for reassurance. I cringed from the contact, but nodded, feeling begrudgingly thankful for the effort he was making. It wasn't comforting, but it was an attempt. "If at any time you want to stop, have a break, whatever, just say so. If you start to feel like things are getting too heavy, please just tell me."

"I will." I gave him a smile that wouldn't touch my eyes, and inhaled deeply. "And… thank you… for the opportunity to, you know, get the truth out there."

"Thank *you*," he said. "Now, let's get you set up."

"Even before the crime took place, there was enough anecdotal evidence to suggest that Ruby Wilcox was deeply disturbed and dangerous beyond belief. Legal action should have been brought against Child Protective Services and the entire school system for their negligence and inability to spot what was essentially a walking time bomb."

– Simon Ward, Dead Behind the Eyes

"… Among the plethora of leaked documents to surface after the trial were Ruby's report cards, years 8–10, which, according to all accounts, reveal a sensitive, timid, but exceptionally intelligent student who had a hard time making friends. She had no criminal background, no record of any violent infractions whatsoever. Nothing in any document or witness statement supports the idea that she alone could have orchestrated the catastrophe at Vincent Street."

– Floyd Wilkinson, Mayhem in Mind: The Untold Truth of The Vincent Street Incident

CHAPTER 7

It started the day I met Mia. But things were already falling apart before then, I think. She was just a whisper in my ear, a helping hand, pushing me over the edge.

It was the beginning of the school term, Year 9, so it would have been mid-September. Everyone was in class, but I was sitting on a bench just on the edge of the playing field with my head in my hands and lightning bolts shooting through my brain. I'd been on the way to the medical room, but the pain made movement impossible, almost bringing me to my knees.

When I was eight, my mum had a car crash and I got a bit banged up, and ever since then I suffered from these little thunderstorms in my head. Most of the teachers at St Monica's knew about my migraines – well, they called them migraines, but that wasn't really accurate. I always thought of them as thunderstorms. The teachers were usually caught between sympathy and impatience whenever the classroom started to feel a bit fuzzy and I had to make a hasty exit. The headaches could last anywhere between ten minutes and a couple of hours, but most of the time, I could get through them by lying down in the medical room with the crook of my arm covering my eyes.

Stress was always the trigger. Two days before this particular headache, I had found out about my dad. When he dropped the bombshell, it broke something inside me that had already been precariously fractured since the accident and the pain taking up permanent residence in my skull. Lying on the bench, my eyeballs felt as though they were being sucked out of their sockets from the pressure. It was like a chisel was wedged in my nasal passage, intent on prying my face open from the inside out. Then those familiar knitting needles jabbed into my eardrums. Sometimes it got so bad that I passed out, and I was hoping to on this occasion because I usually felt better when I came to, but no such luck. I just had to weather the storm, blind and bewildered. My breakfast had climbed aboard a train that was tunnelling up my throat, and without care or caution, I sprayed vomit onto the grass.

"Get it all up, that's it," a vaguely amused voice said, though I was too preoccupied to know where it was coming from. Then, through my tear-sparkled vision, I saw her; nothing more than a silhouette eclipsing the autumn sun, and when she spoke again, her words were clear and almost musical. "What is it? Food poisoning?"

Spitting strings of sour bile, I tried to shake my head, which was a mistake. Hissing, I said, "H-headache."

"Headache?" this stranger repeated, the sunlight touching one side of her face. "You look like a bus hit you. You sure it's just a headache?"

"I get them," I croaked, groaned, and then added, "they... pass. Just takes a while."

"I see," she said, observing curiously.

"It's alright," I said, careful to move only my lips this time. "I'll be fine in a minute." And though I said this as a means of moving her on, the truth was, I *had* begun to feel marginally better. The storm had lost its ferocity, and the world around me – which had begun to resemble a colouring book that some toddler had scribbled over with crayons – was starting to straighten out again. The colours began correcting themselves, and, concentrating on my breathing, I pinched the bridge of my nose, trying to stem the pressure in my eyes.

She was holding a bottle of water toward me. Gratefully, I took it, uncapped it, and gulped. "Thank you," I said, trying to pass it back to her.

"No way," she laughed, sitting down next to me. "You can keep it."

I thanked her again and then we didn't speak for a long time. Her presence served as an awkward distraction to the ebbing pain. Mopping sweat from my forehead with the sleeve of my blazer, I said, "How come you're not in class?"

She shrugged, then cocked a thumb past the main building. "I go to Dumb-Dumb City. Thought I'd take a walk. No biggie."

"Oh," was all I could manage. Now her being there outside of class hours made perfect sense. Dumb-Dumb City was the nickname for a program they ran at St Monica's called The Bramble Huts. It was a place where the neighbouring boroughs sent problem kids – the ones who had been expelled from other schools for a variety of behavioural issues. They were kept very much separate from the good catholic boys and girls at St Monica's, wearing their regular street clothes as a way of distinguishing themselves. That's probably why I'd never seen her around school until that day.

But maybe that isn't quite right, either. In the years since that first encounter, I've thought that maybe I *had* seen Mia before. Now I have vague recollections of coming across her in the lunch hall or passing me in the courtyard between the science building and the gymnasium. As it goes, I'm never able to verify these sightings, unsure as to whether I dreamed them up in the long stretches of boredom between capture and sentencing.

"You need to go to medical?" she asked, and it was in that moment that I got my first proper glimpse of her. A cascade of curly black hair, high cheekbones, eyes like two onyx coins. She was very pretty, except that didn't really sum it up. She was *exceptionally* beautiful, and in our brief time together on that bench, I sensed the aura of unwavering confidence effortlessly oozing from her. There was a maturity about her that I immediately envied.

But she was in the Bramble Huts, which meant there had to be something wrong with her. Though the regular pupils at St Monica's didn't get much chance to mix with the kids in the Huts, there were wild rumours. One boy they reckoned was an arsonist who had burned his local play scheme building down. Another boy who had brandished a knife at the maths teacher at his previous school. A nympho girl who got caught servicing a parade of sixth formers during an unsupervised detention. A whole cast of colourful characters.

"You looked really green for a few minutes," she said, smiling.

"I think I'm okay now." I picked my bag up off the floor, rested it on my lap. I tried for a smile, swallowed bitter saliva, and said, "I just get these" – I twirled a finger near my temple – "from time to time."

"You have a problem in your head?" the girl asked me, handing over a tissue from a packet of Kleenex, indicating to my runny nose.

A problem in my head, I thought. Yep, I guess you could say that. Even at thirteen, I knew there was some wiring loose up there. Had to be. You go through a car windscreen, fall into a coma for three days and live to tell the tale, the music doesn't always play too smoothly after that. Sometimes the record skips. Especially if you'd just had the weekend I'd had, got the news I'd got.

"Had an accident when I was little," I told her, and impulsively scooped the hair away from the side of my head to reveal the crescent scar that ran from the back of my ear to the top of my skull. Perhaps I was trying to prove that I wasn't just some nerd who vomits everywhere for no reason. Or maybe I was bragging, trying to show that, despite not looking like much, I was sort of hardcore. I don't really know why I showed her, but just felt I had to.

"Ooh, that's gnarly. You take anything for them? The headaches, I mean."

There was something so cool and effortless about her, with an underlying toughness that, to a mouse like me, was instantly alluring.

"No. I mean, I do have pills that I'm supposed to take, but it's easier just to let things run their course sometimes. Plus, the pills, they kind of… make you wig out a bit."

"What do you mean?"

"Mood swings and things," I said. "You're laughing your head off one minute and the next…"

The next, you want to kill yourself, I almost said, but clamped shut, and let the sentence fizzle away.

"Right," she said, nodding but already looking away as though the conversation bored her. "Well, I'd better get back. You should probably go to the medical room. I bet they'd sign you off to go home."

It would have been so easy just to leave it there. I've often wondered how things might've turned out if I'd have just taken her advice. I probably wouldn't have had much opportunity to bump into her again. Then, the tragedy on Vincent Street wouldn't have happened. On the same note, I don't think I would have made it through the next couple of years without her, either. In many ways, I met Mia when I needed her most. And I think she knew that too.

"I'm Ruby, by the way," I managed, and the pain was now the distant drumming of a marching band that has already passed through the town. I tested this notion by tilting my head slightly, and when I didn't feel the crackle of lightning, I added, "Ruby Wilcox."

"I'm Mia Swehl," she said.

And just like that, I'd made a new friend. I had no way of knowing how dangerously disturbed she was until much later.

CHAPTER 8

There had been warning signs, little things that I found peculiar.

It didn't take very long to find out how she ended up in the Huts, either. She loved to steal.

I mean, *loved* it.

The first time I noticed her do it, we'd been walking past a fruit and veg shop, talking about something – boys, maybe, music, last night's TV? – and she just lifted a mango from one of the display boxes and sort of, threw it behind her back to her other hand. Like it was a party trick. Like something one of those kids in *Oliver Twist* might do. It was only a mango, right? But it was the audacity that I found… well, sort of fun. Cheeky. It was a mango; who cares?

Sometimes, though, it got to be a problem. We'd cut through a mall on our way home from school and she'd wander into a shop and come out with CD's stuffed down the front of her jeans. I wouldn't even notice her doing it. She had this handbag that she'd lined with foil because apparently it blocked the shop alarms, and she would just fill that bag up. A t-shirt, a hat, a scarf, underwear, sometimes things she didn't even need like a toy car or a water pistol. Stupid stuff. It was like she couldn't help herself; if it was there, then she just had to do it.

There were times when we'd walk through a supermarket or something and I'd watch her like a hawk, hoping to catch her in the act. She'd pick things up, put them down, gesture with her hands, drop an item on the ground. It was all distraction, but I'd keep my attention glued to her, trying to spot the sleight of hand as though she were a magician performing a card trick. But I was never able to, and neither were any of the security guards. It was all so casual.

The only time she ever came close to getting rumbled was when we were in the makeup section of a department store. She was going around trying the sample lipsticks on the back of her hand, spritzing herself with tester perfumes, holding up eye shadows next to her face and asking my opinion about which colours suited her complexion. I was always very jealous of her smooth, olive skin, which completely contrasted how pasty and pimpled my own face was. All those dolled-up women working at the kiosks would watch us warily, knowing we didn't have money to make a purchase.

I hadn't even noticed the security guard coming up behind us. There was a crash, and he grabbed my arm, spun me around, and started yelling in my face, asking to see what was in the bag.

"What bag?" I asked, terrified, wondering if he meant my tatty old backpack. Sure, he could look through that all he wanted. Then I realised what he really meant. That crash I'd heard was Mia's special foil-lined bag, which she'd abandoned at the first sight of the security guard and vanished into thin air.

The guard was shouting and dragging me, and I really thought he was going to hit me in the face if I kept proclaiming my innocence. I was trying to tell him that I didn't steal anything, that I wasn't even planning to, but it would have done no good. Panicked, I scanned the brightly lit aisles for any sight of Mia, but she had disappeared and left me to deal with the heat. *Her* heat.

The guard pulled me past a perfume counter, where an older woman protested the rough handling. "What's the matter with you, dragging her like that? She's only a little girl, for God's sake!" And when the guard snapped toward the woman, unable to let the rebuke go unanswered, I yanked free of his grasp and made a sprint for the exit. I've never been athletic, and I probably resembled a baby giraffe, loping away from the guard. Then I saw Mia by the exit, laughing and waving me on. Her cheerleading lent some strength to my spindly legs, sent a few extra squirts of adrenaline into my bloodstream, because at that point I felt fast – nimble, almost. The store alarms bleated as I passed through, which barely registered with me at the time. It wasn't until later, when I found the silver compact mirror with a sticky alarm on the back of it wedged deep inside my backpack, that I knew Mia had used me as a mule. I wasn't angry, though; she'd said she was going to give it to me as a present anyway. Mia and her presents.

There was one other unusual thing about her that I picked up on almost immediately. Mia didn't like crowds. Or, maybe more accurately, she didn't like *people*, being near them. She got spooky if it was busy inside the shopping centre. Sometimes, when we were on lunch break at school, we'd find a quiet spot, usually on a patch of grass around the back of the main building where we weren't likely to be disturbed. I'd catch her staring off into the distance at the other students but could never read her expression. She always seemed edgy around strangers, was always sizing them up, skirting around them. We'd be waiting at a bus stop, and a man might wander over, not even look our way, and I would feel Mia turn rigid. She would scan the person from head to toe, assessing whether they were a threat or not, her face frowning with the intensity of her distrust. Those black eyes of hers would become skittish, darting around. The only time she was ever truly comfortable was when we were alone; in the park by my house, or sometimes we'd walk through the cemetery and hang out there for a while. Then, of course, there were the scary abandoned buildings that she always seemed to find on her little night-time excursions.

That's why it was such a big deal when I persuaded her to go to the fair with me that day, a couple of years later. Sure, we were almost sixteen and had failed to find any other friends, but getting her to the fair had been a step in that direction. I guess I liked the idea of us branching out a bit, integrating with another group, maybe. Mia's attendance at school was spotty. She always had something else going on, some secret drama that she would never fully divulge, only hint at. And there would be days when I had nobody to talk to at all. There were other girls I said hello to, but I never found it easy making friends. People just always thought I was weird. Aloof, maybe, I don't know. But Mia never did, and that's what made those frequent absences so lonesome.

My mum had been in one of her dark moods. The noise of her scrubbing the kitchen floor had woken me up at about six that morning, and it was usually a good indicator that things were about to go south very quickly. Whenever Mum fell into one of her depressions, she would clean… I mean, *furiously* clean. She'd spend so long mopping and vacuuming and disinfecting that I'd get dizzy and nauseous from the noxious stink of chemicals, tasting the bleach in the back of my throat. Once, during a particularly intense cleaning session a week or so after Dad left, she had thrown a remote control at my head. I'd been sitting in the armchair, watching TV while she was folding laundry. The remote cracked against the side of my face, the back panel broke off and batteries burst from the plastic, opening a small cut near my temple. She had immediately rushed to my side, swaddling me tight, angrily muttering that she hadn't meant to hit me, she only meant to get it out the way while she was folding. She'd been trying to toss it on the couch, and of course it was an accident, even though she'd thrown it like a baseball. And I supposed I believed her, except, a few months later, while I was sat at the kitchen table chipping away at my Geography homework, she decided it would be a good time to start hoovering. "Mind your feet," she'd said, pushing and dragging the hoover across the floor. But as she passed me by, she ran the hoover over my bare foot, and the wheel cracked my big toenail in half. "Fucking hell, Ruby, I said move your feet!" She then proceeded to fetch and apply a plaster to my damaged toe, before making a joke, something about how I had feet like a sasquatch. Incidents like those were easy to dismiss as aggressive accidents, but I never believed they were. She'd always had that nastiness in her.

I have a vivid memory from when I was very young, probably four years old. My dad was away on a business trip – back then, he worked as a book rep for a library school supplier and would often have meetings in different parts of the country, usually staying overnight in a hotel somewhere. I used to get very anxious and cry for hours when I knew he had to go on a trip.

I don't know what set my mum off, but it had something to do with a drawing I'd done. I *think* I'd scribbled two stick figures and told her that it was me and my dad. She had pretended to be impressed by my artwork, and then a moment later, she pretended to be upset that I hadn't included her in the drawing. "Oh, no Mummy? That makes me feel a bit sad." I tried to amend the mistake, telling her that I could add her too and that it wasn't a problem.

The next thing I knew, she had got something from beneath the sink.

"Do you know what this is, Ruby? This is a mousetrap. Shall I show you how it works? Watch. You pull this spring back, and the little mousey eats the cheese. Show me a little mousey, Ruby. There, put your finger there. That's where the little mouse goes."

On the morning that Mum woke me up with her compulsive cleaning, I wasted no time in calling Mia on the mobile phone she had given me as a present about two weeks before. She had told me to check my shed when I got home from school, and there it was, an old, scuffed Nokia with a red ribbon around it, sitting on an upturned plant pot amidst the ancient junk and clutter that my dad had left behind. The buttons were worn down from excessive texting, and the casing was chipped in places. When I asked how she'd come across the phone, she said she found it... in someone else's house.

She was always leaving me presents in the shed. My old house backed onto the common. She would climb the fence and get into the weathered old shed through one of the busted windows. No idea how she managed to navigate all the debris in the shed without breaking a leg. My dad was a hoarder – paint pots, chairs, an old sofa, TV's that didn't work, all kinds of junk.

When I called Mia, she answered after one ring. "Hey, you must be psychic. I was just about to phone you," she said by way of greeting. She didn't sound gruff or croaky despite the hour.

"Really? This early in the morning?" I asked, keeping my voice hushed in case it travelled downstairs and disturbed Mum's frantic scrubbing.

"Don't tell me she's cleaning?"

"Yeah," I said with a short, nervous laugh, picking the grit out of my eyes with nails bitten to the quick. "Something's got her worked up. I can't be around this today. I need to get out."

"I can be at the common in an hour? The real question is: is it too early for vodka?"

I snorted laughter. "Yeah, I think it'll be early by about ten hours."

"Don't be so lame. We can have Bloody Marys with the celery and everything. Make it like breakfast." And before I had a chance to mount any counter offers, she added, "Ooh, or we could have prosecco in the park. A picnic. That better for you, Rube? Classier, I think."

"Nothing says class like guzzling booze first thing in the morning," I said.

"Well, we're ladies of leisure, are we not?"

"When you put it that way, sure, sounds like a plan," I said, biting my lip as Mum's scrubbing began to wane. "Hold on, Mia." I listened, heard the glug and swish of rinse water being poured down the sinkhole, and continued. "But hey, I was thinking maybe we could go to the fair today." When she didn't speak, I said, "Hello? You still there?"

"I'm still here," Mia said. "What's so good about the fair? It's for babies."

"It's just something to do," I said, before quickly adding, "we could have a picnic in the park, chill out, and then just… pass by? We don't have to make it a big thing, but you know… could just be a bit of fun. We don't even have to go on the rides, could just have hotdogs or something."

Her exhale crackled through the receiver. "It's so stupid, but if it's what you really want to do, then yes, fine."

"Don't get sour about it."

"I'm not getting sour," she sighed. "But what madam wants, madam gets. Clearly."

"You're being mean now. I bet you end up enjoying yourself."

"I bet you I definitely don't."

"Grouch. See you in an hour."

The line went dead. I threw on some jeans and a baggy t-shirt, and finished my ensemble with my round, blue-tinted sunglasses, before making my way downstairs. My mum must've heard me coming because she was there to receive me in the hallway, wrapped in a fluffy pink dressing gown, her hands red from the hot, soapy water. Her blond hair, black at the roots and streaked with silver threads, was tied back into a tight ponytail.

"Morning," I said.

She looked me up and down and said, "Going out?"

"Just to a friend's house."

"This early in the morning?" She pulled a packet of cigarettes from her dressing gown pocket and lit one. "What for?"

"To hang out."

Mum nodded, but there was no recognisable expression on her face. For a woman a year shy of her fortieth birthday, she looked so much older, the crinkles around her eyes and the smoker's lines giving her a perpetual tragedy mask. I had a quick flash then of her going to get the bucket of hot water and tipping it over me as I tried to leave, and then claiming she had tripped on her way to the drain.

"Your mysterious friend that's too scared to come over." She nodded, exhaling twin plumes of smoke through her nostrils. "Right. I'll just stay here and do the cleaning. As always."

"I can help," I said hesitantly. "What else... needs to be done?" I asked, knowing the question was redundant. The house was practically gleaming.

"Nothing," she said with a dismissive shrug. She turned away from me and padded back toward the kitchen. "Have fun at the fair."

I almost let it go. For a while, I'd been suspicious that my mum was listening into our conversations, that she was snooping around my room when I was at school, looking through my drawers and under the bed.

"How'd you know I was going to the fair?"

From inside the kitchen, she said, "I heard you on that phone. Always on the phone to your little friend; whisper, whisper, whisper, scheme, scheme, scheme. Go on. Go if you're going."

Then, the swish-swish-swish as she resumed scrubbing.

CHAPTER 9

Mia sat on a concrete bollard in the common carpark, popping gum with a wide-brimmed hat shading her face. She displayed a large bottle of vodka like a trophy, her smile almost as radiant as the sun backlighting her. "What took you so long? We need to get breakfast started!" She was wearing blood-red lipstick that matched her nails and dress. My mum would have undoubtedly called it a whore's colour or something similarly vulgar, but I liked it. I thought Mia looked great.

"I thought you said prosecco." I frowned. I hadn't even been awake for two hours yet, and the thought of glugging back anything stronger than a cup of tea was already giving me trouble. "Oh, God, are we really doing vodka? I haven't even eaten yet."

"If you want me to go to that funfair later, then you need to sweeten me up a little bit. I'll need the Dutch courage. Anyway, I told you: celery." An airy giggle sailed from those crimson lips as she rifled through her tote bag, which still had a plastic security tag pinned to the bottom. "And I've got other things in here too. Pancakes, sandwiches. Lots of lovely things. We're all good to go." She rose from the bollard and casually flung an arm around me in a hug. The mingling vapours of pilfered perfume and the vodka on her breath wafted into my face. She stood back, assessed my appearance over the top of her shades and said, "You look tremendous, by the way. Absolutely outstanding."

"You're a bad liar," I replied, reluctantly accepting the bottle as she extended it toward me, "but a good friend."

"We've got the sun, we've got drink, we've got the whole day ahead of us," she said, breathing deep the freshly cut grass. "Go on, now. You take a sip to get you started."

Even though my stomach was rebelling at the thought of it, I didn't need too much persuasion. I drank, coughed, and hesitantly went back for another slug. Mia cheered as I cringed and capped the bottle, passing it back to her. As the vodka went down, the morning sunshine began to seem brighter, the breeze smelled sweeter.

"There we go," she said, offering her hand for me to hold. "That's already much better, isn't it? Oh, I know it is."

We floated through the streets, passing the bottle back and forth, until we got to the bus stop. By the time the bus came, I was already beginning to feel as though I were a passenger inside my own body and someone else was piloting the ship. The vodka had hit me like a hammer, and when we got on the bus, the momentum only accelerated my giddiness. Mia took out a Walkman, which had a mixtape she'd recorded for us. I listened to one earphone, and she listened to the other as we nibbled pancakes and grapes straight from her bag.

"Sorry your mum's being weird," Mia said, thumbing the bell for the next stop.

"It's alright," I said with a shrug. "When she starts getting like that, I just have to leave. Give her some space."

"It's not alright. You shouldn't have to feel scared of her all the time. She doesn't have the right."

"Yeah, well," I said, but the sentence was stolen by a sigh. I laughed for no reason as my head began to bobble around like a counterweight to my body. "How am I already this drunk? Half the neighbourhood is probably still asleep."

"They're missing out," Mia said, rising from the seat as the bus slowed for our stop. "It's such a wonderful day."

We hung out all day in the park, lying in the shade of a weeping willow, dappled in gold sunlight. Mia made daisy chains and intricate bangles from braided grass while we listened to music on the portable Walkman speakers and read magazines she'd stolen. Somewhere along the way we fell into a deep, alcohol-induced slumber and woke in the dusky late afternoon, slightly sobered but covered in ant bites.

Down the hill from us, the fair was vibrant and strobing. Gleeful screams funnelled through a cacophony of pop music blaring from the various rides. A DJ's muffled voice amplified by a microphone was yelling some approximation of *Scream if you want to go faster!*

"So, I'm thinking," I began, raking fingers through my hair, picking out flecks of grass, "if you really don't want to go to the fair, we can skip it. We've basically got the view here. We can hear everything. Might be too loud down there anyway."

"No." She shook her head, readjusting her hat. "We should try new things. Who knows, there might even be a couple of hot boys down there ready to snap us up," she tittered, fiddling with a blade of grass, sadness passing across her face like a fleeting shadow. She inhaled, smiled bravely, and added, "Like you said, it's just a bit of fun. But, we do have one small item on the agenda to attend to." She reached into the bag, and I groaned. There were four inches of vodka left, and I could scarcely believe we had put that much of a dent into the bottle. My mouth was so dry that my lips chafed against my gums. "Come on. You know the rules. Can't leave it like this."

"You go first," I said, already heady from the booze and dopey from the nap. When it was my turn to drink, I gagged, thought I might throw it back up, but by some miracle of biology, I managed to keep it down. "Fuck this, I'm not drinking anymore. Ever."

Mia cackled, necked the rest of the drink, and threw the bottle in the grass. "Dutch courage acquired," she announced, and helped me to my feet. She felt sturdy, like she was made of concrete, and I couldn't understand how she managed it. That vodka had been brutal to drink, almost knocking me into another planet. The world was a Vaseline-smeared lens, the earth transforming to a waterbed mattress beneath my unsteady feet.

Mia helped me down the hill, correcting me every time I stumbled. The sight of those blurry, dizzying rides did nothing for my equilibrium, and all that screaming was making me both jumpy and sort of nostalgic. I started thinking about that one time my dad took me to the fair when I was a kid. It was a forbidden thing, and he was directly disobeying one of my mum's commands by doing it, but we didn't care. It poured down with rain that day, and we didn't care about that, either, because we were eating candy floss and giggling in the ghost train, having the time of our lives. Dad tried to win me this big inflatable butterfly at the coconut shy because he knew I had a thing for butterflies, but he couldn't manage to knock any coconuts off, even after three tries. Eventually he just said to the stringy guy running the stall, "Hey, how much would it be just to buy one of these things for the little lady?" pointing at the prizes. I don't remember how much the guy quoted, but Dad coughed it up and I had my butterfly, which I ended up calling Benny.

"Mum's going to be really angry when she sees Benny," I had said, terrified at the thought of having my wonderful souvenir snatched away.

"Why? We found it on the bench, remember?" He winked at me. "Some poor kid must've dropped it."

"It's packed here," Mia said, dragging me out of the daydream. She was adjusting her dress, which kept riding up. Her head whipped right and left as she walked, careful not to bump into anyone. She reminded me a little bit of a tiger cutting a path through tall grass. "You don't want to go on any of these rides, do you? I mean, I will if you really want to, but... I'd probably rather not."

"No, just want to have a... look," I said, propping my shades on my head before rubbing my eyes with my fingertips. A constant stream of people flowed in the aisles between the amusements and concession stands, bumping past me. The drink was catching up with me, fast. My stomach threatened to rebel, so I kept my concentration on the ground in front of me. When Mia walked, it looked like her feet weren't even touching the ground. Like she was floating.

Mia cupped a hand over her ear. "What?"

"I just want to have a look around. Soak it up." I stopped, unable to compete with the music blaring from a nearby speaker. I signalled for us to move away, and we trotted further down by the kiddie rides. We carried on to the closest concession stand, which was nothing more than a hut on wheels with bags of candyfloss and toffee apples dangling from hooks. Two puffy women in their forties stood in the claustrophobic confines, sweating over a steaming grill. I remember thinking that working in one of those huts had to be the most miserable job ever, and I also remember feeling lucky in my assurance that I would never end up like them. It's funny when you think about the seemingly insignificant things that stick in your head. The image of those haggard, red-faced women would pop up in my mind a lot in the coming years, when I was hugging my knees into my chest and sobbing in my cell or shivering beneath a scratchy blanket in a hostel with mice running across my feet.

After a bit of exploration, the fair became an abstract painting, the details smudged and bleeding. Everything was moving too fast, unbalancing me. Coming here had obviously been a mistake. There was more than a good chance that the vodka was going to make a comeback, but I'm not sure I cared.

When I think back to what happened next, it always plays out in slow motion. The fair's crammed with people, and there are a lot of passing faces that I think I recognise from school, but none of them stop to say hi or even acknowledge me. I'm walking along, bobbing like a balloon, being nudged and barged, and deafened by the speakers, blinded by the lights. The colours come at me in a kaleidoscopic assault, flashing and throbbing. The artwork on the sunbeaten rides becomes almost hallucinogenic, freakish distortions of things I vaguely recognise – or *think* I recognise: Mickey Mouse on the teacups, Pinhead from *Hellraiser* on the ghost train, a suggestively erotic blond who looks a bit like Pamela Anderson winking on the side of the Waltzer. Screams cut through the air, reverberating as the rides go around, and my heart kicks like a donkey each time. The red-faced women sweating over greasy meat and onions. I'm going to be sick. Mia is walking by my side, and she's watching my face as we walk, and in my peripheral vision I see – or sense – that she's smiling at me. Maybe she's just made a joke that I didn't catch. She's sucking on a candy pacifier that I didn't see her steal. Spinning, lights, jagged laughter, a man's voice muffled over a microphone, but everything is slowing down, isn't it? A stand full of stuffed toys, another hut with packets of popcorn, candyfloss.

Right. I'll just stay here and do the cleaning. As always. I ask Mia if we can stop for a second, I need to catch my breath because I feel weird, and it's just as this thought tries to take form and make some sort of agreement with my mouth that I see him.

My dad is at the fair. And this is the reason why I'm here, isn't it? To remember that one special day we had. But he's here, I've just seen him, walking with a woman, laughing, locked in conversation that doesn't include me, having a great time, creating more wonderful memories.

He's trying to forget me.

"Dad!" I yelled so loud that I felt the cords stand out in my neck, the word burning my throat as it leapt from my lips. I couldn't compete with the clamour of the fair, but seeing him through the crowd was as sobering as a swift slap in the face, partially clearing my head. "Daddy!" I screamed it this time, the tempo of the world speeding back up to something like normal. I waded past the people blocking my path, stumbling around until my coordination failed me and I slammed down onto the ground. Renewed by an almost electrifying sense of urgency, I scrambled back to my feet, distantly aware of Mia following and calling after me.

With my vision blurred by the drink, keeping track of my dad was almost impossible. People kept pushing by, and I had to reset my step at all the sudden, jarring interruptions. Searching for my dad among the chaos of the fair was like getting to grips with an ever-changing optical illusion. The woman he was with didn't matter to me – in fact, I was almost happy for him; anything had to be better than my mum, after all she did to him. And still, I couldn't deny the bonfire of jealousy burning a hole in my stomach. I just needed to see him, hold his hand, hug him as tight as I could.

"Ruby, stop a second." Mia's voice, soupy in my ears, barely registering against the thumping techno music.

Swimming against the tide of fairgoers, I began clawing my way past them, earning staccato bursts of abuse and threats of violence that I didn't acknowledge. I had one goal: to get to my dad. I hadn't seen him since he walked out on us almost three years before, and I knew that if I could just talk to him, remind him that I was still that little girl he bought that inflatable butterfly for, then...

"Where is he?" My feet anchored in the tough grass by the bumper cars. I reached out to a random passer-by for support, who swiftly yanked free of my clasp, almost toppling me. "Mia? Mia where is he?"

She looped an arm around my waist and whispered into my ear, "It's okay, hun, breathe. Don't panic."

"Where is he? Where is he? Where? He was right there!"

"Right where?" she asked, rubbing my shoulder.

When I went to raise my hand and point toward the queue at the ice cream van, it felt as though I were holding a bowling ball. My arm dropped back to my side. "I just saw him walking with a woman right there. He was in line at the ice cream van. He *was*."

I know that's what I wanted to say, but didn't quite have the verbal dexterity to articulate it. Instead of wasting time fumbling through the sentence again, I shrugged out of Mia's clutches and pushed away from the back wall of the bumper cars and made a determined beeline to the ice cream van. Slowly spinning on the spot, gathering a panoramic view of my surroundings, I searched for my dad, but he was gone, lost in the ocean of faces. My eyes ached with the heaviness of oncoming tears, and I wanted to scream very badly.

"Come on, Rube. Let's get back," Mia soothed, her hands lightly guiding me along.

"No, I have to stay and find him. I have to..." But I couldn't finish. The dam broke, and I fell to my knees, sobbing.

CHAPTER 10

I often had nightmares about the accident, but that night after the fair, they were especially vivid.

I'm nine years old in the back of the car. Mum is driving fast, and I am not wearing a seatbelt. "Leave it off," are her exact words, though even as a young girl this feels like a strange command, especially considering she's still wearing hers.

The moments just before the crash are hazy, but I do have an opaque recollection of the tyres screaming as the world spins out of focus. Gravity pulls me to the side, and I brace for impact. My bladder fails me, and warm piss soaks my crotch. Mum raving madly. I can't even understand what she's saying as the car spins. There is an almighty boom as we hit something and I lurch forward, cannon-diving through the windscreen. A heavy, crunching pain over my skull as my head shatters the glass. Then I'm on the cold, wet asphalt, the shock numbing me from head to toe, my entire skeleton encasing in ice. From my grounded vantage point, I can see tree branches bending in the wind on the other side of the road, can hear someone screaming but know that it isn't my mum. Then the blood seeps into my eyes and the picture fades, but I can smell the burnt rubber, the metallic tang of my own blood, the ozone odour of the oncoming storm. The stink of petrol.

Something is seriously wrong with me, and I cannot move. I'm dying.

Then a random jigsaw piece revealing a kind nurse in a hospital, smiling as she stands over me. I can't smile back because there's a tube in my mouth. And can only see her through one eye because the other is blindfolded by bandages.

My dad shouting, the fury of his voice only dampened by the doctors and nurses working in tandem to calm him down. Someone is threatening to call the police. My good eye rolling toward the disturbance, but the footage is lagging, the sound trailing a few seconds behind the action. Then I either hear, or *dream*, my dad screaming "You could have killed her–"

My mum's voice, cold and hard, cut through the dream, snatching me out of the hospital bed I had been bound to for over two weeks.

"… know you're awake."

I thought it was just the dream reconfiguring, some mercurial layer of the nightmare changing in its usual strange and unpredictable way. But my bedroom was silent, so I must've imagined it. Exhaling, I relaxed, and was on the verge of slipping back into uneasy sleep when she repeated, "I know you're awake."

She sounded as though she'd spent the night gargling rocks. I turned to the armchair in the corner of my room and could see a firefly bobbing in the darkness, could smell the cigarette smoke, and was seized with fear. She had almost set her bed on fire twice before by falling asleep with a lit cigarette. Sometimes I think she was deliberately trying to burn the house down.

"Mum?" I asked, my tongue, pebbled with dehydration, glued to the roof of my mouth. In the few hours of sleep that I'd had since coming home from the fair, the vodka had turned my brain into a pin cushion.

"You've been screaming in your sleep," she said. There was no hint of comfort or reassurance in the statement.

"Um... alright," I cleared my throat and said, "I'll try not to again. Sorry if I woke you."

I heard her exhale a plume of smoke and imagined a dragon sitting on the armchair, its throat thick with phlegm. Her breathing was deep and slow. "Do you know what you've been saying?"

"Of course not," I groaned, now able to smell the vomit in my hair from when I'd puked on the way home.

"You said, 'She did it on purpose, Dad.' What's that supposed to mean?"

"N-nothing," I stammered. The way she was talking, it made me feel like spiders were crawling all over me. Sitting up, a shotput rolling in my stomach, I said, "I was just having a bad dream."

She rose from the chair and, for at least half a minute, stood as still as a mannequin. Her slow, methodical breathing was the only sound to be heard.

"I'll try and be quiet," I said, starting to feel as though I were still at the fair and my bed was the carriage of a rollercoaster.

"You're going to have a very bad hangover in the morning," she said, and whirled to leave. "Don't make a mess. While you were out living your life, I was cleaning the toilet. That's just the way of it, isn't it? You go out and have fun, and I deal with the shit. Story of my fucking life. No more screaming."

She slammed my door as she left.

* * *

Mia's parents were a bit of a grey area.

Mia lived on the Barker Lane estate. It's been knocked down now, but it had a very bad reputation in 2002. A female police officer got killed chasing a suspect through that building, and that's what it had been most well-known for at the time, before... *our* thing. Anyway, Mia always came to my house, usually waited by my back gate, or sometimes in the shed.

I never went to her flat. I always offered, but she told me not to. Said she didn't mind travelling to my neighbourhood; that it was nice to get away. She hated being at home with her mum. That's another thing that brought us closer together, I suppose. Except, my mum was Princess Diana compared to what I'd heard about Mia's mum.

They fought a lot. Physically. Sometimes, Mia would turn up to school with bruises, scratches, and even bitemarks that she'd cover up with foundation. When I'd ask how she got them she'd say she had a *dispute* with her mum. That's what she called it. A dispute. Even when we first met at thirteen, it didn't take very long to realise she was being abused. And then there was the other thing Mia always mentioned, about the men. Mia told me that her mum had given birth to her when she was only fifteen, which seemed insane to me at the time, and ever since she was young, her mum had always brought boyfriends over to the flat. That's why Mia always wanted to get out. That's why she went looking for other places to stay, how she found out about all those abandoned buildings she used to go creeping around in. That's how she got so good at breaking into houses.

There was only one time before the whole Vincent Street thing happened that I remember seeing the other side of Mia. Her true face. It was on the Monday after the fair. While

I was licking my wounds, feeling sorry for myself because I couldn't reach my dad, Mia went home, and something even worse happened to her.

She had a dispute with her mum.

I'd been waiting for her in the empty hallway by my tutor room, sitting on the floor next to my locker. It was lunchtime and all the other pupils were either in the canteen or scattered around the school grounds.

I hadn't even heard her approach. The smell hit me straight away. Mia hadn't bathed; her perfume and cigarette smoke fragrance had been replaced with the stale sweat living in her rumpled uniform. I looked at her, momentarily confused, and saw her face through her lank, greasy hair. One eyeball was completely bloodshot. The side of her jaw was puffy and decorated with a greenish bruise that gave her a sickly pallor. There were little red pockmarks in her skin that hadn't scabbed over yet.

"Mia," I whispered. "Your face?"

"Don't," was all she said. There were teeth marks on the back of her hand.

We cut out the back entrance, which was forbidden because that's where the staff car park was. I asked about her face again, figuring that she wasn't going to give up an explanation unless I pushed her for one. "Did your mum do that?"

She nodded but said nothing. Even though some morbidly curious side of me wanted the details, I left it there.

"Did you go to the hospital? Your jaw could be broken."

"It's not broken. I can move it and talk, can't I?" The swelling impacted her speech, giving her a lisp.

"Can you eat?"

"I managed a flapjack this morning, but it hurts to chew."

"Fuck," I said under my breath. "You should go to the police. I'll come with you. Hasn't any of the teachers in the Huts said anything? You need to make a report, and–"

She shook her head and somehow managed a ghastly smile through her misshapen jaw.

"I can't believe she would do this to you," I said. "How *dare* she? What are you going to do?"

"I'm not staying there anymore. I packed up some shit and left."

"Where?"

"One of the flats is empty on the ground floor. They haven't boarded it up yet, so I popped the back window and went in there. Only problem is it doesn't have electricity or water. That's why I smell like a dog."

I palmed my face, barely able to believe what I was hearing. God, it took everything in me not to start bawling, I felt so bad for her. "Jesus, Mia, you can't go on like that."

"So, what am I gonna do? Move into your place? Sleep in your shed?"

"I mean, you can. If it was up to me…"

"I know." She waved my rambling away. "The flat I'm in is fine for now. I just wish it had water, even cold water, so I could wash myself. I used the toilets at Safeway's to have a quick whore's bath, but it's not enough. No deodorant. Will have to remember to pick some up today."

"I can't even believe you made it to school today," I said, genuinely in awe of her. She was a survivor, and I couldn't help but admire her for that.

"I didn't know what else to do. Can't just be on the street all day or I'll get picked up by the truant officer, and all they'll fucking do is take me home. And I can't sit in that flat all day without a TV and nothing to do."

"You're tough as nails, Mia, you know that?"

"I don't feel it."

"You are. I wish I was half as tough as you, I really do."

We came to the zebra crossing and were just about to step out into the road when an approaching car honked. The car was supposed to give way to pedestrians, but the driver had other ideas, coming within five feet of running us over. Startled, we both jerked to a stop and spun toward the driver like a couple of deer in the headlights. The driver was an animated blond woman in her early forties, flapping her hand at us and mouthing obscenities as though *we* were in the wrong.

And that's when Mia exploded. There was no warning, no steady build-up, no time to stop and think about what was happening. She just walked to the driver's door, opened it, and grabbed two handfuls of the woman's hair. The woman screamed, clutching at Mia's wrists, trying to break free of the grasp. Her knee hit the horn, and a long, angry blare sounded. Mia clawed the woman's face, trying to hook her fingers into her eyes. The sheer ferocity of the attack stunned me to my core. Mia was trying to blind the woman; I was sure of it. She was like a pit bull that had locked its jaws. The only thing keeping the woman in the car was the seatbelt, which in hindsight was very lucky. If Mia had got her onto the floor, I don't know what would've happened.

Mia now had both hands around the woman's face. The woman was shrieking and bleeding from her nose. Mia's mouth opened wide, and she was going to bite into the woman's head, just sink her teeth right into her skull. The only thing that stopped her was the driver in the car behind.

"What are you doing over there?" the tall, bearded man asked, piling out of his car, leaving his door open.

Mia released the whimpering woman and spun on the man. I didn't even see her pull the knife – didn't even know she had one. I just saw the sun gleaming on the blade as she extended it out toward him.

"What are you going to do, you fucking cunt?" she snarled at him through clenched teeth. "Come here and I'll stick this in you, you fucking pig bastard."

I'm not sure what scared the man more: the knife or the possessed look on her face. Either way, the Good Samaritan retreated to his car and quickly slammed the door behind him.

"Put that away, Mia," I managed to say, but I was shaking all over. I was trying to snag her attention, but her eyes were fixed on the bearded man. Meanwhile, the woman she had attacked sped off down the road with her driver's door still open. I urged Mia out of the road, keeping my hands on her arms. The hot charge of adrenaline had turned the muscles in my legs to play dough.

That whole exchange had taken less than twenty seconds.

"Take your hands off me, Ruby," Mia said in a low, controlled voice when we were around the corner and away from the main road. I released her, suddenly very conscious that the blade was still out.

"Mia, they're going to call the police," I said in a wobbly voice.

"So what?" she asked, finally folding the blade and putting it back in her pocket. "What can they do to me?"

As far as I can remember, that was the last time Mia attended St Monica's.

CHAPTER 11

The thing that set everything off sort of happened out of the blue. This was a couple of weeks after Mia went berserk on that lady in the car. It was the last day of term before the summer break, which was coincidental but not really significant – at least, I don't think so. Later on, when I was cross examined, I remember the prosecutor saying something about how I felt tremendous pressure because I was about to go into my final year at school, and that this added to why we ended up at Vincent Street. But none of that's true.

If we hadn't finished school early because it was the last day of term, if I'd been on a different bus, if I'd been reading a book, if I'd been talking to Mia, then I wouldn't have seen him at all. But it was fate. I was predestined to see him. There really is no other way to describe it. I was sitting at the back of the bus, head resting against the window, sort of just watching the world go by in the bright, optimistic summer sunshine. It was a journey I'd been on hundreds of times before. You could have dropped me off at any stop along that route and I would have been able to make it home with a blindfold. And on this afternoon, the bus was passing that stretch of shops along Cresthill Avenue. I don't know what's there now, but back in June of 2002, there was an ice cream place, a newsagent, a video rental shop called Apollo, and a laundrette.

My dad was sitting down on a bench in the laundrette, absently watching a washing machine. There was no mistaking him: his posture, the way he had his legs crossed and his foot dangled. Even the clothes he wore: the short-sleeve shirt, brown shoes – loafers. I immediately sat up as though jolted by an electric current, and my hand whipped out to press the bell. The bus was already pulling away from the stop, so I thumbed the bell a few more times, *ding-ding-ding-ding-ding*, and shouted for the driver to let me off. Barging through the busy lower deck, elbowing the other St Monica's pupils out the way, I frantically announced to the driver that it was an emergency. When he ignored me and continued driving, I flipped up the plastic case covering the emergency button to activate the doors, pressed it, and jumped off the moving bus. I landed on my feet, but the momentum sent me sprawling across the pavement amidst a string of panicked pedestrians. My knee had smashed against the floor, and I scraped my face on the concrete. But both those ailments were muted by the roaring urge to move, to get back on my feet and dash to the laundrette before my dad could vanish from my life again.

My heavy school shoes clip-clopped clumsily as I floundered to the laundrette door, the sun baking me inside my uniform. When I swung the door open, my dad's head whipped toward me as though a bomb had exploded, and there was a passing moment where neither one of us seemed to quite recognise the other. It was definitely my dad, but he had changed so much in the two years since I'd last seen him up close. His face had a droopy, forlorn quality to it, the skin loose as though it didn't quite fit him properly. He had dark pouches beneath his watery eyes, and there was so much more salt in his hair than there was pepper. Besides that, he had lost a lot of weight. He'd never been a big man, but he'd always had a small paunch that I often used as a pillow whenever I lay down on the couch next to him. Now, his meagre frame swam inside clothes that seemed as though they should belong to someone else. He was a sad, rumpled old scarecrow.

"Dad," I shouted, panting. The word had come out in an excited, panicked rush, too loud and sudden to be part of any comfortable conversation. Luckily, we were the only ones inside the laundrette, but it wouldn't have mattered to me if the place was full of customers. The moisture had evaporated from my mouth, and I had to work hard to swallow. "Dad, what the fuck?"

"Ruby," he began to say, shaking his head. When he stood up, I heard his knees click. "Oh, Ruby, this isn't a good idea."

"What are you talking about?" I said, feeling the mercury in my internal thermometer rising. "Where have you been? Mum said you moved to Blackpool."

His tongue slithered from between his thin lips, his face taking on a spiteful, pinched expression. "Did she?"

"Yeah. Said that you were up there drinking yourself stupid and… Why haven't you called me?"

He looked away as though he had clothes spinning in one of the other machines. "This is not the right time or place to have this conversation."

"I haven't seen or heard from you in two years." My voice warbled and cracked, and when I blinked, tears dripped from my lashes and ran down my flushed cheeks. "Did I do something wrong? What is it? Just tell me."

He regarded me with a peculiar mix of softness and pity before the spell broke and his features hardened. He pressed a button on the washing machine to stop the cycle and flung the door open. Hot air buffeted from the drum as he scooped his half-dry clothes into a laundry bag.

"I saw you at the fair last month," I said.

"Fair?"

"Yeah. I was calling you and you couldn't hear me and…"

"It's better that we just leave things the way they are," he said, refusing to look at me. "Everything is broken, and we can't fix it, so let's just leave the pieces where they are and move on. The only way we can get past it all is if we forget and move on."

"Forget? Dad?" I clasped his wrist and felt his arm turn rigid at my touch. "Dad…" I breathed, barely able to see through the tears. "How could you do this to me? How could you just walk out and not even call?"

"Because we need to forget it all," he said, his voice rising, thick with emotion. "You don't think this hurts me, too? You don't think this has…" He slapped a hand over his face and clamped his teeth together, a scream revving in his throat. "This has killed me, Ruby. It has *killed* me."

He dropped the laundry bag and slammed the washing machine door so hard that it clanged and flung back again, the sound shuddering through the laundrette. Panting now, his shoulders were bunched, and I just had time to notice that his hands were clenched into fists before he punched the machine. Once, twice, and the third time he struck it; he left bloody smudges on the peeling plastic casing.

The outburst frightened me, but I didn't falter or step back. My dad had never hit me, and I could never foresee a scenario in which that would change.

"I could come and live with you," I said. "I don't want to live with *her*. She's got worse since you left. I hate her. I could live with you, Dad. I wouldn't be any trouble, I promise. You know I wouldn't."

My dad covered his face with his swollen, bloody hands and remained like that for at least a minute. I kept expecting the owner of the laundrette to wander in and raise a complaint about my dad's behaviour, but nobody did. With his face hidden, I heard him discreetly crying, probably embarrassed that he had broken down in front of me. It was the first time I'd ever seen him cry. This was where we were supposed to hug. This was where we both fell apart and bawled our eyes out and declared our unyielding love for one another. This was where we forgot the nightmare of these past few years and made a solemn promise to never leave one another again, to build a bridge over those choppy waters and live happily ever after. And in a film or a book, that's exactly what would've happened. Except for one thing. He *wasn't* crying.

He was laughing.

"Oh, Ruby," he said, my name muffled against his palms. "Ruby, Ruby, Ruby."

"What's going on?" I asked, and it were as though a freezing-cold breeze had blown in, chilling my blood, encasing my heart in a thin layer of frost. I began to crumble.

His hands dropped away, and he tilted his head back, directing his laughter at the pocked and scuffed ceiling. He stopped a moment before fresh waves of hilarity swept over him, the giggles swelling and tumbling from his lips in high, hyena yips.

"What's so funny? Stop it, Dad," I pleaded as gooseflesh broke out across my cheeks. "You're scaring me, stop it."

When his laughter receded, he wiped his eyes with his fingertips and cleared his throat. "She hasn't told you, has she?"

"Told me what?"

The muscles in his jaw tensed. His complexion darkened, and he clamped his lower lip between his teeth, shaking his head. "That fucking bitch. That fucking *cowardly* bitch," he amended. He bent over to zip his laundry bag, leaving a stray sock behind, and looped the strap over his shoulder. "Best thing to do is just forget everything, Ruby. Forget it all. It's the only way."

With his focus trained solely on the door in front of him, he sidestepped the bench he'd been sitting on and headed out. The instant explosion of panic almost caused my heart to punch through my chest. I ran around the bench to intercept him before he got to the door, wrapping him in a hug and squeezing as tightly as I could manage. A pungent waft of beer enveloped me as I held onto him.

"No, Dad, don't go. At least let me know where you're staying. We could meet up and have lunch or something. Don't go, *please*." My pitiful appeal came out in a jumble as he worked at prying loose from my grip. He was slipping away, just like that day when I was thirteen, watching the argument between my parents unfold as I sat at the top of the stairs, silently willing him to stay. "Please Dad, just tell me what to do."

With a single thrash, he broke free of my embrace, thrusting his bony hands out and clutching my shoulders to keep me at arm's length. "Stop it, now," he commanded in that same authoritative tone I was familiar with; that was the voice he used when I'd been naughty, when I'd jump on the sofa or had answered back with something cheeky or rolled my eyes at him. "Just stop this, Ruby. It can't go on any longer. It..." He shook his head, sagging slightly. He gave me one final appraisal, tears dropping freely from his hooded eyes now and running over stubble. The way he was looking at me, *dissecting* me, was like an arrow through my heart.

When his hands dropped from my shoulders, it felt as though I might sink right through the linoleum. I watched him leave the laundrette without glancing back, and this time, I did not try to follow. Bawling, almost choking on my tears, I stood there, misery mooring me to the spot. Those familiar bubbles began popping in my head, and if I didn't sit down soon and regain my composure, I was going to faint.

Just as the laundrette began to lose solidity, someone walked through the door.

It was Dad. He'd changed his mind, come back to reconsider my offer, to apologise and tell me he'd been too hasty, that the emotion had got the better of him. That was fine, the emotion had got the better of me, too, and it was only natural, all things considered. Sniffling, I smiled so wide that my cheeks ached.

"Ruby," he said, blinking a lot but not quite able to look me in the face. He held his hand out – either to prevent me from interrupting, or to stop me from getting any closer, I wasn't sure. "You know what, you're a big girl now. You're almost sixteen–"

"I'm finishing school soon," I added hopefully, as though it might strengthen my case.

"Stop talking. Just let me speak." He blinked hard as he said this, his eyes briefly fixing on me before flitting away again. "All I ever tried to do is protect you."

"Yes." I wiped snot from my nose and nodded frantically. "Of course. I get it."

"I always had my suspicions about your mother. *Always.* She's not half as clever as she thinks she is. And for the love of God, I should have walked years ago. You were the only thing that made me stay as long as I did."

"I love you, Dad," I said, and it came out almost like a cat mewling.

Ignoring the declaration, he continued: "The crash. You know, don't you?" He saw me scrambling for an answer, stuttering through my confusion. His face soured, eyes squinting. "I was going to leave back then because I had my suspicions about her, and… about you. But after you got hurt, how could I walk out then?"

It felt like someone was standing on my chest. When I tried to speak, only a strained whisper came out.

"There was nothing wrong with those brakes. Do you know what I'm saying? Nod your head if you know."

I nodded.

"Good girl. But you deserve to hear what I think – what I *know* but could never prove. Do you want to hear it? You're old enough to understand it now, but make sure you want to hear it, because once it's out, I can't take it back." Every word was laboured, his shoulders rising and falling with the strain of speaking.

"Just tell me," I said, drying my eyes on my blazer. "Whatever it is."

"Alright. Your mother thought that if you were gone, I'd stay with her. That's why she crashed the car. That's why your seatbelt wasn't on and hers was."

"Jesus Christ, Dad…" A shiver rode up my spine, culminating in a dull pop inside my head that instantly made me giddy.

"I'm not your father, Ruby. I'm sorry for how this has turned out for both of us, but if I can give you anything – anything at all – it would be this piece of advice: get away from her. Do you hear? Get away as soon as you can, because she's nothing but poison. She didn't get you with the crash. But she'd probably try again. I wouldn't put it past her." He opened his mouth to say more but decided against it.

He left, seeming pummelled and dazed as he wandered away.

I knew then that I'd never see him again.

CHAPTER 12

I don't remember how I made it back from the laundrette that day, but Mum was sitting in the armchair by the window when I got through the front door. Cigarette smoke hung like a phantom over the living room. The TV was on and turned up loud, but she wasn't watching it. She was just sitting there, staring at the wall opposite, lost in a trance.

I let my backpack drop to my side and remained in the hallway, waiting for her to acknowledge me. When she didn't, I said, "I've just seen Dad."

"Oh?"

"Yeah," I said, the rims of my eyes stinging, the front of my shirt damp with tears. "Sorry, I mean the man you let me think was my dad."

There was something almost reptilian about the way her hand slowly hovered to the remote and turned the TV off. The sudden silence was more invasive than the overloud soap opera dialogue.

"You have no idea what you're talking about, Ruby. You have no concept of the real world."

"Don't I?"

"No, you don't." A cone of ash dropped from the cigarette and fell onto her lap. She began muttering to herself, shaking her head. She said something about me living in a fantasy world, but I didn't catch all of it. This is how she was acting behind the wheel that day when she drove us off the road. A whisper of fear echoed in me as those sepia-toned Polaroids fanned through my memory: the broken glass, the wet tarmac, one hand trying to curl into a fist, the stink of burnt rubber. Petrol.

"You tried to kill me in that crash."

"This again. Aren't you bored of making up these little stories, Ruby?"

"It's not a story. For a long time, I thought maybe I was remembering everything wrong. But I wasn't. Dad even said so. And I knew it. I knew you did it on purpose."

"Richard is a fucking drunk," she spat. "And if he thinks I'd put myself through that crash to stay with *him*, then he's even crazier than you are."

"But you did. He was going to leave you because he found out I wasn't his daughter. And you thought of a way to solve that problem. You ruined our lives!" Now I was beginning to see the funny side in it all. It was no wonder my dad could barely look at me; I reminded him of the betrayal. I was the living, breathing personification of his gullibility. I have fair skin and bright red hair, and my dad has olive skin and black hair, and there had to be a punchline in all that, didn't there?

"You have clothes on your back, food in your stomach, and a roof over your head, don't you? Ruined your life? Go and tell that to someone in Bosnia who's just had bombs dropped on their house. Go and whine about how hard your life is to the people who lost family in nine-eleven." She twisted the cigarette out in an ashtray, and said, "I have given up everything for you, Ruby. You have no idea. *No* idea. It's *my* life that's been ruined. *Mine*. You still get to go out and do whatever you want. But I don't have that luxury, do I? Oh, no. I'm stuck here. In this fucking house. With *you*. And let me tell you something, Ruby: you're no trip to Disneyland yourself, not with all your selfishness and your headaches. You *are* a fucking headache. So what man is going to want me? I'm just going to sit here and shrivel up and die lonely while you go about your business, ungrateful for everything! Who would want me?"

"Are you going to admit it then?" I asked.

"Admit what?"

"The *truth*." The words rocketed from my mouth, but Mum didn't even flinch. She just continued sitting there, unmoving, like a frog waiting for a fly to pass so it could flick out its tongue and catch it. "For God's sake, Mum. You tried to kill me; the least you could do now is tell me the truth."

"Oh, I tried to kill you, that's right. I'm a murderer now on top of everything else, am I?"

"Dad even said so," I hissed.

"Let me get this straight, Ruby, now that you're such a big grown-up girl who knows everything about everything. I – your mother – crashed the car on purpose to kill you. And I did this so that Richard would stay with me, yes? Right so far? Good. So why didn't he tell the police that, Ruby? Hmm? Why didn't he get in touch with the social services, if I'm such a monster? Do tell me, I'd love to know. This is just such a fascinating insight into how your mind works, it really is."

"Because..."

"Because that's not what happened," she yelled. "He's a drunk, and he wants to say whatever he thinks will hurt me – and you. You got that through your head? Your sweet beloved Richard isn't the saint you think he is, either." She stopped, globs of foam gathering in the corner of her mouth. "Here it is then, Ruby. Are you ready? I had an affair," she said, but there was no shame or embarrassment in the admission. It was simply a statement of fact. "You are the result of that affair. And believe me when I tell you, if I could turn the clock back and save myself the bother..."

The callousness in which she relayed this stunned me. I hadn't moved from the hallway, and she hadn't deviated from the armchair. Her face was pinched and petulant, and she was sucking in her cheeks the same way she did when she was building up to explode. She was also rocking, very slightly. "Richard couldn't have children. We tried for a few years before you were born. We went to a specialist, and we were both tested. We were told it wasn't a complete impossibility, but that the odds were not in our favour, even with IVF. Do you know what IVF is, Ruby? Of course you do. You know everything."

"So, you betrayed him."

Raising her chin haughtily, she said, "If I hadn't, you wouldn't be standing there right now."

"Trust me, I wish I wasn't."

"That makes two of us. Oh, you look so offended, Ruby. Don't worry about all the allegations you've thrown at me already. What's the matter, that hurt your feelings a little bit? A big grownup like you? Good. Because I've worked my entire life to spare your feelings. What about me? What about my feelings?"

I was vibrating with anger. My heart was pumping too fast, the blood rushing to my head. The stress of the conversation sending strange signals of pain and discomfort throughout my body.

She tapped out another cigarette from the packet, placed it between her lips and sparked up. Black snow was falling in my vision, burying the picture. Closing my eyes, the floor fell away from me, and I began floating, teetering on the edge of oblivion. My legs wouldn't obey my command to move, and so I half-stepped, half-fell onto the stairs to alleviate the burden of my weight. I was going to pass out again, could feel the ticklish numbing sensation through the fault line in my skull.

No, don't you dare take the easy way out, I thought, blinking exaggeratedly to restore some clarity. *You finish this with her now. No fainting. No faint…*

Everything adjusted and snapped back into focus. I took a deep breath and retrained my hateful gaze on her.

"Ah, here we go," she said, rolling her eyes. "Let me guess: this is where you pass out? Get a new routine, Ruby. You're boring, you really are."

"Attempted murder," I said slowly, renewed by the strength those words gave me. "You were speeding–"

"I wasn't speeding."

"–and you were crying your eyes out and you were saying that it was all over and–"

"The roads were wet, Ruby. We were driving in a storm."

"–and you told me I wouldn't need a seatbelt because–"

"That's not what happened, Ruby. I always told you to *wear* a seatbelt and you always unclipped it. I would never tell you not to wear one. I'm not a fucking lunatic."

"–because I was going to heaven, and it wouldn't be scary because–"

"RUBY!" She shot up from the chair and slapped me in the side of the head, sparks jumping from the cigarette. "Stop this right now. What the fucking hell is wrong with you? That isn't what happened."

Her strike barely unbalanced me. "It is," I said, icily, rubbing my head. "I remember *everything*."

"Then you remember it wrong! You always remember everything wrong. We were driving in a storm. Yes, I was crying. I'd had a huge fight with your" – she was about to say *dad* and then corrected herself – "Richard, and the brakes were no good; a mechanic told him that he needed new brake pads, and he never got them fixed because he was so fucking cheap. The roads were wet, and that fox jumped out in front of the car."

"There was no fox," I argued. "You can hit me as many times as you want. It won't change the truth. And I believe Dad a thousand times more than I believe you."

She looked at the cigarette and stubbed it out. "I'm so difficult to live with," she began, a nasty smirk slashing across her face. "All I do is cook and clean and make sure this place is a home, for you – the little princess who sits in her room all day and night, dreaming up new ways to be mad at the world. Don't worry about Mum. Don't worry about how I have no friends, no boyfriend, no fucking company all because of you. Well, you're sixteen in a few months. That's old enough to get a job. That's probably old enough to start renting a place of your own, I'd imagine."

"It is. And I intend to."

"Perfect." She sat back down with a sense of triumph, as though I had walked into one of her traps. "Why don't you go now, then? Go on, get a move on. I think that's a great idea. I would love to see your attitude after a week of working all day, and then paying bills, and trying to find the money to eat after that. I think you'll find that being a grownup is a little trickier than it fucking well looks."

"I'll take my chances," I said, knowing that I was rising to the bait, knowing that this was exactly what she wanted.

"Go on, then." She waved toward the door. "You've got it all figured out, I assume? Make a head start if that's what you want. I won't stop you. A dose of the real world might be just the thing you need. After all, I'm so scary to live with, I might try and kill you in your sleep. Isn't that about right? Excellent, this works out for both of us, then, doesn't it? Maybe without you carrying that dark cloud around with you everywhere, *I* can finally have some fun for a change. Some happiness. Because let me tell you something, Princess Ruby, I haven't been happy since the day you were born. All you've ever brought is misery with you."

There was no point in arguing any longer. Instead, I picked up my backpack and thumped upstairs. Once in my room, I tipped out the bag, emptying my textbooks and pens onto the carpet, and began filling it with essentials: underwear, a change of clothes, a toothbrush, and hairbrush. The whole transaction took less than two minutes. When I descended the stairs, the front door was open in anticipation of my departure, and my mum was no longer in the living room.

"You haven't even asked," Mum called from the kitchen. It sounded like she was smiling, goading me. "You haven't even asked who your dad is. Your real dad."

No, I thought. *And I'm never going to give you the satisfaction of holding that information over me.*

When I left the house, I could hear Mum laughing and cheering. *Celebrating*. "Good luck, Princess Ruby," she screamed into the empty living room. "Good fucking luck."

There was only one person I could count on. I removed my phone and composed a text message.

Mia, I need you.

CHAPTER 13

The sky was mottled with lavender clouds by the time I arrived on Barker Lane. It was difficult not to feel neurotic as I crossed the courtyard, jumping at every sound that echoed through the warren of landings and underpasses.

Clusters of kids hung around the benches and lurked in the darkened doorways like jackals awaiting prey. I moved quickly and purposefully, keeping my head up, looking straight forward. I took a seat on a nearby ledge that skirted the large, patchy yellow lawn in the centre of the courtyard and thumbed a quick text to Mia to let her know I was there.

In the distance behind me, I heard the shattering of glass reverberating off the walls followed by gales of laughter. Someone had probably broken a milk bottle, or a car window, or a phone box, who knew? Another smash, more laughter. What were they doing? I turned and squinted through the stretching shadows, trying to make out the activity, but all I could see were scurrying silhouettes.

Then I heard another sound. Footsteps approaching to my right. A girl was walking toward me, her fur-lined hood concealing her face. I got to my feet, but before I could say anything, her hand lashed out and clasped me around the wrist. A grunt of surprise and confusion left my mouth and was about to graduate to a scream when the girl pulled the hood down.

The relief cascaded over me like a waterfall. It was Mia.

"My heart," I said when I was able to speak again. "My heart just exploded. Oh, my God."

One corner of her mouth curled up into a smile. "You finally made it."

"Yeah." I laughed, one hand on my chest trying to sooth my booming heart.

"Come on." She motioned with her head for me to follow her. She led me around the main building, following a high wall that bordered the ground floor's back gardens. She stopped by a wheelie bin that had been strategically placed against the garden wall and, with little effort at all, clambered on top of it. "Do you need help up?" she asked.

"No, I think I can do it," I said, before attempting to hoist myself up. Seeing that I was struggling, she grabbed me under the armpits and pulled me onto the wheelie bin.

She then climbed over the wall, landing on a sofa in the back garden before dusting her hands off. I followed behind her, awkwardly plopping down onto the rain-rotted sofa, almost tumbling face first into the knee-high grass. The streetlight on the other side of the wall gave just enough illumination to reveal that the back door of the flat had a heavy metal grille over it. However, a small rectangular window remained unprotected. The glass had been smashed out of the frame, presumably by Mia, who warned me to watch myself as I wriggled in after her.

The stink of festering mould and damp rose to greet me as I negotiated a bathtub on my way in. The darkness swallowed me. Mia removed a lighter from her pocket, lit a candle, and took me into her living quarters, using the flaming wick to light the dozen or so other stubs of candle dotted around.

She sat down on her mattress in the corner of the room and picked up a container of Chinese food. How she could even think to eat in this place was beyond me. Behind her, the same metal grilles covered the windows.

Mia offered me some of her food and a can of beer, both of which I declined. Then she said, "You'd better tell me what happened."

Before I could get to that, though, I said, "Mia, what is this place?"

"It's where I come to hide out," she said, with a giggle that reminded me of tiny bells jingling together. "What do you think?"

The jittery candlelight revealed plywood walls camouflaged in sinister graffiti: rudimentary sketches of devil faces, monsters with jagged teeth, naked women with enormous busts. And writing, twisty and looping, scrawled in long, nonsensical sentences.

"It's scary," I said.

"You get used to it. Anyway, less about me and more about you." She squeezed my fingers. "What's going on?"

I told her about the fight with my mum. She listened without interruption, chewing and swallowing, chewing and swallowing. Gradually, a hot flush of embarrassment began to flare up in me as I detailed the argument. Mia washed her food down with a long pull on the beer can and said, "Everything happens for a reason, Rube."

"What does that mean?"

"It means that me and you are two sides of the same coin. Look at us now: the girls who nobody wants. You think I come down here and hide out by choice? No, but it's the only way to get away from home. And now you're here with me, and that's the way it should be, isn't it? And just for the record, I think your mum is right."

"What?" I couldn't believe what I'd just heard.

"She's right. We've got to make it on our own now. You know that, don't you?"

"I guess so," I said, more sulkily than I had intended.

"No, there's no *guess so*. Your dad split on you, your mum literally kicked you out." Mia leaned in, the candlelight becoming embers in her wide, black pupils. "It's just you and me now. Right?" I became aware of the small sounds that perforated the darkness, positive that I could hear vermin squeaking and scurrying around, searching for scraps.

"Unless you want to go back to your mum's?"

"How can I?" It came out hoarsely, and my head began to swim with dizziness again. Sweat pushed through my pores, and the scratching seemed to rise in volume. How many rats were in there with us? "But I can't stay here. And neither can you."

"I know," she said, taking her last mouthful of Chinese before tossing the carton. I heard it hit the floor, and then the foil scraping against the bare floorboards as it was dragged away. "This was only temporary until I got my head together. I've been working things out." She carried the candle across the room to a bulging bin bag on the floor. After rooting through it, she eventually returned with a toiletry bag and handed it to me.

"What's this?" I asked. My first thought was that she was offering me a spare toothbrush to use, that her plan was to leave this flat and sleep in the park or something crazy like that.

"Open it," she said.

Holding it next to the candlelight, I unzipped the bag and saw a tangle of gold: bracelets, necklaces, a string of pearls, a watch with an expensive-looking leather strap, a beautiful jewel-encrusted brooch in the shape of a butterfly. Aside from her treasures, there were notes crumpled in there, maybe as much as two hundred pounds.

"I've been going into houses," she said, and the simplistic phrasing of her crimes threw me off. "Nearly got caught yesterday, too."

"Are you serious?" I asked.

"I went a couple of blocks away and saw this big house that had a driveway, but no car," she began. "And you know something else? They had these huge bay windows with their curtains wide open so you could stare straight into their living room." She was almost panting with excitement as she relayed her misdemeanour. "There was nobody in. I waited on the other side of the street and couldn't see anything stirring inside. So, I got over the back gate, broke out the kitchen window and picked the place clean."

"Was this at night?"

"No way. Middle of the day." She chuckled gleefully.

"Swear to God."

"On your mum's life," Mia said, laughing again, and this time I reluctantly joined in. There was something eerie about hearing her tell that story without being able to see her lips move.

"This is so… intense."

"It's survival," she clarified. "I've been sleeping in this place for weeks, hiding out from my mum so that her friends can't get their hands on me. I'd rather die than that. Breaking into these big houses… it's nothing. And what's a few missing things to them compared to what I – what we – go through. It's a means to an end. And I think…" She broke away, grabbed my hand in the dark. "I think we can make it to Blackpool with enough to set ourselves up for a while, at least until we find work. Then you can track your dad down – I mean Blackpool can't be that big, and–"

"He was never in Blackpool," I told her. "Mum just said that. We went there on holiday when I was a kid. Had a great time. Fuck." I rubbed my head. "It's one of the best memories I have. And she's ruined that for me too."

Seeing my distress, Mia held my hand, and almost instantly that urge to begin bawling evaporated.

"We can start new memories of our own," she said gently. "Good memories. Better memories. Memories you deserve. How about it? We'd only need to do one more house, and I know the perfect place. It's big, isolated. We can get in and out easily, and we're bound to come away with a decent haul. I mean, you have to see this house, Ruby. It's begging to be broken into."

The word 'we' flashed through my head like a beacon.

For the moment, I said nothing, just continued mulling her proposal over, unable to quite believe what I was hearing.

Two days later, we broke into the house on Vincent Street.

"It's often debated and widely accepted that there would have been more murders. Ruby Wilcox is the personification of true, unbridled evil."

– *Simon Ward, Dead Behind the Eyes*

"Nobody is born evil, if such a thing as evil exists in the first place."

– *Floyd Wilkinson, Mayhem in Mind: The Untold Truth of The Vincent Street Incident*

"Alright, people. No matter where you are in the country this morning, I want to wish you a wonderful start to your day!"

– *George McDermott, Wake Up, UK*

CHAPTER 14

After that first day of shooting, a car picked Henry and I up and dropped us back at our scruffy hotel room that overlooked the motorway. In bed, after I'd emptied the minibar, Henry asked if I felt any better.

"No," I told him, bunching the blankets in my fists, worried that the room was about to start tilting and twirling. "But we haven't really got to the bad stuff yet, have we?"

No. That came today.

Peter Fidditch waited for us beneath the entrance's awning, smoking a cigarette. Aside from us, there didn't seem to be anyone else on the premises. Fidditch waved the driver to come closer to the entrance, and when Henry and I exited from the car, Fidditch flicked the cigarette into the mud.

"Morning," he said, shielding his eyes from the sun, which had made a rare cameo appearance from behind the curtain of clouds. "How are you today, Luanne?"

"I'm very well, thank you," I said, expecting him to continue with the pleasantries before walking us in. But he didn't. That cheery optimism that seemed to exude from his pores started to wane, and he became gravely serious.

"Luanne, I was wondering something. And of course, like everything else, feel free to say no," he started, leading us into the building and toward the greenscreen. "But I have some more photos I'd like you to look at before we begin this next section of the story."

We stopped at the laptop behind the camera setup. Before he even logged in, I knew what he wanted to show me.

"It's the Vincent Street house, isn't it?" I said, the muscles in my face becoming almost painfully taut.

"Yes," he confirmed. "As I say, you don't have to look at them, but–"

"What would the purpose be?" I sliced across his fumbling, feeling as though my bowels were filling with ice water. A centipede of pain lightly skittered through the bad side of my skull – the side that had cracked and almost shattered when I went through the windscreen.

"There was absolutely no mention of this in any of our correspondences," Henry said, pushing his glasses up the bridge of his nose, the dough of his soft face hardening as he came to my defence. "I'm not sure I like this. This could be extremely traumatic for Luanne."

"I understand that," Fidditch said, patting the air between them in a placating gesture. "But perhaps it's essential to the documentary for her to see the house again. They're not the crime scene photos, if that's what you're thinking. I want Luanne to relay her story with as much detail as she can remember. But it has been twenty-five years. The photos could be helpful."

"You think it will help me relive it," I said, "which will bring out a more dramatic performance from me, I suppose."

"That's exactly right. It needs to be authentic. As sadistic as it sounds, I need to get you as close to that week in 2002 as possible."

"She remembers it all in very vivid detail," Henry said. "You needn't worry about that."

"I'm not worried," Fidditch said with the first hint of annoyance. "Luanne, it's up to you. But I know you don't want to run from the truth anymore. Facing the photos is part of it. If it really does become too much, then by all means, we can stop."

"You don't have to whip me into an emotional frenzy to get some kind of authentic reaction. It's going to be emotional enough as it is," I said.

"That's not what I'm trying to do at all," he replied. "Obviously, I know it's unpleasant, but I honestly think it's necessary."

Nodding, feeling oddly walled in between Fidditch and Henry, I inhaled and said, "Fine. You're the director."

Fidditch seemed to analyse my response, and said, "Luanne, I know you have trouble trusting people. But everything we've done throughout the process of this documentary is for the good of the truth – the truth that the entire world is ignorant of."

"No, I get it," I said, feeling as though this was all building up into something far more awkward and stressful than it needed to be. "I don't like it, but I don't like any of this. I wish I didn't have to tell this story. I wish none of it happened. But it did, and so here we are." I released a shaky breath and wrung my hands together, trying to get some sensation back in them. A dull numbness was migrating through my body. It wasn't entirely unpleasant; perhaps it was a defence mechanism, protecting me from the relapse of this trauma. "Let's not just keep talking about it. Let's rip the scab off and get on with it."

"That's the best way," Fidditch said, and opened the laptop lid. He clicked a folder on the desktop labelled VS HOUSE PICS.

"Luanne, are you sure you're alright with this?" Henry asked, his palm resting on my lower back. "I had no idea about this. If you've got a bad feeling about it, we can just stop with the photos. This wasn't in the contract."

A bad feeling. What a choice of words. I'd had a bad feeling ever since the man I thought was my dad had left me. Every day since then, a storm cloud had drifted over my head, perpetually pissing down on me. Today was no different.

"Henry, let's just get this done," I told him. "I just have to get the story down. That's my only choice. The pictures can't hurt me. I see the house every night in my dreams anyway."

He nodded, and there was perhaps even a mild stirring of relief behind those thick frames.

Fidditch began clicking through the gallery of photos. An acidic burp burned the back of my throat as I looked at them. I was struck with a tremendous sense of fear and sadness. I could feel the muscle beneath my left eye start to twitch involuntarily.

"Henry," I called uncertainly, holding out my hand for him to take.

"I'm here," he cooed. "I'm here. Do you want to stop?"

The laptop screen became a time portal. I was immediately shuttled back to 2002. I was in the house with the chequered floor tiles in the hallway, and the large, leafy rubber plant by the front door. I could only hear the tremble of my breath as my heart galloped painfully in my chest, and blood rushing in my ears like the hush of the ocean. Fiddich was talking, but I only knew this because I saw his mouth moving.

The floral gold decal against the lime green of the hallway walls. The framed and signed *Gone with the Wind* movie poster hanging on the wall just before the entrance of the kitchen. The chunky, solid silver frame of the floor-to-ceiling mirror before the living room. Even the house phone – sleek black plastic with a neon green halo, seeming futuristic even twenty-five years later.

"This... hard I kn... ake as much... need..." Fidditch's voice tuned in and dropped out as though we were on a bad connection, and not three feet away from one another. He gestured to the chair in front of the green screen. Fidditch's assistant, the gangly woman, bobbed in the background, watching me closely, one hand to her mouth as she nibbled her thumbnail nervously.

Little rockets fired in my stomach, and I started to feel as though I might have the first stirrings of food poisoning or was maybe teetering on the edge of an episode of diarrhoea, because my insides had turned to mush, and Fidditch was still talking, and I think I was nodding.

"Can we hold on a second," I tried to say, but wasn't sure how much of the sentence came out. The sickness was in the base of my throat, ready to creep up and explode from my lips if I so much as opened my mouth a hair's breadth wider.

"Luanne?" Fidditch mouthing the name, those blue eyes suddenly alive with concern, his hands outstretched toward me.

Henry came into view, his brow deeply furrowed. "Luanne? Look at me, love."

"The living room is wrong..." I said again, trying to regulate my breathing through my nostrils. *There was a huge picture above that fireplace.* Henry's hands seized my wrists. *George McDermott and his wife, cuddling their young daughter who was smiling through missing front teeth... They looked... so happy... so happy to be together... loving each other... That little girl's face.*

I heard some approximation of "She's going down!" from Fidditch, and then felt all the muscles in my body give up on me, one by one. The strength fled my legs and my knees buckled under me. In the process of falling, my head rolled back and I was confronted by the blindingly harsh studio lights, searing into my soul. Commotion now as Henry, Fidditch, and the gangly woman rushed into view, all gawking over me, tenting me from the lights.

"Water, get her some water," I could see Henry saying.

"She's alright," Fidditch announced. "I don't think we... to... ambulan... ive her time to..."

And then it came. The shattering of glass in my head, sending shrapnel confetti through my brain. My teeth clamped against the pain as the diamonds of glass slit everything inside me and my toes curled so violently that they popped at the joints. Then, like a fog bank, the darkness rolled in, shrouding my feet before enveloping my legs, my body, and then...

CHAPTER 15

I sat up, bamboozled, as my motherboard rebooted and my senses came back online one by one. First a ringing in my ears as the volume levels adjusted. Then my eyesight unblurring as the soundstage snapped back into focus. The taste of pennies in my mouth and the smell of aftershave, thick and cloying, vaguely spicy, foreign, and expensive.

"There she is," Fidditch said. He was knelt by my side, Henry flanking opposite.

"Have some water, Luanne," Henry ordered, and I complied, draining half the bottle as soon as it was offered. My stomach still swished and churned, a heavy weight rolling in my bowels that was unsure as to whether it wanted to work its way up or force its way down.

"Luanne, sweetheart," Henry said, clearing a bead of sweat from my forehead with his hand. "Look at me, love. Look here." He clicked his fingers, much to my irritation, but seemed satisfied when I was able to focus on him. A thin, guarded smile twitched on his lips and quickly disappeared. "Right, I think that's it for today."

"Well, hold on a second," Fidditch said, running his fingers through his hair. "Let's not get drastic just yet."

"Drastic?" Henry said, letting go of my hand and standing to his full height, which was significantly taller than Fidditch.

The showdown resembled a dad squaring off against his adolescent son. "She dropped like a sack of cement, for God's sake. She could have cracked her head open."

"I'm okay," I muttered. "I didn't faint. I'm okay."

Fidditch pursed his lips, his eyebrows arching condescendingly, as though bottling a retort to Henry that might escalate the situation further. Fidditch glanced over at the gangly woman, who watched the scene unfolding warily but was quite happy to take a backseat to the action. Was Fidditch waiting for her to jump in and act as referee?

The stage became a hollow arena of silence. Nobody quite knew what to say, or whether to say anything at all. The group's body language seemed to suggest that they would defer to me to make the decision. And so, I did.

"I'm okay," I said again. "I didn't faint. Just got a bit overwhelmed. Honestly, I'm okay."

"It's not okay," Henry grumbled, but that momentary flash of fire had lost its ferocity. "You could have hit your head."

"Don't worry about that. I've got a tough head. It's been hit by worse." I extended my hand. "Henry, could you help me up, please?"

When I got to my feet, Fidditch and the gangly woman gave me a stilted round of applause, as though I'd performed some miraculous feat.

"Was that one of your… what do you call them, Luanne? These little fainting spells?" Fidditch asked. "What I mean to say is: did you just faint, or was it like, you know, when you were younger?"

"I didn't faint," I repeated. "It's just… haven't had breakfast, it's hot in here, the photos. My legs went, that's all."

"Right." He nodded, and an almost excited impatience overtook him. "But was it similar to when you were a kid? Is that how it was?"

Henry huffed at the question. "Can we give her a couple of minutes to get her bearings before interrogating her, please?"

"Yes, sure." Fidditch threw his hands up and took a step back, muttering something under his breath.

"Is there a bathroom here?" I asked.

Fidditch turned to the gangly woman, who spoke to me directly for the first time. "Yes. It's a bit of a walk. Shall I show you?" The words were clipped, and her precise enunciation could only have been the result of good private schooling.

"Yeah, sure," I said. "Lead the way."

"If you need anything…" Fidditch began to say, but I cut him off.

"Yes, I get it, I will let you know." I raised a hand to silence any further offers of assistance. "Right now, I just need to get my legs under me."

The gangly woman reminded me of someone who might work at an amusement park – Disneyland, perhaps. Her dyed black hair was cut into a severe bob. She wore almost comically large glasses with round pink frames, and a billowy polka-dot dress that hid her thin physique. Her fire-engine red lipstick was stretched in a hopeful, eager-to-help smile.

"What's your name?" I croaked as we broke away from the set, feeling as though I were wading at sea rather than walking.

"Oh, um, Adelpha," she said. "And sorry." She offered me her hand. A thick plastic bracelet hung around her wrist that should have been kitsch, but on her seemed stylish in a hipster sort of way. "I'm sorry, we haven't been properly introduced. I keep expecting him to." She made this last admission quietly even though we were far away enough from the set for Fidditch not to overhear.

"Right, I think Peter mentioned you, actually. That name's ringing a bell. Nice to meet you. Properly, I mean," I said, wiping my palm on my jeans before shaking her hand, which felt small and fragile when encased in my own. "Oh, Jesus, my head feels like it's on a flight to the moon. Can we just um…" I stopped, exhaled, waiting for my balance to return.

"Would you like to sit down again?" she asked.

"No, no. Let's just keep walking. That helps get rid of the pins and needles. So, are you the, uh… the sound person?"

She walked me to the end of the soundstage and opened a door, which led to a small, dark corridor, illuminated by a single caged light. The corridor would have failed every fire safety protocol if an inspector had swung by to investigate; the narrow walkway was a maze of crates and wire bales, random equipment such as spare clunky overhead lights, monitors, and even cameras, all of which were probably inoperable, left to rot in the cool, moist air.

"Oh, I'm sort of a jack of all trades, master of none. I do sound and a lot of the admin stuff," Adelpha said, stepping over a large roll of bubble wrap. "So, like, I booked your hotel, your cars, and things like that. Has everything been okay, by the way? I've been super nervous that there would be problems with the hotel or something."

"No, it's all been fine. The hotel's very… nice."

"I'm so relieved," Adelpha said, stopping at a chipped and peeling door. "Here you are. There's one slight thing to mention that I found out this morning, though," she said, opening the bathroom door and reaching into the darkness. There was a click-click-click. "The light doesn't work."

"Really? Oh. Well." I was about to suggest that I could hold it in but didn't think I could. Though I didn't much like the idea of sitting on a frigid toilet seat and spinning out in the dark.

"I could wait outside if you want? It's super creepy back here." And before I could protest, she walked a few feet back down the corridor and said, "I'll just be here."

When I was finished, I met Adelpha back in the corridor.

"How are you feeling now?" Adelpha asked.

"Better. Thanks."

"Do you take anything for it?" she asked.

"Oh, I used to be on some medication that helped even me out when things started to feel wobbly, but…" I was losing my train of thought. I stopped, waited for my memory to catch up, and continued. "But I haven't needed to use it in so long. I rarely get dizzy these days, and I haven't had a real fainting spell in years."

We walked a few steps without speaking before she stopped short of the door that would lead us back into the soundstage. "Um, Luanne, can I just say something?" Her wide anime eyes blinked hopefully behind the lenses. "I think it's really cool that you're doing this. The documentary, I mean. We're all really… impressed." She looked down at her feet and shook her head as though regretting the compliment. "Sorry, I just wanted to say that. It's not right what they're doing… the Netflix thing. The real truth deserves to be told."

And for a second, I was sure she was about to burst into tears. I wasn't used to getting compliments, and I never knew what to do with them on these infrequent occasions.

It wasn't something I was entirely comfortable with, and so I just smiled and thanked her, muttering that it wasn't a big deal, when we both knew it was entirely the opposite.

"We should get back," she suggested, and led me to the greenscreen, where Fidditch and Henry awaited my arrival.

"You look much better," Fidditch said, nodding enthusiastically. "You've got some colour back. I think maybe it was just the shock. Would you agree?"

"Yeah, sure," I mumbled, and cleared my throat, the surface of my tongue feeling dry and scaly. Henry gave me the water bottle, and I swigged and swallowed.

I was midstride to the chair when I suddenly stopped. "Actually, before we begin, would anyone mind if I had a drink? A proper drink I mean?" Fidditch wasn't forthright with his answer, and so I felt compelled to add, "I'm not talking about getting loaded; I just mean, a small knock. Just for, well…" I held out my quivering hand. "That's nerves, by the way, not the DT's. I'm not a drunk."

"We don't have any alcohol on the set," Fidditch said.

"I do," I replied. "In my bag." At this admission, Henry clutched hold of the bag tightly and furnished Fidditch with a guilty look, before breaking eye contact completely.

Fidditch glanced across at Adelpha, perhaps hoping for some input that might save him the awkward lecture he was about to deliver. Adelpha mirrored Henry and found something more interesting in the toes of her patent shoes.

"I don't have any objection in theory," Fidditch began, shaking the curls out of his eyes and crossing his arms. He coveted the annoyance with a neutral expression but couldn't stop his cheeks flushing or hide the steeliness that had sharpened his eyes. "But I suppose ethically, there's an argument against it." He paced pensively for a moment, mulling over his words, before settling on: "I wouldn't want you to drink because it compromises the validity of your story."

Anger, hot and sharp as a soldering iron tracing my guts. My fingernail worried at the ragged wound in the corner of my thumb where I'd unconsciously peeled a rind of skin away the day before. "Sort of like it becomes inadmissible in court?" I asked. "That type of thing?"

"In a sense," he said meekly, massaging the tension that had apparently crept into his neck. "Look, I'm not implying anything. I'd just... rather you didn't. I know how difficult this next part is, and–"

"You don't know anything. So stop saying you do."

The lividity in his cheeks spread through his face like a fever until he was glowing. Henry shuffled from foot to foot, wringing his hands together.

"A shot isn't going to hurt," Adelpha suggested. When Fidditch looked over at her, seemingly surprised that she had spoken out of turn, she added, "if anything, it could very well be just the thing Luanne needs to get through the story. I think it's a fair request."

Adelpha straightened and pinned her shoulders back in a caricature of confidence, and yet it appeared to work, because Fidditch acquiesced with a single shrug.

I sat down in the chair, already feeling the lure of sleep as Henry removed the bottle and passed it to me. I took a healthy slug and sighed as the brandy burned through my chest.

"So," Fidditch's voice cut across the set, slashing the silence that had settled in the aftermath of my drink. "Vincent Street. Take us through it."

CHAPTER 16

In the two days before we broke into the house on Vincent Street, I convinced Mia to stay at a cheap bed-and-breakfast, which she paid for with the profits from her previous endeavours. Back then, you didn't need ID, an email address, all the rest of it. If you had cash and looked sixteen or older, which she definitely did, then you were guaranteed a place to lay your head. And it wasn't like we were trying to stay at The Hilton or anything like that, I mean, this was just some shitty little dive in King's Cross called The Continental. We both knew that we needed something permanent and stable, and that if we could just get some breathing room, then things would run just like a well-oiled machine. I had been turning over the idea of trying to rent somewhere – not officially of course; we were too young to do that legally, but there would probably be ads in shop windows, landlords looking for tenants who would take us on face value as long as we paid a deposit up front. To make this daydream a reality, we would need a steady income, legal or otherwise.

That was the only reason why I went along with it. I swear. I didn't want to hurt anyone.

Mia said she picked the house on Vincent Street because it was big and fairly secluded. "Some rich guy lives there," she'd told me over a dinner of takeaway pizza that we ate straight out of the box while in bed at the hotel. "We can sneak in, clean the place out and he probably won't even notice anything's missing, not if we're careful. And think of this" – she sat up on one elbow, tossing a crust into the box – "we pawn any jewellery, take the cash to the train station, and buy our tickets to Blackpool. We're out of London that same night, so even if this prick goes to the police, we'll be gone."

"What if he comes home while we're inside?" I asked.

"He won't," she said, with such a note of finality that it really seemed as though she had everything figured out. "I'm not just going into this blind, you know. I've done my homework."

"Meaning?"

"Meaning, I know when he goes to work and when he comes home." When I asked how she knew, the simplicity of her reply quelled any further questions on my part. "I've watched him," she said.

After that, I wasn't sure I wanted to know any more.

The morning it happened, we left our stuff at the hotel and took a taxi down to the high road in Dollis Park, which was about ten minutes' walk from the house we planned to burgle. It was a lovely warm day; the sun was shining, the sky was blue, and the grass and leaves had started to get that almost iridescent pop of colour that signalled the start of summer. It hadn't really dawned on me that we were actually going to go through with this daring plan we'd been discussing for the last two or three days. I suppose somewhere in the back of my mind, I believed we'd find a way to talk ourselves out of it; that we'd skip the stress of a home invasion for some alcohol and ice cream in the park.

We passed a petrol station along the way. The nervous tension had been clawing at my stomach, and I had become so thirsty that I couldn't even draw enough saliva to spit.

"Wait a second, let me get something from here," I said, turning into the station.

"Be quick," Mia said, lowering her shades to eye me. Was she angry with me? Or maybe she was just as apprehensive as I was.

"Yeah, sure. I'm just getting a drink."

"We can get drunk after," Mia said, sidestepping a car that had pulled up to one of the pumps. "I don't think it's a good idea to try and get tipsy before we go in."

"No, just a normal drink," I said. "I'm thirsty."

She stood on a concrete island that separated a row of pumps and watched as I ventured through the automatic doors. The air conditioning was a blessing as it blew on my skin, and I took a couple of seconds to indulge. Then I went to the freezer, picked up a strawberry and ice-cream flavour Panda Pops, and took it to the counter.

As I was fumbling in my pocket for the coins, the cashier said, "What are you doing down here?"

My head snapped up. I didn't immediately recognise the girl; whenever you saw someone outside of school wearing something other than a blazer and tie, it was always like you were encountering a completely different person. To add to the confusion, this girl – Becca, her name badge read – was wearing a different uniform: a bottle-green polo top and black cap. She was in my year, but I think we were only in the same History class together.

"Oh, hi," I said, spilling my money on the counter.

Becca scanned the bottle but didn't smile. "What are you doing all the way down here?" she asked again. Dollis Park was only about an hour away from school on public transport, not exactly the other side of the world. But when you're a teenager, your boundaries are a lot smaller. Dollis Park might as well have been another city, or another country for how unfamiliar it felt.

"I'm just, uh… visiting a friend." I said, wondering if she was ever going to ring the till up and give me my change. I suddenly felt a desperate urge to just forgo my fizzy drink and run out of the station as fast as my legs would carry me. "You, um… live down here?"

This was the first time we'd ever spoken to one another. In school we had absolutely no interest in each other, but now, in the real world where social circles were a lot more mercurial, we were forcing small talk.

"No," she said, finally tapping buttons on the till. "I've only been working here since start of the holidays. My dad drops me."

"Right." I took the drink and spun on my heels. "Enjoy the rest of the holidays," I said, almost floundering down the aisle.

"Don't you want your change?" she asked, in a sort of nonplussed, vaguely irritated way.

"No, it's okay, keep it," I blurted, flapping my hand in a wave before almost bumping into the automatic doors as they opened. Skipping now, I hurried to meet Mia at the pumps, only casting a quick look back at Becca when we were on the street.

"We've been spotted already," I said, struggling to coordinate my hands long enough to twist the cap off the bottle.

Noticing my difficulty, Mia relieved me of the bottle and did the honours. The cap twisted off with a hiss, and I snatched the bottle back, gulping the pink liquid greedily.

"What's the matter with you?" Mia asked. "Spotted by who?"

"The cashier in there. She goes to St Monica's. We have History together," I said, stopping to take another sip. "And she's in my Home Economics class," I remembered, with a sudden flush of panic. "We have to call it off."

"No, Rube. Don't be crazy."

"What do you mean, crazy? I've been spotted in this neighbourhood by someone from school."

"So what? It's a free country, isn't it?"

"But..."

"But what? What does it matter?" She put her cool palms on my shoulders and looked into my eyes. The sun caught her face, illuminating her features, adding a warm glow to her unblemished beauty. "Honey, look at me a minute. It doesn't matter. We're not going back to school. You're never going to see her again. We're going to Blackpool, like we've always said we would."

"Yeah but..."

"No," Mia said softy. "It's only a big deal in your head." She tapped the side of my skull playfully and giggled. "It's not a big deal at all. But we need to do this, alright? We do this and then we go to Blackpool. Yes? Hey, look at me. Yes?"

"Yes," I said, reluctantly.

"You're tough, Ruby. Look at me. You can do this. You're tough and you're made of steel."

"I don't feel it," I croaked, suddenly on the verge of tears. Even as I let her guide me away, I still couldn't believe we were doing it. I didn't want to break into anyone's house. I wanted to go back to bed and watch TV. I wanted to go swimming or get a milkshake or go to the cinema. I didn't want *this*. But she persisted. She held and stroked my hand, pulling me along, guiding me, and the whole time she was just talking nonstop. Telling me how wonderful Blackpool was going to be, all the boys we were going to meet, the nightclubs we'd visit, the matching tattoos we'd get.

She practically dragged me through a park with a large pond occupied by swans, through a field populated by daffodils and dandelions, and into a charming, picturesque suburban neighbourhood. None of it felt real until we were on Vincent Street.

You took one look at that street and knew all the residents in those big, detached houses were extremely well-off. I mean, they didn't even look like *houses* because the size of the buildings suggested dozens of people could live in them, like they could be broken up into half a dozen single apartments on the inside. There were only about six or seven houses on the street, but they all had these huge, well-tended front lawns, some with ponds and elaborate statues, with two or three cars in each driveway: Aston Martins, Mercs, Jaguars, Range Rovers. One of the gardens even had a boat hitched to the back of a large truck. All gleaming like they'd just rolled off the showroom. No rust-eaten Ford Fiestas or clapped-out Renault Clios down there.

Just us being on that private street was suspicious enough. If one of the residents had stepped out of their house or had a peek through their window and seen us, then it would've been over, and that's when I think it finally sank in. We were really going through with this.

"That one," Mia said, pointing to the house that sat alone and regal at the end of the street. It was a marvel of modern architecture, unabashedly unique in comparison to the neighbouring houses. From the outside, the structure resembled three glass cubes sitting atop one another, through which you could just about glimpse shades of the affluence within. Most of the main walls were made of glass, which did little to conserve privacy.

"You have to be joking, Mia," I said, acutely aware that the vein in my neck was pulsing as though straining to cope with a sudden rush of blood to my head. Navigating the inclined pavement was making me breathless, and my calf muscles were bunching from the effort. "That's not a house. It's a fortress."

"Don't be silly," she said, so cool and casual that the spell immediately broke, and I saw the house for what it really was: just a building with a few extra bells and whistles, now seeming garish as opposed to glamourous. "And don't worry about the gate," she said, nodding with her chin to the black and silver railings that culminated in two double doors with the initials GM in wrought iron at the front. "We're going over the back wall."

"Oh," was all I could say, and again, the explanation helped demystify the whole process. "Easy as that, then, huh?"

I tried to match the light, graceful flow of Mia's stride, but wasn't able to coordinate my limbs. She walked with the lithe ease of a cat, as though she owned the house. There wasn't one noticeable sign of apprehension in Mia's movement or expression. And perhaps that was the secret to a successful burglar: keeping your cool, pushing all those meddlesome anxieties away so that you were in complete control of the situation. She even whistled, which made me laugh, turning my internal pressure valve and releasing a much-needed whisper of steam. "Mia, this is insane."

"It's really not that big a deal," she said as we approached the lane that would lead us around to the back of the house.

My head was on a swivel as we cut down the lane, making sure that nobody had seen us, my palms secreting sweat as the adrenaline flooded my system. “From the street, you have that big gate, which is a pain in the arse to climb by the look of it, but around here” – she pointed to the rear wall where a smaller gate allowed entry to the back of the property – “we can climb this no problem.”

Before she attempted to, though, she halted by a large hedge that kept us concealed from the rest of the enclave and pointed into the yard. “There’s a camera aiming straight down at the garage; you see it? But there isn’t one pointing at the back gate or at the garden. When we climb over, just follow my lead and we’ll steer clear of that.”

My eyes darted around, trying to find error with Mia’s information, but as far as I could see, there was indeed only one camera. There was, however, a burglar alarm, visible near the roof of the second floor. “How will we get into the house without tripping that? If we break something, it’ll go off.”

She cupped her hands over her mouth and chuckled gleefully. “You can’t see it?”

“See what?” I asked.

“Our way in. Come on, I’ll show you. Just stay close.” She grabbed the railings atop the wall and began clambering up.

“Wait, wait,” I whispered as she ascended, one leg now over the railings. She was halfway in, halfway out. “We can’t do this, Mia.”

“Yes, we can. Come on, Ruby. It’s fine.”

“Someone’s going to see us,” I protested. The side of my head began to ache as though that section of my skull was hardening to concrete.

"They will if you just stand there," she said sternly, but there was a smile hiding just behind her frown, as though she wanted to laugh. "Come *on*. It's easy. Who cares?"

"Why don't I just be the lookout?" I said, bristling with fear that our whispered conversation would travel down the street and alert the neighbours. "You're better at this sort of thing than me."

"No. We can get through the house quicker if we work together. Come on, Rube, I can't do it alone." She didn't wait for me to lodge a counter argument. She just jumped down into the back yard, and I had to tiptoe to see her through the railings above the wall.

"Mia," I moaned, stretching her name until my voice threatened to betray me.

"Ruby, listen to me," she said firmly. "You can do this. You're strong, you're clever, you're fast. We aren't going to get caught. Do you hear me? We are *not* going to get caught." Her wiggling fingers appeared between a gap in the railing. I linked them with my own. "Come on. There's nothing to be afraid of. Tonight, we'll be in Blackpool, under the bright lights. That'll be nice, won't it? Fish and chips, a stick of rock, candy floss?" she tittered, and stroked my hand. "Look at this house, Ruby. Whatever we take, he can afford to buy again." Perhaps she felt the trepidation in the stiffness of my fingers, because she added, "It's either this or go back to your mum's. And you don't want to do that, do you? Not after all the lies. Not after what she did to you and your dad. You don't deserve that."

That was the decider. That was what got me climbing up the wall and over the railings. When I dropped down into the yard, Mia embraced me, laughing naughtily into my hair. "This is going to be so much fun."

CHAPTER 17

It was the first and only time I'd ever seen a back garden with a swimming pool. There was a separate building off to the left of the main house that looked a bit like a big shed but was actually a sauna. On the deck, a jacuzzi. The garden seemed to stretch the length of a football field. It had a whole playground set, complete with swings, a slide, a climbing frame, and Astroturf. *He has kids,* I thought, and this somehow made our intrusion feel that much more of a violation. But by the time Mia had slunk up to the open window of the conservatory, I'd already changed my stance on that particular train of thought. These children lived in a mansion. They had a playground and a swimming pool in their back garden. They weren't to be pitied. Their parents had probably never tried to kill them in a car crash or invited strangers over to abuse them. And my initial guilty reluctance began to morph into bitter determination.

With the guile and ease of a gymnast, Mia pulled herself up through the conservatory window, flattening her body down like a cat to fit through the gap. When she was on the other side of the double-glazing to me, she climbed on the sofa in the conservatory and did a victory dance, twirling and clapping excitedly. "Come on in," she urged, and my heart kicked in my chest at the volume of her voice. "This place even *smells* expensive!"

She was right, too. After I struggled through the gap in the open window, I was met by a fresh, floral fragrance that had an unmistakable chemical undercurrent. The house had been recently and frequently cleaned, and as we drifted out of the conservatory and into the lavish, sleek kitchen, I saw vases containing arrangements of brightly coloured flowers on the counters.

"Look at this," Mia said, walking her fingers along the black marble counter. She opened the sleek, shiny fridge, which was void of magnets and fingerprints or anything fun and inspected the contents. "You hungry, Rube?"

"I feel like I'm going to shit myself," I said, through a mouthful of thumbnail. "Come on, let's stop messing around."

"Sure you don't want an omelette?" She removed two eggs and did a mime of juggling them.

"Put those back," I said. "Mia, my stomach's doing cartwheels."

"Then use the toilet," she said, replacing the eggs before wandering around into the hallway. "I'll bet there's one on every floor." She opened a door beneath the stairs to reveal a spacious bathroom that looked like it wouldn't have been out of place in a five-star hotel, not that I'd been to one. It had a sunflower showerhead and a clawfoot bathtub, a mirror surrounded by tube lighting, and a twin sink. Mia whistled, impressed. "I'll bet those taps are expensive. You think we can get them off?"

"I hope that's not a serious question," I said, hanging back, keeping my attention trained directly on the front door. From my vantage point, I could see the outside gate and had a good view of the rest of the street, and even a smattering of the city beyond.

Sunlight drenched the interior of the house through the glass walls as we continued to explore. We poked our heads into the living room, but a quick survey revealed nothing of interest. We couldn't get that obnoxiously large TV out the door. Mia grew bored and was about to head back out into the hallway when something caught my eye: a large picture of the family that lived in the house, hanging above the fireplace toward the far end of the living room. At first, my eyes processed the dad, wife, and daughter – who was probably seven or eight in the picture – without much interest. I was turning away when I decided to look again, my attention snagged by the man. Handsome, strong jawline, piercing blue eyes, and a stylishly messy mop of strawberry blond hair. Like a Ken doll come to life.

"Oh, my good God." The words tumbled out my mouth, the shock rooting me to the spot.

"What?" Mia asked casually, looking over her shoulder.

"Mia, do you know whose fucking house we're in?"

She joined my side, following my gaze to the picture above the mantlepiece. "Yeah, the guy from TV."

"The guy from TV," I parroted in disbelief. "The guy from TV, Mia? George McDermott? That's what the GM on the front gate was?"

"So what?"

"So what?" I almost screamed, suppressing the urge to grab Mia by the shoulders and shake her until she became as panicked as I was. "You didn't say this was George McDermott's house."

"Well, you didn't ask."

"Because it didn't occur to me to. I thought this was some stranger's house, not – I don't know – one of the most famous people in the country!"

"Who did you think would live on a street like this? In a *house* like this? A butcher? A bus driver?"

"I didn't... I d-didn't..." I began stammering, unable to articulate how incredibly bad this scenario was becoming. George McDermott was on billboards. He was in coffee adverts. My mum watched him on *Wake Up, UK* every morning without fail. The man was a national treasure. And here we were trespassing in his family home.

"Should we give him special treatment because he's on TV?" Mia asked. "So, what if he is? What difference does it make?"

"I don't know. It just seems... *scarier* knowing that he lives here."

"Hey." She placed a finger on my chin and turned my head toward her. "There's nothing to be afraid of. I'm right here with you, aren't I?"

"Yeah, but..."

"No buts. We're in this together, aren't we? So, it's George McDermott's house. Who gives a shit? Tonight, we'll be in Blackpool laughing our arses off about all this, and tomorrow we can watch *Wake Up, UK*. That'll be a trip, won't it?"

"Mia, you're crazy," I said, shaking my head. "Someone could come in at any minute. We need to get out of here."

"Okay, okay. No more joking around. You're right. Let's just do what we came to do."

We ascended the floating staircase to the next floor, where my trainers sank into the thick, plush carpet, leaving dirty footprints behind. I had a vision of George McDermott coming home from a hard morning of fake laughter and celebrity interviews, only to find evidence of our intrusion leading up the stairs. Then something more urgent occurred to me, like a bucket of ice-cold water crashing over my head, shocking my system.

"Shit. Fingerprints," I said, holding out my hands. "We've been touching everything."

"So what?" Mia said, not even faltering in her step as she entered a spare bedroom that resembled a Harrods showroom – the blandest space in the house so far. "You don't have any prints on record."

"Do you?"

"I'd be wearing gloves if I did." She ran a finger along a bookshelf and then inspected it for dust.

I wanted to say more. Yes, our prints weren't on record *now*. But once George McDermott realised his house had been invaded, he would call the police, and they would dust the prints. And what if the police turned up the heat on the investigation because it was a big celebrity who had been burgled? What if the police somehow got wind of us and...

"Mia, I think I'm going to have a panic attack," I said, leaning against the wall, struggling to swallow.

"Don't be dramatic," she said, smiling. "Just breathe. Take it easy, silly."

"It's going to be all over the news."

"What is?"

"This – *us*. George is going to go to the police, and it'll be in the papers. *Breakfast Presenter has House Burgled*. They're going to catch us, I know it."

"Ruby, you give *them* too much credit. Now come on. Pull yourself together. We're having fun, aren't we?"

She took my hand and we went along the hallway, searching the rooms in order. We came across a girl's bedroom, which was larger than the living room of my house. The walls were bubble-gum pink, and there was a fairy and unicorn theme going on. It reminded me more of a giant birthday cake than a bedroom. A brigade of oversized stuffed teddy bears mingled with a crowd of Barbie dolls. A four-poster double bed with glittery rainbow drapes occupied the middle of the room.

"I'd bet if we bagged up all these toys and sold them at a car boot sale we'd make a fortune," Mia said, kicking a big, fluffy polar bear across the carpet. She picked a snow globe up from the top of the dresser drawer, shook it, and then let it fall from her hand. It hit the carpet with a thud that made me flinch.

"What a boring fucking house," Mia said, brushing past me on her way back out into the hallway. "Good stuff's gotta be in the master bedroom. Would you say so, Rube?"

"Yeah, I guess," I said impatiently, following her as she continued the investigation in another spare bedroom that looked like it was only there for cosmetic purposes. I doubted anybody actually used this bedroom at all. "Mia, what time is he supposed to be back here?"

"I don't know," she said with a carefree shrug as we came to a games room with leather couches, another gigantic television, a snooker table, dart board, and bar in the corner. "Fancy a cocktail?"

"No," I said irritably. "What do you mean you don't know when he'll be back?"

"I mean I don't know. *Wake Up, UK* finished about half an hour ago, so I'd say we've got about an hour before he pulls up. Depending on traffic, of course. That's even if he comes straight home. Might go somewhere else, see a mistress. Who really knows? I'm not his secretary."

"Then let's *hurry* this up," I hissed. She made a cartoonish shocked face at my outburst, and it took every bit of restraint I had not to erupt. The muscles across my chest tightened with tension, and my fingernails bit into my palms as I closed my hands into fists.

"The best way to keep calm is to realise–"

"Oh, shut up," I said, stepping around her to cross the landing. The floating staircase continued up, but there was another room across the way from the games room that we hadn't checked. Using the sleeve of my hoody, I depressed the doorhandle and entered what I thought was going to be the master bedroom, but I was wrong. It was a shrine to the man himself. I was immediately haunted by framed publicity photos of George McDermott throughout various points in his career: a still from the eighties, wearing a suit with large shoulder pads, his hair cut into a mullet. George standing in front of a map of the UK from when he worked as a weatherman, flashing a radiant smile. George with his hand around his wife's waist on a red carpet, waving at paparazzi. A blown-up and framed magazine cover of *Lady Essentials*, depicting George in a fitted suit, his hair dyed brown, posing as though he were in consideration to play Bond.

A glass cabinet housed several trophies and awards. On a separate display were various items of merchandise that bore George's likeness, including a lunchbox from his stint presenting *Canteen Catastrophe*, a twelve-inch doll in a rectangular box, t-shirts, and a vinyl of a single called *So Bad at Being Good!*

"What a creep," Mia said, fingering a selection of keyrings that were neatly arranged on a table with George McDermott mugs and a boardgame of *Nutmeg Rush!*, a football-themed show he used to host. "He's got his own personal museum. She picked up a ball-point pen, clicked it, and threw it back on the table. "None of this shit's worth anything. Except maybe to him."

Ascending the stairs, we immediately emerged into a loft, which was used as the master bedroom. We'd been in the house for at least fifteen minutes now and our pockets were still empty. I hadn't even seen anything I thought was vaguely worth the trouble of stealing. If we searched the master bedroom and came up dry, then all this stress and anxiety was over a wasted effort. Then what? Look for somewhere else to rob? No. I couldn't put myself through this again.

"Here's where the magic happens," Mia said, sounding bored. The wall-to-wall windows offered a panoramic view of the neighbourhood and the smog-smudged city skyline on the horizon. At the same time, though, the bedroom was almost uncomfortably warm, the sun's heat concentrating directly on us as though we were ants beneath a magnifying glass. The cosmetic appeal of the room was greatly outweighed by the reality of inhabiting it. "I'll search the wardrobe, you do the drawers on the nightstand." She pointed across to a dressing table. "Jewellery there. Fill your boots."

Crossing the room, I spotted another one of George's awards on the bedstand. It was an elaborately detailed bronze bust of a comedy mask. The words 'British TV Personality of the Year 1993' were inscribed on the base. This coveted award was almost ten years old. Why wasn't it downstairs with the rest of his accolades? Could it be that this had been the pinnacle of his career thus far, that he was still chasing those heights?

On the dressing room table, I found an array of makeup and several jewellery boxes. "Rolex," I said, opening the first box, before getting distracted by strings of pearl necklaces that were casually strewn over the table. *I could just take these,* I thought, picking the necklaces up, my face instantly flushing with heat. My throat felt constrictive, limiting the air supply to my brain, and I thought I might actually spin out right there. It was probably the most expensive thing I'd ever held, and I could just take it. "Christ, it's hot in here," I said, dragging the back of my hand across my slick forehead.

"How you getting on over there?" Mia asked on her knees, opening shoe boxes, presumably hoping to uncover a pile of cash.

"Jewellery, yeah," I said, suddenly very thirsty. I opened the dressing table drawer and saw a velvet display case, upon which a dozen or so women's rings were housed. Diamonds, sapphires, winking and casting rainbow prisms in the sunlight.

"Well, well, well," Mia said. "I've found something."

I looked over, holding the ring case, and saw Mia holding a large polythene bag of white powder. "You're joking. That's not... *coke,* is it?"

"What, hidden in a shoebox at the back of a wardrobe? No, definitely not," she said, with a mischievous grin. "Of course, it is. These celebs are all at it. How do you think he wakes up so early?"

"I guess we know why they sleep on a different floor to their daughter, then," I said. "Look, there isn't going to be any money here. They probably just use credit cards. But there's lots of jewellery. I don't even think we should take all of it. I mean one of these rings is probably... I don't know, but it's expensive." Mia continued rifling through the shoeboxes as I spoke. "Mia?"

"If there's coke, I bet you there's other stuff, too. Pills, probably. Where there's coke there's usually pills." She scuttled around on all fours, searching beneath the bed.

"Mia? Did you hear what I said?"

"Oh... my... God!"

"What?"

Mia pulled out a clear glass box inside of which, at a glance, appeared to be six or seven dildos of various shapes, sizes, and colours. She tipped her head back and cackled hysterically. "Who do you think they're for?" she asked. "His wife or him?"

"Put that back," I nagged. "Who gives a shit? Mia, we've got the jewellery. Let's get out of here."

"Coke and dildos," she said, wiping tears from her eyes. "What kind of parties you think they have? Fun ones, by the look of it."

A bead of sweat dripped from the back of my head and slid the length of my spine.

"I'll bet you if we keep rooting around, we're bound to–"

A sound distracted us both. We froze.

It was the front door opening downstairs.

The double-glazing of the bedroom had blocked all outside noise, and neither of us heard the car pulling into the back gate. And we didn't see it either because we were distracted with the stupid fucking dildos.

Now someone was in the house with us.

George McDermott was home.

CHAPTER 18

The jangle of keys being tossed onto a table. A long, loud yawn. A *thud-thud* that I couldn't identify at first, but later realised was George kicking his shoes off. The muted footsteps, socks on hardwood, going into the living room. A pause, then the enormous sound of that cinema screen TV being turned on, an advert for car insurance blaring through the house. My heart became a brick in my chest, sinking right through the centre of me. I wanted to pee very badly.

"Mia," I whispered. "What do we do?"

She held up a hand to hush me and cocked her head, trying to track his movement downstairs. She motioned for me to follow her toward the bedroom entrance, but the muscles in my legs had liquified, making movement impossible. Noticing my difficulty, she clasped hold of my arm and dragged me to the opening in the floor that we had come through to enter the bedroom. From there, we had a skewed view of the first-floor landing, and a sliver of the ground floor reception. We stood there a moment with bated breath, neither of us daring to fidget for fear we'd give ourselves away. When George emerged from the living room a minute or so later, we caught a quick flash of him, enough to send spikes of panic through me. Now my muscles had solidified and locked up painfully, cramping with apprehension.

"I think he's gone to the kitchen," Mia said, her palm flat against my stomach to prevent me from doing something stupid like bolting down the stairs.

"What shall we do? Make a run for it?"

"No." She shook her head. The fact that Mia didn't appear the least bit panicked did nothing to ease my fraying nerves.

"Then what?"

She didn't answer. Her face became a blank mask while she watched the stairs, and as I stood there, literally quivering, I was almost impressed with how composed she appeared.

"What, Mia? What are we doing?" A feeling of pins and needles numbed my skull, threatening to graduate into something monstrous. Rapid fluttering began in my belly, like a kaleidoscope of butterflies had been set loose. "He's in the house; we have to do something."

"Hide," she said.

"Hide?"

"Not the wardrobe," she said. "He might come up and change his clothes. The bathroom," she pointed to the en-suite. "In there."

"No, I don't think that's a good idea. I think we should–"

The shock of seeing George ascend the stairs stole the rest of my sentence. Thunderheads forming in my brain. A deep booming migraine began stirring.

"Bathroom," Mia ordered. "*Now*."

My legs felt like sandbags as we scurried over to the en-suite, our feet sinking in the lush carpet. Just as we got to the door, I heard George say something aloud, but didn't quite catch the specifics. He had stopped ascending halfway up to his bedroom, and I knew why: he'd seen the muddy footprints.

"What on earth is this?" He was near now, and his voice was clear enough to be heard even with the blood rushing through my ears.

Mia clasped hold of my wrist and pulled me into the bathroom, closing the door to a crack behind us. There was absolutely nowhere to hide in there. If he decided that he needed to piss, he would be met with two strange girls in his house. And then what would happen? He'd call the police and we'd get arrested. Or we'd try and flee and probably get caught anyway.

George began talking, and at first, I thought it was directed at us. Sounded like he was still on the stairs. "Have you been here?" he said. My body tensed tightly, my guts twisting themselves into knots. "What do you mean what am I talking about?" he said. "Have you been by the house? Which one? Vincent Street, obviously."

He was on the phone, but this revelation brought no reprieve.

"... Because there's fucking mud tracked all through the place. It's on the stairs, I'm only just noticing it now, but it's everywhere. Have you had someone come by while I was working? Well, I don't know, do I? That's why I'm asking. Believe me, I'm not calling for my health."

"Mia," I said as my eyesight drifted in and out of focus. "I think I'm going to pass out."

"No, you're not. Don't you dare."

The hinges of my knees felt weak, as though they might give out at any second.

"The gardener doesn't come every week," George said into the phone, growing more annoyed. "Not unless you've booked him in – have you? Right. And even if he was booked in, he wouldn't come in and start roaming about the house, would he."

"Mia..." The bathroom was dimming.

"It's not a leak, Kristen; it's mud. I'm looking at it now, it's everywhere. It's footprints... In the house? You mean like a burglar? Oh, shut up will you. Yes, alright, sorry to have wasted your precious time." His footfalls accelerated as he bounded up the stairs.

My knees buckled out from under me, and I grabbed the edge of the sink just in time to stop myself smashing down on the tiles and cracking my face open. "Mia, I'm going to black out..." I was saying this, unsure as to whether she could even hear me or whether I was speaking the words at all. The lights turned out and I felt myself plummeting inward. Mia was stroking my cheek, her fingers icy cold against my hot face.

"I'm going to pass out. Don't leave me here," I uttered, and it felt like the air was vibrating around me.

"Rest," Mia said, her lips brushing my ear. "I'll take care of it."

CHAPTER 19

I woke to the sound of screaming. I was lying on the bathroom floor, my head pillowed by a fluffy towel. Mia was standing over me, her hair covering her face. She was panting and smiling.

"There you are," she said, chest heaving. "Feeling better?"

My mind was momentarily muddled. I didn't know where I was, or why I was on the floor. Then, as the seconds trickled by, the sludge sifted away, and everything came back to me in a cinematic collage; us climbing the back gate, wriggling in through the conservatory window, the pink unicorn bedroom, the dildos, and…

"George," I said, the soundtrack of screams now making sense. I sat up, too quickly, and felt the house tumble around me as though it had been picked up and spun by a tornado. My equilibrium was slow in correcting itself, so Mia helped me up and onto the edge of the bathtub.

"… Fucking crazy bitch…" George wailed miserably.

"Don't listen to him," Mia said sweetly, waving the sound of his distress away. "Just concentrate on me." She held up a finger, attempting to get my focus, but it only served to distract me. Her finger was red.

"You're bleeding," I said.

"Not my blood," she replied, smiling almost shyly.

"What's happening? Is that George screaming?"

"Yeah." Mia grabbed a towel and wiped her hands, leaving a red smear. "You passed out. He was coming up the stairs. I had to."

"Had to what?"

"He would have come in and found us anyway," she said, ploughing over my enquiry. "What do you think he would have done to us? We found his coke. He wouldn't have let us leave. He was going to hurt us."

"What did you do, Mia?"

"I hurt him first." She shrugged tentatively.

"Fucking hell." My head rolled back.

"Ruby, he wasn't going to let us leave. I promise you. If he didn't beat the shit out of us, he would have called the police and we'd both be on our way to prison. You *know* that. Tell me you know that. I had no choice. I was protecting us." She grabbed my face and tilted it so that I met her doe eyes. A spark of excitement danced in her pupils, but there was vacancy there too. It was almost as if she was looking *through* me, and this unmoored me in a way I still can't explain. Perhaps it was the first time I truly realised that there was something deeply wrong with Mia, something that had always been there, hiding in plain sight. How had I missed it?

The truth was, I *hadn't* missed it. I had always known.

I just didn't care.

"Sorry I called you a bitch… Can you just phone me an ambulance, please," George disrupted the moment, freeing me from Mia's spell. "I don't care what you take. I won't report you to the police, I promise. Just… my leg is… it hurts really badly. It's broken… my ankle. Please, for Christ's sake."

I pushed off from the bathtub, sidestepped Mia, and began out into the master bedroom, the ground feeling spongy and treacherous underfoot. There was a good chance my legs would fail me at any second because they refused to cooperate. Just walking across the room seemed to take an extra mental effort that I wasn't accustomed to.

"Don't go down those stairs, Rube," Mia said urgently, hurrying to prevent my descent. I peered down the stairs and saw George lying there, his face a crimson mask. Blood saturated the white carpet and sprayed the glass wall in the landing behind him. "He's only seen me. He doesn't know that there's anyone else here. Just let me handle it."

"Handle it? His face has been smashed in. Mia, we're in so much trouble," I squealed.

"Only if we get caught."

I didn't even have time to wonder what she'd hit him with before I saw the bronze comedy bust lying on the floor by the top of the stairs.

"Oh, God, Mia." I palmed my forehead, the veins in my temples wriggling.

"Rube, there was literally no other choice," Mia said, losing that apologetic edge and growing more defiant. "Tell me: what choice did I have? He was in the bedroom, and I could hear him talking to himself, like he knew we were in the bathroom. You were passing out, and I had two options–"

"Let me think for a second," I said.

"–I could either just stay cooped up in there with you or I could go out there and get the jump on him. So that's what I did. I ran out, picked up that stupid fucking trophy and–"

"Mia, *please*." My hands locked into claws of frustration as I cut her short. "For the love of God, please just let me think."

She opened her mouth to say something more before swallowing it back. She exhaled through her nose and began pacing, hands on hips.

"My leg… it's broken. Please, I need an ambulance. And my head… there's blood everywhere. Please, take what you want…"

"SHUT UP!" Mia roared, her words tearing through the house but dying when they reached the double-glazing. The home's architecture made the acoustics weird and muted. "Shut the fuck up before I come down there and cave the rest of your stupid fucking skull in!"

I was awed and more than a little terrified at her rage, mesmerised as she exploded. Her ivory skin had marooned from the effort of screaming, and her voice had deepened, sounding almost masculine, the veins standing out in her neck.

When she was finished, I padded back to the bathroom, got a towel, and used it to pick up the bronze award. It was heavy, George's blood running through the fissures and grooves of the mask. I wiped it thoroughly with the towel before replacing it on the nightstand.

"Ok, here's what we should do," I started, my mouth feeling as though it were coated with sandpaper. "We go downstairs, we wipe everything we touched. And we tell him… we tell him that if he tries to call the police on us, then we'll let them know about the cocaine in his house. Yes, that's right, let's take a photo of the coke. And the dildos. Because the dildos will embarrass him, and we can say… We can say we'll go to the newspapers if he tries to press charges on us. We can just threaten him and…" I struggled to fill in the rest of the plot holes. Even if he took our blackmail at face value – assuming our little bargaining chip was worth his silence – how would he explain his head being split open, or his leg being broken? He was on the TV every day. "The police or whoever might think this is part of some drug debt or something. That might work, Mia. That part of it might work. I mean, will people actually believe him if he says two girls… two little girls like us broke in and beat him up and robbed him? No, of course not. And even if they do, then how would they trace it back to us? There's no way."

Emotion sifted through the blank slate of Mia's face, animating it ever so slightly. Her eyes shone with cunning, and a small smile appeared on her lips. "You're so clever, Ruby. You always think of everything. God, I love you so much, honestly."

I exhaled and saw black dots on the edge of my vision. With a scrunch of the eyes and a vigorous shake of the head, the dots dissipated.

"Anyway, enough worrying about that fucking idiot downstairs. How's *your* head?" Mia asked.

"It's okay, I think." Which was a lie. The stress of this scenario was teasing the thunderstorm. I could feel it pulsing behind my eyes. "It's not my head we need to worry about right now. He's really quiet down there. I can't even hear him moaning anymore."

Mia shrugged. "Maybe he passed out."

We peeked from the top of the stairs. George wasn't moving.

"How hard did you hit him with the award?"

"I don't know," Mia said, defensively. "I just picked it up and swung it at him. Thumped him in the head. He tried to grab me, and we wrestled a bit, and he fell down the fucking stairs. His problem. Shouldn't have touched me."

A zoetrope of the scene played out as she described it, but all I could think of was how heavy that bronze award was, and how much blood was on and around George's face.

"What if he's hurt really bad, Mia?" The thought threatened to eject the contents of my stomach onto the bloodstained carpet. "What if he's got a fractured skull or slipped into a coma?" A quick flash of the car crash interrupted my thoughts: my cheek against wet tarmac, the rev and screech of tyres, the stink of petrol. "Fuck, Mia, what if he's dying?"

"He's not dying," Mia said, with the confidence of a veteran doctor. "No chance. I didn't hit him hard enough. He's probably just passed out because of the blood."

"Well, we have to check," I said reluctantly, even though the very thought repelled me. "And we still have to wipe the place down. There's no way we can leave it like this."

"Sure," Mia said, being agreeable just to placate me. She stepped forward and hugged me suddenly, and I became aware of the slightly bitter smell rising from her. Not sweat, but something unpleasant that I couldn't place. Her usual fragrance was a melange of stolen perfume, chewing gum, and strawberry lip gloss. "This is just a little bump in the road. We can still be in Blackpool tonight. Tomorrow afternoon latest, I'd say."

When she pulled away, I saw that the stress was apparently having an impact on her, too. I hadn't noticed the light bruising of tiredness beneath her eyes, her hair fraying with an almost greasy shine. It might have been the harsh sunlight blazing in through the glass walls, but very suddenly, Mia appeared older. Much older.

He was going to hurt us. And she had been hurt before, hadn't she? Her mum's boyfriends. Why did I have the feeling that this could have been avoided? Why did I have the feeling that this is exactly what she wanted?

It didn't matter either way because we were both mixed up too deeply in this trouble now.

"Come on," I said, "let's see if he's okay."

"Wait." Her hand struck out, whip-fast, and claimed my hand. "Don't go down there bare faced."

"Bare faced? What do you mean?"

"He's only seen me, remember?"

That's right. I was in the bathroom, passed out on the floor. This might have ordinarily stirred up a wave of embarrassment, but given the circumstances, I had never felt more justified in blacking out. Some internal moral high ground wanted to protest Mia's plan, to assure her that we were in this together no matter what. But I hadn't been the one to come up with this crazy scheme. I hadn't picked this house. I hadn't attacked an important celebrity and pushed him down the stairs. Our portions of blame were not equal in this. Not even close.

"Here, I found this when I was looking through his things." She went to the wardrobe and came back with a lacy, black sequined mask, complete with bunny ears. It looked like something you might find in Victoria's Secret. "He's got a few of these things lying around in there. All kinds of masks. Maybe he had a Halloween party. Put it on."

I did it without a second's thought. Then I grabbed the towel and followed Mia down the stairs, wiping the wall as I went.

CHAPTER 20

George was splayed out like a starfish on the landing, his blood appearing almost black against the white carpet. A gust of déjà vu swept through me as I stared down at his face, his handsome, familiar features just about recognisable through the crimson. Here, beaten and injured in his home, he was stripped of all the shine and glamour that celebrity afforded him. He was just a weak, broken man now – no foundation to even out his skin tone, no dazzling artificial smile, no witty remark to throw into a conversation to crack-up his co-stars.

He was in a bad way. His right foot tilted askew from his outstretched leg, but it was the blood that worried me the most, the metallic stink of it, that coppery taste in the air.

"What should we do?" I asked, unwilling to leave the security of the stairs just yet.

"It's your call. You know any CPR?"

"No, of course not. But isn't there something you're supposed to do when people are bleeding like this? Like, I think we're supposed to sit him up or something."

The nausea again, swirling strongly inside me. The fear unglued me from the stairs and brought me down to George's side, my fingers finding his wrist, pressing for a pulse. "He's alive," I said with the weakest tremble of triumph, and felt the crushing weight of inevitability ease slightly. I looked across through the open doorway of the games room. "There's a sofa in there. Let's get him on it."

"Leave him, Ruby," Mia ordered. "Why are you making all this work for yourself? Let's just leave him here."

"We can't leave him," I said. "Not with a head injury. Not until he wakes up and we know he's alright. You can't play with a head injury, Mia. I should know."

"Fuck that," Mia spat. "And fuck him."

"And we still have to wipe this place down," I said, the mask feeling constrictive against my face as sweat soaked into the sponge lining. "We still don't know what condition he's in. Mia, if he... if he's in a really bad way, then we're... God, I can't even think about it. If he dies on us, we are *fucked*. Are you understanding that?"

"You're right. Of course, you're right. I'm sorry." She relented too quickly, and the apology had no weight behind it.

"And what about if someone comes home? His wife, kids, all that?" That fizzy feeling in my head, blood rushing to my brain, the colour tipping out of the world. The migraine crackled, and I felt pencils turning behind my eyes. "Mia... it's going to happen again. I'm going to..."

Her hand swept across my face, the clap loud in my ears. The darkness slithered away.

"Sorry, I don't want to hit you," Mia said, stroking the spot on my cheek that she'd just slapped. "But I can't have you flopping over every time you get spooked."

"You hit me? Seriously? I can't help it," I said through gritted teeth. "It's a medical condition."

"I know, honey, I know." She took my hand, kissed it reassuringly. "I know you shut down when things get rough. I know it isn't your fault. I just don't like it when you go away like that." She tried for a smile, but what had once been charming and sweet now came across as ghoulish. "Listen, if anyone comes to the house, we'll... we'll deal with it. But he isn't expecting his wife."

"How do you know?"

"They're divorced. Don't you watch any TV, Rube?"

Now that she had reminded me, I realised that I *had* known this. I probably picked this useless knowledge up through osmosis from one of my mum's magazines or from the TV. Something like that.

"Let's get him up," I said, my cheek still tingling. I stumbled behind George, trying to avoid stepping in or touching his blood, but it was impossible. Securing my arms around his upper chest, I strained to heave him, while Mia took hold of his legs. Even working together, it took a tremendous effort to budge him a few feet. The stress of carrying my half of the burden wrung sweat from my pores, and I tried not to look at his face while we manoeuvred him through the games room. Cringing as his warm blood coursed over my hands, we made it to the sofa and, with a final effort, heaved him onto it. I propped his head on a mound of cushions and caught a glimpse of the plump, glistening welt above his eye that had ballooned to a fleshy tennis ball.

Without thinking, I tried to remove my mask. Mia stopped my hand and said, "Leave it on, just in case," then twirled a finger toward the windowed walls.

"Is his head supposed to be tilted back? Or is that just for nose bleeds?" I said, mostly to myself, knowing Mia didn't give a shit.

"Well, you've fluffed up his pillows for him. Shall we get him a blanket and a cup of tea now?" Mia asked, still breathless from the exertion of carrying him.

I didn't answer the rhetoric, but instead traced the ellipses of blood that trailed from the bottom of the stairs and through to the games room. I ran upstairs to retrieve another towel from the en-suite bathroom, wetting it in the sink before bringing it back for Mia. "Press this on his head."

"No," she said, pushing my hand aside. "I'm not his nurse."

"Mia, please," I said, exasperated. "Just try and stop it from bleeding." She let my outstretched hand linger a moment before snatching the towel. "Just wait with him. I'm going to go back and give everything a wipe."

"That's going to take you ages," she said. "And it's pointless."

"It won't be pointless if he reports us and they get a forensic team to go through this place."

"God, you and that big imagination of yours. A forensic team? And so what? Our prints aren't on file, remember?"

"No, not yet," I snapped, sick of her constant contradictions, tired of her unwavering carelessness. "But what if they seize all the CCTV footage of the buses that did the rounds this morning, and we get picked up? Or some other camera on the high street that we didn't know about? And what if we get caught and they take our fingerprints and match them to something in the house?"

She blew a strand of hair out of her face and furnished me with such a bland expression of indifference that it made me wonder why she was being so relaxed about everything. Wasn't she finding it hard to breathe, wasn't her chest tightening, her stomach cramping? How could she be so… so fucking normal about it all? And just when I neared my threshold, when I thought there was a real possibility that I might lurch at her and claw her face with frustration, she smiled again, showing those perfect, straight white teeth.

"You're right. Of course, you are." Delicately, she touched my elbow and said, "There's a reason you're in the top classes at school and I'm in Dumb-Dumb City. Because you're bright. I'm sorry. I know I'm impulsive."

You're not impulsive, I thought, struggling to navigate her constantly shifting moods. *You're the most calculated person I know.* She was manipulating me – and I suppose she had always been manipulating me in some way or another, but it was only there, in that moment that I really felt it. The *push*.

"Go on, you clean up. I'll keep an eye on him."

Glad of the dismissal, I left the room, eager to be away from them both. I was just about in the hallway when I stopped and said, "Yell if he gets worse."

"I will."

Heading back upstairs, I started in the bathroom. With a towel over each hand, I began vigorously rubbing everything down, moving as fast as I could manage. I cleaned the edges of the bathtub, the sink, even the tiles where I'd been lying, before advancing into George's bedroom. Why hadn't we thought to bring gloves? Why were we in this big, preposterous playset of a house in the first place? And why… *why* had I gone along with such a stupid plan? This was never about getting enough money for Blackpool; it was about doing something bad, getting a charge of adrenaline, lashing out.

When I started on the dressing table, I saw the strings of pearls again, and the carelessly discarded ring display case. Now the idea of stealing something after all the carnage we'd caused made my gorge rise. There was no way I could rob this man after we'd ambushed him and put him out of action for the foreseeable future. No way he could turn up on *Wake Up, UK* looking like the Elephant Man with his leg in a cast. Wouldn't be great for his public image.

While I was wondering whether fingerprints could be lifted from fabric, rubbing down the dildo case, I happened to look over into the walk-in closet. My thoughts had turned to how I was going to run the towel over everything in there, as Mia had undoubtedly pawed through all the garments on the racks, when I saw the box. It was visible on a shelf just above where Mia had parted a row of suit jackets that were still in plastic from the dry cleaners. My attention stuck on it for a couple of seconds before I returned to rubbing and wiping.

Then I looked over at the box again. It had been deliberately tucked away, out of sight. Why had George taken the time to cover it up when he left the dildos and coke out so openly? I could have just ignored it and carried on.

And yet I couldn't. I just had to look.

I got up, my legs working with less urgency now as I went over and into the closet. Reaching up on tiptoes, I grabbed the box and pulled it down from the shelf. It was some kind of chest. There was a keyhole at the front, and I assumed that it would be locked before I tried the buttons to either side of it. But it wasn't locked. It popped right open, overflowing with Polaroids. The pictures spilled across the carpet as I lifted the lid, but it took me a few seconds to focus and understand what I was seeing.

There were naked people in every photo, some of them wearing masks just like the one I had pressed against my face. Scenes from parties, the smiling participants grinning and toasting to the camera with champagne flutes. I fanned through the photos and saw sex, immortalised in just about every position I could have imagined at the time: group couplings, close-ups, tongues, fluids. I spotted a picture of a potbellied middle-aged man snorting a line of coke from the counter in the en-suite bathroom, while another man gave the camera a thumbs-up. Then, of course, I started to pick out the star attraction like a lewd game of *Where's Wally?* Sometimes he wore a mask, and sometimes he didn't. In one photo, he was receiving a blowjob from two women while he sat on a couch in the living room laughing.

A part of me wanted to call down to Mia, to share this pornographic discovery and giggle and sift through every scandalous scene. But a larger part of me wanted nothing to do with it. These were his photos. His property. Hadn't we violated him enough? Yes, it was gross to me, and vulgar and demeaning, but it wasn't any of my business. These were private pictures of consenting adults. Mia didn't need to see them. I scooped the pictures back into the box and closed it with a click. Then I returned the box to its place on the shelf and spread the suit jackets across to conceal it.

I'd been so wrapped up in the photos that I hadn't heard Mia talking to George in a low voice.

Whatever she was saying, she didn't want me to hear.

CHAPTER 21

The carpet blanketed my footsteps. I crept down the stairs, stopping in the hallway so that I remained out of sight from the games room. Sweat stung my eyes, and I lifted the mask, propping it on my forehead, vaguely nauseated at the thought of who might have worn it before me.

Mia was growling at him, her anger raising the volume of her voice, but I could still only make out snatches of dialogue. I heard the words "worst', "life', and, more clearly, "fucking pig'.

George gave a long, awful moan in response.

When Mia spoke next, it came out in an enormous, hateful scream:

"CONFESS YOUR SINS, YOU FUCKING PIG! TELL ME! TELL ME! TELL ME!" Her voice was beyond manic; it had deepened until it was unrecognisable, the venom thickening her words. "YOU'RE GOING TO TELL ME! YOU'RE GOING TO CONFESS EVERYTHING! FUCKING PIG! FUCKING DISGUSTING DIRTY CUNT OF A PIG!"

My hand flew to my mouth, the fear freezing me in place. My heart boomed like a sledge slamming against my ribs. Gooseflesh broke out across my cheeks, up my arms, and down my legs. A throbbing, tightening knot in the centre of my chest.

I had never been so afraid in my entire life.

The only response George gave to her outburst was a series of muffled sobs.

Calmer, but no less spiteful, Mia said, "What is it that you don't understand, Mr Superstar?"

In a low, barely decipherable slur, he managed, "What do you want…"

"*What do you want…*" she mimicked, matching his cadence. "Shut up, you fucking stupid pig."

"Mia!" I called, but her name sounded as though I'd said it underwater, the stairs feeling bendy and unsolid underfoot. The house began to feel as though it were rolling like a giant marble.

She appeared on the landing, closing the door behind her, cutting off the sound of George's garbled sobs. There was an almost guilty look on her face that she tried to assuage with a smile.

Almost.

"Better you stay out here, Ruby," she said, breathing hard, tendrils of hair plastered to her pale, blood-flecked face.

"What are you doing to him?"

She didn't answer. Only stared.

"We need to go now. This has already gone on too long. It's already got too out of control, Mia," I snapped. "You're scaring the shit out of me the way you're acting. What's going on with you?"

"We can't leave yet."

"Yes. We can. We can just go out the back door, the way we got in."

"Won't do. We haven't finished here yet."

"Yes, we have. We're only going to make this worse – if that's even fucking possible to do at this point." I tried to say more, sputtered on the words, and started again. "Mia, what are you doing to him in there?"

From the games room, there was a loud thump, followed by a stifled howl.

"Don't go anywhere," Mia said in a voice that sounded like gravel being crunched underfoot.

Mia looked sick, as though she'd been stricken with an aggressive strand of flu since we'd entered this house.

From the games room, another thump, another muffled cry.

"He's trying to get to the balcony door," Mia said. "Just wait there. Don't come in. You're not going to want to see this."

"Don't do it, Mia. Just leave him. There's still a chance we can get away with this if we just go now."

It was at that very point, as Mia turned to go back into the games room, that we changed our lives irrevocably. I should have done more to try and stop this madness. I should have wrestled her away from the door or fled and made an anonymous call to the police, but even if I did, I'm not sure I would have saved George's life. Still, I should have tried. But I had no idea that Mia had gone into that house with murder in mind. I didn't even understand what was happening, or how everything had unravelled so fast.

The scene shudders out like stop-motion animation. Mia wiggling her blood-slick fingers in a wave before turning away from me and going back into the games room. As the door clicked closed behind her, my knees buckled out from beneath me and I fell like an ironing board on my face. The air billowed out of me in a great gust. The carpet mushed against my cheek. I could feel my heart beating painfully against the floor, my temples pounding. A wave of heat flashed through my body, my migraine nesting in the base of my skull.

I'm dying, I thought. *The stress has sped my heart up and it's going to explode and I'm going to die in this house.*

The world began to fade.

Mia was talking to George again. I'm certain that this wasn't an auditory hallucination. She was asking him to confess.

He made some approximation of, "Confess what?" I'm sure that's what he tried to say.

"Confess your sins."

George's jagged scream thundered through the house. Even though I was quickly sliding downhill on my way to unconsciousness, the ferocity of his anguish made the fine hairs on the back of my neck rise. Now I wanted to sink into the abyss, to be away from this nightmare that I was powerless to prevent. Thumbtacks pushing into my brain. The pain bordering on unbearable.

"Don't you recognise me, George? You know who I am. Say my name. Go on, confess your sins and tell me who I am!"

George sobbed.

"You do. And unless you tell me your secrets, confess your sins, then…"

George screamed again, but it broke off halfway through.

"TELL ME!"

Fireworks in my head. The curtain came down.

CHAPTER 22

When I swam back to the surface, Mia was sitting on the stairs with her back to me. She was rocking, ever so slightly. I lay there for a while, waiting until my heart didn't feel as though it were trying to punch through the floor beneath me, then pushed myself up. That fainting episode seemed to have hit my mental reset button, because I was momentarily caught in a whirlwind of confusion again. Where was I? Yes, a house… George McDermott's house, that's right. Why was I still here? Because I'd passed out. Right, but before that? A reel of memories played out, quickly getting me up to speed: the conservatory window, the dildos, the coke, the box of photos, George…

"Where's George?" I asked, and the very act of speaking brought about such a sense of profound dizziness that felt like I was stuck atop a mechanical bull.

Mia didn't answer, just continued to rock.

"Mia?" I said again, getting to my knees. "What's…"

When she turned to look over her shoulder at me, her face was awash with blood. For one terrifying instant, she resembled a polar bear that had just lifted its muzzle from the gore of a seal carcass. The blood had clotted in her brows, her unblinking eyes staring at me as though entranced.

"What have you done, Mia?"

"He wouldn't do it..." she said, bringing her fingers to her lips. "He just wouldn't admit it."

"Admit what?"

She shook her head profusely. Blood flicked from her hair and spattered the wall next to her. "It had to come from *him*. He had to admit to it."

A cold, greasy breed of dread claimed me, and suddenly my stomach plummeted.

Then I remembered: he'd been screaming about his broken leg and his battered face. Why wasn't he screaming now?

"Did he pass out?" I asked, looking toward the closed door of the games room, where a bloody red handprint stood out against the white wood.

"He was supposed to tell the truth, but he wouldn't... he wouldn't confess to what he'd done."

Without caution, I pushed the games room door open.

I cannot begin to describe the horror I saw in that room. One coroner testified in court that his remains no longer resembled a human body.

My mouth snapped wide open to scream, but my lungs refused to cooperate. Instead, I made a series of loud panting noises that wavered in pitch. I had never heard myself make anything close to those sounds before.

Or since.

Amidst the carnage, I saw the British TV Personality of the Year award lying there, gleaming bronze and red in the sunlight. She must have gone upstairs to retrieve it. How many blows would it have taken to make him look like *that*? I had no way of knowing.

"What... what... what... what..." I couldn't get the sentence to form; it was like revving a broken-down car in the hope that the engine would turn over.

"Don't feel bad for him. He deserved everything he got," Mia said softly behind me. When she exhaled, the breath stirred the hairs on my neck.

"You… you… kill… kill…"

"Yes," Mia said. "Because he wouldn't do the right thing. He had one last chance to redeem himself, and he chose not to."

"B… b… blood… blood…"

Standing close behind me, her heavy breaths fluttering my hair, she made me think of a different animal: a bull, snorting in a pen.

"M-M-Mia." I couldn't move. Couldn't talk.

"Now it's time to go," she said softly. "Come here. Ruby? Come here to me."

Gently, she turned me around to face her, and I put up no resistance. The stink of George's blood was like a visceral cologne, sharp and abject. She put her hands – her wet, red hands – on my face and appraised me before pulling me in for a hug.

"I thought he was going to admit it," she whispered into my ear. "I'm so sorry, Ruby."

"What have you done to us, Mia?" The bank overflowed, and when I cried, it came in terrible, hitching gags. "Why, Mia? Why? Why?"

But she never answered. She just hushed and soothed. Hushed and soothed.

When she had coddled me long enough, she pulled away and said, "It's all over now."

All over now.

How wrong she had been. That was only the start.

CHAPTER 23

"Luanne?"

I'd shed a river of tears over Vincent Street in the past. Now my eyes were dry and itchy. I ran my hands over my face, masking it from the crew. There was a horrible dry taste in my mouth, as though I'd been chewing on cardboard.

"Luanne," Fidditch said again, waving a hand to get my attention. "Are you with us?"

"With you?"

"Yeah. You sort of… went away there for a sec. It spooked us," he finished, with a small, nervous laugh.

I palmed the side of my skull and searched for Henry. It took a few seconds for my vision to catch up with the movement, and when the blurriness subsided, I saw Henry with his fist pressed against his mouth. Poor Henry couldn't hide a thing from me; his face was an open book. He was terrified.

"Henry, are you alright? What's wrong?"

"I'm not sure," he said, frowning deeply. Beneath the intensely bright lights, he seemed so much older, as though the weight of my past were pressing the vitality right out of him. "You sort of went into a bit of a trance, there. Your eyes were open. But you… you weren't here. You just stopped talking and… you seem okay now, though, right?"

"That's... right," I said hesitantly, hoping it came across as casually flippant as I'd intended. Then a bolt of lightning zigzagged through my head, the pain seizing me. "Ugh, is that it for today?"

When I didn't immediately receive an answer, I looked over and saw Adelpha whisper something to Fidditch. Then, he said, "Do you think we could go on just a bit longer?"

"How long have we been going for?" The soundstage didn't have a clock or any windows, so there was no natural lighting to mark the passage of time.

"It's only coming up to one," Fidditch said.

Henry was about to step onto the set, then hesitated, not wanting to get caught in the camera's line of sight. "I think maybe that's plenty for today."

Fidditch stared at Henry until Henry backed down from the challenge and looked away like a timid dog. Then Fidditch returned his attention to me. "Luanne, can you give us any more today? I mean, I don't want to make you feel... unwell, but I'm just worried that if we break here, at such a pivotal moment, then we'll lose the fluidity. I think the momentum might be difficult to pick back up if we prolong this."

"I have quite a bad headache coming on. We haven't even stopped for food, have we?"

"Is that a question or a statement?" Fidditch said with a slight laugh, although he seemed genuinely curious. Henry licked his lips and watched me closely.

"No, we haven't had lunch yet," I said slowly, as though it had been a trick question. Though, if truth be told, I honestly couldn't remember. If a fucking troupe of circus bears had come through the sound stage clashing cymbals and riding unicycles, I wouldn't have noticed. I was so tightly locked into the story that it had felt as though I were there, back in that hot, stuffy house that stank of blood.

"Are you hungry?" Fidditch asked. "We can stop for food if you like?"

"No, I'm not hungry."

"Then, perhaps I might suggest something." He pointed to the camera, and Adelpha turned it away from me. "Henry, Adelpha, would the two of you mind if I had ten minutes alone with Luanne, please?"

"What for?" Henry lurched like a dog at the suggestion.

"I'd like to discuss one or two things about Vincent Street. I don't intend to film this conversation, and it will be easier for Luanne and I to discuss without an audience, if it's all the same."

"Well, I'd like to stay, *if it's all the same,*" Henry challenged.

Raising his eyebrows, Fidditch puffed his cheeks out and looked to me to make a call.

"If you're not filming it, then I can have my brandy," I said.

"Fine," Fidditch shrugged. "What I have to say won't take very long, but I just feel like I need to have a direct conversation with you about it. I don't want Henry – or Adelpha, she's very close to this story too – to have any input on this."

"Sure, I don't care," I said. "Henry, do you have that brandy handy?"

"Hey, you know what?" Fidditch interrupted. "I may have told a tiny fib when I said that we didn't have any alcohol on set. The truth is, and this was intended to be a bit of a surprise for the end of the shoot, but I have a couple of bottles of champagne out back. I was saving them for when we wrapped, but you know what? I can always get more. Adelpha, be a gem and fetch me the–"

Adelpha offered him a bottle of champagne and two plastic flutes. "Way ahead of you."

"You are a miracle, Adelpha, thank you." Fidditch twisted the cork off with a fizz, poured us both a flute. "Adelpha, why don't you give Henry a tour of the grounds. And crack that other bottle open while you're at it. You both deserve a drink, too. We're all in this together. In the trenches."

Henry was about to leave when he came over, bent down, and gave me a hug. He whispered, "If you start to feel uncomfortable, just yell for me, okay? I won't be far."

I kissed his cheek and watched him and Adelpha disappear. When we could no longer hear their footfalls and stilted conversation, Fidditch said, "I know we aren't finished yet, but I want to give you a toast, Luanne. You're doing a brilliant job. And really, you're quite inspirational. To have gone through all that shit, to have endured so much trauma… hats off, honestly." He raised his glass and drank. "Fucking hats off, for real."

"Is there a problem, Peter? I'm sensing there is," I said, sipping the champagne. It was the good stuff, expensive. Another sip and my head felt lighter, my muscles looser. I could have quite happily sat there and sucked down that whole bottle.

"Not a problem, as such." He parked himself in a chair opposite me and crossed his legs. "I just want to get a few things straight in my own head before we move on to the next portion of your story. You see, I have to make sure that I'm understanding every little detail, because if I'm not, it could really reshape the documentary in a negative way. Also, getting everything straight in my head will help when it comes to the editing.

"Now, your story – your *truth*, shall I say – is" – he broke off, sighed with contemplation, and continued – "it's one of the most polarising tales in the history of British crime. But, as I see it, the way you've told me, there are two points that are really going to stir up a lot of doubt in the validity of the story."

"Go on," I said, cautiously.

"You and Mia break into this house. You claimed not to know it was where George McDermott lived. You go through the place searching for something to steal and hit a jackpot in the master bedroom. Then George comes home unexpectedly and you… faint?"

"From the stress, yeah. Because it was scary. That's how it happened. I was terrified."

"And while you were otherwise unaccounted for, Mia attacked him. She hits him with an award, he falls and breaks his leg. But you were passed out through all of this?"

"I have a medical condition."

He raised a finger. "We'll get to that in a sec. Now, you come to, and you hear him swearing and hollering, and you lift him onto the sofa in the games room. Then you… faint again, and it's when you're unconscious the *second* time that Mia killed him."

"Yes," I said, sitting up straight in the chair. "That's exactly what happened. Just as I told you."

"And you see the conundrum that this version of events presents the audience?"

"Version of events?"

"Sorry. I know it's true, Luanne. You don't need to convince me. Adelpha and I are Team Luanne all the way, okay. We wouldn't be doing this – going through all this trouble, risking a tsunami of bad press, risking the wrath of the British public – if we weren't a hundred percent behind you. But the fact remains that in your two bouts of fainting, the two most significant parts of the crime occurred: the initial assault, and then the murder. It quite conveniently absolves you of any blame. Now, again, I know you're telling the truth about how it went down. I just need to get this absolutely crystal before we move on. It will help the audience understand." Finished, he turned his hand over in a gesture meant to convey that it was my turn to elaborate.

"The only time I touched him was to pick him up and get him on the sofa. And I only did that because I didn't want him to lie there bleeding on the floor. I thought if we got him up on the couch… I remembered something about having people sit upright when they're bleeding, that the blood flow would be better and… I was trying to help him."

"You're not supposed to move someone with a bad head injury," he murmured, almost to himself – a throwaway line to reel me in.

"Yeah, I wasn't a trained nurse," I snipped. "I was just trying to do what I thought was best. Blood was pouring out of him. I thought if we got him upright–"

"I'm not accusing you of intentionally hurting him," Fidditch said. "I know it was Mia that killed him."

"Then what are you accusing me of? Because it definitely sounds like there's an accusation here."

"Nothing at all. Don't misunderstand me. Just… allow me to play devil's advocate for a moment, alright? I'm going to ask you the same thing the prosecutor did: Isn't it *convenient* that you blacked out during both bouts of violence, thus rendering you…"

"I didn't witness any of it. Only the aftermath. And as you've obviously read the court transcripts, why don't you try quoting from my defence team instead of the prosecution? My solicitor told me that I am as much a victim of Mia's insanity as George McDermott was."

"Well, I mean, that's not strictly true. You're still alive and breathing."

"I was *groomed.*"

"Yes, I know, look." He picked up the champagne and filled my glass until the foam spilled over the rim. "This is a judgement-free zone. What is it the kids say now? We listen and we don't judge? I know you were only in that house because your mum practically drove you there. I'm just thinking about potential issues that might arise if they're not addressed now."

"We went in the house. George came home. I passed out."

"Twice," he agreed, nodding.

"Twice."

"So, in a way, you're not even really a credible witness to the crime. I mean, you didn't see Mia actually hurt him, did you? Even when you were conscious?"

"That's right."

He went into his backpack, which lay just off to the side behind the camera and retrieved a small moleskin notepad. "For the record, just so we can work this into the documentary, what is the name of this condition you have?"

A beat.

"Vasovagal syncope. Stress-induced fainting. After my crash, when I woke from the coma, some of the wiring up here" – I rapped my knuckles lightly against my skull – "wasn't connected properly. The fainting spells are an emotional misfire. My body's way of protecting me when things start to… Look, I've had it since I was ten years old. If you want me to get a copy of my medical records, then I can prove it."

"I see." He jotted something down, and then scratched his head in thought. "When was the last time it happened, when you fully blacked out?"

A few heartbeats passed before I answered. "The last time it happened was in the house on Vincent Street."

"Really? Never since?"

"No. I've come close a few times, but never gone fully under."

There was, for a flicker of a second, a flash of distrust in his face, but it was gone as quick as it had arrived. "This is just me doing my due diligence. Nothing more."

Standing up, I paced the set, almost feeling a tear in the fabric that segregated the past and present. Now I could smell blood, I could smell Mia's perfume as though she had just spritzed me at a department store counter. There came an awful internal heaviness, like my blood was setting to cement, and I had the unreasonable idea that I was trapped in that building, that I'd wander off and find myself in some sort of never-ending optical illusion.

"I have this weird idea that you don't believe a single word I've said since we started filming. My fainting is well documented."

"Respectfully, Luanne, the reason I asked about the medical condition is because I've only ever had a second-hand account of the Vincent Street Incident. Remember, Adelpha and I have researched this case thoroughly. We've read every single piece of literature, every statement, every transcript, watched all the bullshit documentaries and reconstructions. This is just me crossing the T's and dotting the I's, making sure that the condition wasn't something the press invented."

"And you believe me then? You believe me when I say that Mia killed him."

"Of course. Haven't I said that all along? That's our whole stance on this film. We know Mia did this, and we know you took the fall for it. In our opinion, after spending hundreds of hours researching and discussing the case, that's the only way it could have gone down. I just need to make sure I can convey that in a way that will make other people understand too. Remember, we're changing the whole narrative, and we have to do it correctly. Here, have another drink." He got up with the bottle and began toward me.

"I don't want one," I said, brushing past him. I resumed pacing, trying to shake this persistent sense of déjà vu. "I need to leave. Now."

"Sure, we can take a break. That's fine." He stood up and started to fidget.

"No, not a break. I have to go. You're trying to make a fool of me."

"Absolutely not. Luanne, that is the very last thing I would ever do. I'm not sure what else I can say to persuade you that we are not your enemy. We *believe* you. You are the victim in this. We want to help. We want to proclaim the truth."

"How do I get out of here, Mia?"

He stopped in place as though he'd trod on a bear trap, his face briefly twisting into a grimace.

"What's your problem?" I asked, feeling my palm moisten after massaging my neck.

"You just called me Mia."

I coughed to clear the dead leaves in my throat, and said, "No I didn't," and before he could open his mouth to argue, I said, "And even if I did, it's because I've been talking about her for the last... however many hours. It's called a slip of the tongue, or aren't I allowed to be human?"

"Of course, you're right." His strained features relaxed and gave me a whimsical, placating smile. "Why don't we take that break? I was wrong to try and squeeze so much juice from you, without breaking, Luanne. Please forgive me."

"I'm going to get some air."

Henry and Adelpha were smoking by the entrance, watching as the torrential rain fell in sheets, filling the potholes in the uneven car park beyond. They didn't see me approach, but I had enough presence of mind to observe their interaction, the way they seemed so at ease in each other's company.

I watched them transform upon my approach. The way they straightened up was like two lovers caught in an affair.

My eyes flicked from Adelpha to Henry, then back to her.

"Hi, Luanne. How's your headache?" she asked. "Is everything okay now?"

"Fine," I said, and for the first time, I noticed something familiar in her. Probably paranoia, but she had such a distinct look, and I was suddenly sure that we had previously met somewhere before. A journalist, I was almost sure of it.

Henry touched my elbow and I pulled away. "What's the matter?" he mouthed.

Ignoring him, I said to Adelpha: "Where do I know you from?"

She apparently hadn't heard me, or thought I was speaking to Henry.

"Adelpha?" She looked up from the phone, the screen reflecting in her glasses. "Where do I know you from?"

She angled her head, confused. "Sorry, I'm not sure I follow."

"We've met before, haven't we?"

"No."

"No?"

Her face brightened with optimism. "I'd definitely remember if we'd met before." Her eyes widened, and she cast a quick glance at Henry, as though awaiting his input.

"You been on TV before?" I asked. "Maybe that's it. I saw you on TV."

"No." She shook her head. "I was interviewed by my uni's YouTube channel after I graduated. I came back to do a couple of guest lectures about practical film studies. But I much prefer being *behind* the camera." When she smiled it completely transformed her unusual face. Her red lips pulled back, lifting her cheekbones, which seemed to blush on command. "I'm going to step back inside. Luanne, shout if you need anything, alright?"

I didn't answer.

Henry shuffled closer to me. "Luanne, are you–"

"Henry, stop asking me the same question over and over. Please."

"Sorry. It's just… no, sorry. It's stupid. You've had a hard few days. I need to be more sensitive to that. I'm sorry."

"Did you research her before you let me sign the contract for this film?"

"Research *her*? Adelpha specifically, you mean? Well, I checked out the company, their previous works. It's all on their website. I told you all this, Luanne. This is the biggest thing they've ever done though. I mean–"

"She's lying," I said. "That woman Adelpha is lying. I do know her from somewhere. She's a… she's been on TV, or something like that."

"She said she hadn't."

"I've *seen* her," I reiterated as firmly as I could without snarling. "I don't know why I didn't notice it before, but now it's sinking in."

I was expecting him to shoot me down in his calm, diplomatic way, using some synonym of paranoid to describe my intuition. But he didn't. "In her bio, it says she *was* a freelance journalist before becoming a filmmaker. Could that be it? Maybe she reached out to you for an interview. Something like that?"

"Yeah." I rubbed my forehead. "Yeah, could be."

Half an hour and a brandy-laced coffee later, I returned to the greenscreen.

There was a moment of tense silence as Fidditch conferred with Adelpha. They spoke briefly before he clicked his fingers and returned to address me directly.

"So, Luanne. You wake up. George is dead. Mia hugs you and tells you everything is going to be alright. What happens next?"

CHAPTER 24

"It's not going to be alright. Are you fucking crazy, Mia? It's not going to be alright. Why would you do this?" I asked. I couldn't stop shaking.

"He deserved it," was all Mia kept saying. That, and, "He should have just confessed."

The panic I experienced at that point was something otherworldly. It was an out-of-body experience. I was separated from myself, from the house, from the world. On the outside looking in.

It really only occurred to me in those few minutes after waking up that Mia had experienced some kind of mental breakdown. I thought that she initially attacked George to protect us. But what she did to him after that... There isn't any rational explanation, and the only thing that I've been able to come up with since is conjecture, but I think it's still valid: Mia had been wanting to kill someone for a long time. She'd bottled this rageful impulse, keeping it locked up until it festered and grew enormous within her. I saw a glimpse of it back when she had attacked the woman in the car at the zebra crossing, and though Mia's reaction had shocked me, I'd found the episode easy to dismiss. Mia had just been brutalised by her mother. I could understand why she flipped out and went nuts when the woman almost hit us with her car. But this? She probably realised that we were looking at prison time for striking and sending George McDermott tumbling down the stairs, and then found a real chance to unleash her inner monster. It was always going to happen. It was just a matter of *when*.

"You should go now," Mia told me, sitting back down on the stairs. "Wash your hands and face and go through the back. Don't get on the bus. Walk home. It'll take a while, but do it."

In a very weak, distant voice, I asked, "What are you going to do?"

"I'll go when I'm ready."

After a minute or so, I nodded, then located a bathroom down the hallway where I washed myself, trying to clear as much evidence from my body as possible. I scrubbed blood from my hands and face, trying to contain the crimson spray within the sink and prevent it from spilling over. It stained the crevices of my palms. When I was finished, I stepped out and called again. "I'm going now. Are you coming?"

"No. I'm going to wait until dark. You go now, Ruby. It's not a good idea to leave at the same time."

And even then, after everything that had transpired in the time we'd spent in the house, I didn't want to leave her alone. Yet my desire to be away from this place – to escape the stink of death – was stronger than my loyalty to Mia. There was no reason for me to stay and share the blame for what she'd done. If I was guilty of anything, it was trespass – not even burglary, as I hadn't taken anything. So, I fled, almost plunging down the stairs in my haste to leave.

The pavement pulled away from me as I padded down the streets in a daze, my legs moving on autopilot. I passed three phone boxes along the way, and each time, I hesitated, wondering if I should bite the bullet and make an anonymous call. Those battles of conscience only lasted a few seconds, as I mentally mapped out what would unfold if I did phone the police. The enormous gravity of the situation made the warm summer air feel thick as gelatine as I waded through it. But perhaps I should get a head start on Mia, I thought. The way she had been behaving, that look of wild, animal insanity in her eyes, did not fill me with any degree of confidence that she could get out of this unscathed. Her carelessness would lead to her capture, and for all I knew, she would drop me in it as the main culprit.

But maybe not. Mia was more street-smart than me. Even as unhinged as she appeared to be now, she'd still know how to keep her head down. The scale of this crime was going to stun the nation, and that the investigation was bound to be the biggest ever launched in this country. But I clung onto the idea that I could escape this tragic nightmare intact, that if I just lay low and pretended that everything was perfectly normal, then it would deflect any suspicion. It didn't matter that my DNA was all over the house. It didn't matter that I'd *touched* George. I hadn't really done anything wrong. I'd tried to help him.

Halfway home, I remembered that I'd left my bag at The Continental. We'd paid for another night, but I didn't think I could stand to stay there again. No, now seemed like a good time to try and get back into the rhythm of ordinary, everyday teenage life, and that didn't include fretting inside a hotel room, being cannibalised by my conscience. I had to get back in my mum's graces and pretend that everything was just as it should be.

The extra journey back to King's Cross didn't bother me, even though I felt like a patient about to go into the operating theatre not quite fully anesthetised. Crossing my arms to conceal the bloody patches on my top, I skipped up the steps and into the hotel. There was nobody on reception, so I just peddled back to the room, grabbed my bag, changed my clothes, and hiked it out. I had thought about leaving Mia a note, but even if I had wanted to, my hands wouldn't hold still to perform the task.

It was late afternoon by the time I reached my house, clumsy and disorientated as though I'd been backing vodka all day. Patting myself down for a key, I gave up and thumbed the doorbell, noticing the red lining of my cuticles. When my mum opened the door, I could not bear to look her in the eyes. It wasn't fear of *her* that had my vision trained on the patterned carpet, but rather, the absurd idea that she'd be able to read the guilt in my pupils.

She didn't move out of the way to allow me passage, nor did she say anything. She was happy to stand there and wait for me to grovel, to let me beg for forgiveness, to prove that she had been right all along: I wasn't an adult, I was just a silly little girl.

"I'm sorry," I said in a hoarse whisper. "Please… can I come in?"

In a low, drunken rasp, she said, "Ah, the wanderer returns. My little Princess Ruby. I'm *so* surprised by this visit. I thought you were gone for good. No? Not the case? That's so weird, isn't it? You're back. Well, I'll be the first to say that it is a huge shock."

Staring at the doorstep, I said, "Please can I come in, Mum?"

"Come in where? This house? *My* house? Why do you want to do that? I'm a mad person, remember? I tried to kill you – or kill us both, wasn't that it? Oh, who's really keeping track of the details?"

"I… made a mistake."

"A mistake about what? I didn't try to kill you, then? Is that what you're saying? It's just you seemed so adamant about it the other day."

You did try to kill me, I thought, the blood rushing hotly to my face. *You snapped my hand in a mousetrap when I was little and then you crashed the car on purpose and put me in a coma.* But all I said was, "I made a mistake."

"Did you? Hmm. Well, mistakes are easily made, aren't they?" She moved to allow me passage, and then put her hand across the threshold as I tried to step inside the house. "Aren't they, Princess Ruby?"

"Yes," I whispered.

Satisfied that I'd suffered enough, she sidestepped.

The house stank of bleach, stronger than I'd ever smelled before.

She walked back into the living room to continue watching television. She didn't say another word to me for the rest of the day, and that was fine by me. I had enough to think about.

That night, instead of getting into bed, I crawled under it and lay there. As childish as it was, it felt better to be hidden away, safer. Every time the snapshot of George's smashed face tried to invade my mind, I scrunched my eyes closed and forced it away. I checked my phone, wondering if Mia might have texted me, but she hadn't. I wanted to message her very badly but resisted the urge. A part of me felt the need to seek her out, to get our stories straight and ensure that we were on a level playing field; I needed to know that she accepted full blame for the murder, and that she would absolve me of all involvement, should the need arise. Yet, I also felt the deepening need to distance myself as much as possible from Mia. If she got caught, then I hoped she would do the honourable thing and leave me out of it.

I wondered how long it would take before somebody realised George was dead. He was expected live on TV at 6 am the following morning, so I supposed everything would come crashing down soon enough.

I just had to hold tight until then and see what happened after that.

There would be no sleep for me that night. Or for many nights to come.

CHAPTER 25

The only reason I got out from beneath the bed the following afternoon was because I thought I heard a noise in the shed. It sounded as though something heavy had fallen over in there – a box, an old chair, a can of paint, I wasn't sure. When I looked out the window, I couldn't see any sign of disturbance but knew that I'd heard it. Mia had snuck into the shed. Was she going to use it to hide out? No, she couldn't, for both our sakes. We had to stay separate now; all those dreams of running off and starting a new, grown-up life together ended the moment she cracked George's head open with the award. What was she thinking coming here?

Continuing to watch the shed, I sat on the conundrum for a while, wondering what to do. Ultimately, though, I knew if I didn't seek her out, she'd probably come up to the house at some point, and that was the last thing I needed.

On my way to the garden, I passed the living room and saw my mum watching TV, a cigarette burning between her fingers. She said something to me, bringing my progress to a halt. When I asked her to repeat it, she replied "You heard what I said." This was destined to be an argument, and so I decided not to engage any further, but instead relented with a simple, "Okay, Mum," before heading out to the garden.

There was a single window on the front of the shed, but

the sun was bouncing straight off it, preventing me from seeing inside. As I neared, I squinted but could only make out the mountain of mess beyond. There was another thud, like something being moved – or tossed – followed by a rustle. This wasn't a fox or a pigeon that had found a way in through the rotten asphalt roof. Someone – Mia – was in there. What was she doing? Leaving me another present?

Unbolting and opening the door, releasing a fusty breath of damp and the ancient smell of rain-swollen wood, plastic, and disuse, I peered inside. Dust motes danced in the shafts of sunlight piercing through the holes in the roof.

"Mia?" I whispered, but there was no response. I stepped inside, braving the labyrinth of junk, and headed to the back to investigate further. I had definitely heard something in here. She usually got in through the shattered window in the back, but as I neared, I could see no sign of her.

Had I imagined it? Had the sleep deprivation and anxiety pulled a trick on me? I couldn't be sure, and I didn't have long to contemplate it either way, because when I returned to the house, I could hear my mum bawling. I thought she was laughing until I heard her moaning, "No, this can't be," over and over.

From the hallway, I saw that my mum's daytime drama had been interrupted by an urgent news broadcast. The TV revealed an ariel view of George's glass house, filmed by a helicopter hovering over the property. The surrounding area was packed with forensics in white suits, police cars, and paparazzi.

"No. Oh, my good Lord, no, please," Mum was saying, and in the outpouring of emotion, her waxen face had begun to wobble with the tremors of her grief. "This can't be happening."

The words were like punches, returning fire at my beating heart. My ears were only able to pick out bits and pieces of what the reporter was saying, as most of my concentration was centred on remaining upright.

"What's going on?" I asked, clutching onto the doorjamb, the words like cotton balls in my mouth.

"This can't be happening." She shook her head. Her complexion had become blotchy from crying, and as she thumped across the living room to me, I had a strong urge to run, to get away from her and this house as soon as possible. For a split second, I thought she was going to try and hug me, and my body became rigid as a board.

"They're saying on the news that he's dead."

Her hysterical reaction was as unsettling as the inevitable news itself. I knew that my mum watched *Wake Up, UK* with almost religious devotion, but this was something else. I'd never seen her like this. Even when my dad left, she was stoic and unmoving, refusing to reveal so much as a hint of emotion.

The reporter was unspooling the information they had thus far: TV presenter, comedian, and all-round national treasure George McDermott had been found dead in his home just hours ago. He was due on TV this morning, and when he failed to arrive or answer his phone, friends and colleagues grew concerned. A welfare check was conducted, resulting in the discovery of his corpse. Police weren't willing to comment at this time, but foul play was suspected.

"Foul play," my mum muttered. "What does that mean?" She was aiming her question at the TV, not me. "What does that even mean? Did he kill himself? Is that foul play? Why aren't they saying more?" She clawed at her tatty cashmere cardigan and then flopped over the sofa as though in prayer at a pew in church. Her back convulsed as she wept into the sofa cushion.

Feeling lightheaded, I sat down on the sofa next to her and watched the news play out, though I wasn't really taking any of it in. A layer of reality had peeled away, leaving only this distant, fragile perspective from which I viewed the world. A shivery feeling of déjà vu echoed through me as I watched George's house, wondering how long Mia had decided to stay in there after I left… and what else she might have done.

The nausea washed up inside me, and every reservoir of strength had now run dry. This time yesterday, I was in that house. There could be millions of people watching this broadcast, but only two people in the whole world knew who was responsible for the mayhem that unfolded. This knowledge brought no advantage, no sense of power; instead, it created an intense, suffocating pressure that made it difficult to think and breathe.

My mum straightened up, supporting her head in her hands, staring into the fabric of the sofa. "How can he be dead? Did he kill himself? Why won't they tell me?"

Even though her questions were clearly rhetorical, I felt as though I should say something – anything – but I couldn't. And I couldn't just sit there, watching my life fall apart in real time, so I got up to leave, deciding that hiding under the bed was probably the best place for me.

When I was halfway up the stairs, my mum burst into the hallway. "Ruby, where are you going?"

"Upstairs."

"No, you need to come back down," she said, blotting her tears with a ragged tissue. She groaned as though physically in pain, and said, "Right now."

"Why?"

"Don't ask me why," she said in a shrill voice that was like a drill bit grinding through a sheet of steel. "Just do as your told, will you? For once in your life, just do as you are told and come down. Now."

"I don't want to watch the news," I said, whiny and petulant. "I'm going to read."

In a viperous hiss, she said, "You get down these stairs before I fucking drag you down, Ruby. Right this instant. Do it!"

"What's going on?" I asked, thumping my feet as I descended. She probably thought I was sulking, but the truth was I still didn't have full control over my body just yet. I wanted to go back into that living room and listen to the news broadcast about as much as I wanted to jump into an alligator pit.

Muting the TV, she pointed at the couch next to the window and said, "Sit there and wait a minute," before heading to the kitchen. When she returned, she had a bottle of gin and a regular drinking glass. She half-filled the glass and gave it to me. I stared at it as though it were poison until she swigged directly from the bottle. Even then, I wasn't sure. Sometimes, when my mum would plunge into one of her dark places, she often remarked, "I should just swallow some pills and go to sleep for good." She always said it to herself but made sure I was within earshot to hear it.

"Drink," Mum ordered. "Don't play coy with me now, Ruby. Your room always stinks like a brewery. Now get that drink down you."

"What for?" The glass felt slippery in my grasp. I wanted desperately to place it on the coffee table, but knew this would be a terrible move given the mood my mum was in.

"Because you're going to need it. Now drink."

I wasn't going to protest anymore, especially considering my body was yearning for the alcohol. She watched stone-faced as I took a sip and swallowed, hissing as the liquid went down.

Nodding her approval, she took a moment to gather herself, sucking in a deep breath.

"Before you were born, I worked at the Maypole Broadcast Service head office," she said. The aftermath of her emotional breakdown had left her grim face red and swollen, her eyes bloodshot slits. "Did you know this? Have I ever told you that?"

"I think Dad did," I said, keeping the glass by my mouth, the alcohol fumes funnelling up my nose. "You were a secretary."

"I was a *PA*," she corrected, affronted by the error. "Personal assistant. That was a very sought-after position back in the eighties. MBS was a prestigious company, and they paid really well, even at my level – even during a recession."

Fearing that this was going to turn into a rambling lecture about why it was important for me to do well in school so I could go on and get a decent job, I drank more gin. To my utter surprise, Mum topped my glass up. Then I knew exactly where this monologue was headed. It was going to sound something like, *If a popular and well-respected celebrity like George McDermott can die at any minute, then we all can. That's why it's important not to waste any time moping around in your room, blaming the world for your problems.*

"MBS produced a lot of TV shows, including *City News Report*. My boss, Frederick Chapman, was the director. And George McDermott" – she paused, gulped from the bottle –

"was the host. He'd go around London, talking about stocks and shares, investment banking, all sorts of things."

"You… knew him?" I felt like a kid again, going down one of those tunnel slides at the park, except it was going on forever.

She nodded. "Yes. In fact, when George was headhunted to present *Chasing Limelight,* he resigned from *City News Report* and asked me to be *his* PA. I agreed."

The glass began to quiver in my hand. I drank to steady it. "Is that why you're so upset?"

Ignoring my question, she continued. "I worked with him for about a year. And during that year, I got to know him well." Her glistening eyes sought understanding in my own, before she emphasised, "Really well."

"Where's this…" Sliding, dizzy. "Where's this going, Mum?"

… I won't report you to the police, I promise. Just… my leg is… it hurts really badly. It's broken… my ankle…

"On your eighteenth birthday," she said, before her face screwed up in an effort to avert the oncoming swirl of emotion. She bit down on her lip until it turned white. "There's an account set up for you. When you turn eighteen, you'll have access to it. A hundred and fifty thousand. That's what I managed to get out of him…" She snorted humourlessly. "Hush money. A pittance to him."

"Don't say any more," I said, the sentence quavering uncontrollably. "I don't want to know."

The heft and weight of that TV award. George's head, resembling a ruptured pumpkin, thick, dark blood pouring out of his skull. The games room dripping viscera, looking more like an abattoir.

"You have to know, now." She drank again and then exploded. "Do you think this is easy for me to say? Do you think I want to be stood here saying this?"

CONFESS YOUR SINS

Clutching the arm of the sofa, I tried to pull myself off the couch, but my limbs were riddled with pins and needles. "So, he's the reason…" I started to say. "This George guy is the reason Dad left."

Dad. Dad left.

Not your dad, though.

Your dad's dead.

You just helped kill him.

"Richard and I had only been married for a couple of years when it happened, and already we'd been having problems. And, in a way, I suppose I…" She closed her eyes and exhaled, and the resentment worked her features into a bitter mask. "I suppose I fell in love with George. It is possible to love two men at once, Ruby. And it's also possible to have two men love you back at the same time. That's a dilemma you will probably never have to deal with, but–"

"Enough!" I clamped my hands over my ears. "I don't want to hear it."

"Fine," she said. "Do you understand what I've told you?"

"Yes."

"And you don't have any questions?"

"No, for God's sake, no. I want to go now." My feet were completely numb as I got up. My eyeballs felt as though they were pulsing from the pressure. In the distance, somewhere over the hill of my skull, thunder rumbled. The lightning would strike very soon. As I attempted to flee the living room, she blocked my path.

A white-hot rod of lightning scorched my skull, leaving a metal taste in my mouth as though I'd been chewing on a tuna can, pulling a strangled cry from my lips.

"Ruby, are you…"

Everything began to dissolve.

"Ruby," my name sounded slow and cumbersome, *Rhoooobheeee…*

She caught me before I hit the floor, her unusually strong arms wrapping around my waist. The film didn't cut off, just momentarily skipped, and slowly began correcting itself in my head.

"You stop that, Ruby," Mum snapped, her smoky breath on my face. "You stop that fainting routine. There's nothing wrong with you. If anyone should be fainting, it's *me*."

YOU'RE GOING TO TELL ME! YOU'RE GOING TO CONFESS EVERYTHING!

"I need to get out for a bit," I said, when I found enough wiggle room to break free. "This is a lot, right now. Can I just…" I put my hands up and stepped back as though she were aiming a weapon at me.

"I didn't want you to find out like this. God almighty, I don't know if my life is a comedy or a fucking tragedy. I mean this." She waved at the TV. The cameras were still filming from George's house, cutting between a reporter on street level and the shaky aerial footage. "He did love me, you know. And like it or not, you were the result of that love."

"Who else knows?" I asked, because until a couple of minutes ago, I had no clue that George McDermott was my biological dad. But Mia did. That had to be why she chose his house. That had to be what she was trying to get him to confess.

How could she have known? And why was she so bent on having him confess it to me?

If she knew, why didn't she just tell me herself?

"Your dad – Richard, I mean – he found out you weren't his, obviously. Doesn't know about George, though. Richard didn't want to know whose you were. He's prideful that way – wouldn't want anyone to know that he'd been tricked for all these years." Her eyes passed across me. "He wouldn't want other people to know he was raising someone else's bastard."

She had been expecting a rise out of me, but there was too much chaos going on inside my head for her remark to sting. "Other people must know, Mum."

"It's not something I went around broadcasting. I'm not a slut, you know. And anyway, George's fucking solicitor made me sign an NDA to get that money. A non-disclosure agreement. I'm legally not allowed to tell anyone. And by the way, you should be on your knees thanking me for doing that, because it's money I negotiated for you – not that you'll appreciate it at all. And not that I got a fucking penny out of it, they made quite sure of that. Richard found out when I tried to re-negotiate the terms of our arrangement. I had this idea that maybe raising George's lovechild might be worth significantly more than we'd first agreed, and maybe I should get something for all the work I'm basically doing alone. That's when Richard found the papers."

Oh, and I'm sure that wasn't an accident, I thought. *I'll bet I know exactly how it happened. You and Dad got into an argument and suddenly he just stumbled upon the solicitor's letters. You just loved that, didn't you.*

"And did he… tell anyone? George, I mean."

"It wouldn't have been in his best interests," Mum said, slowly bringing the bottle to her lips. "He already has a family. A wife, young daughter."

I know. I saw their picture above the mantlepiece yesterday when I broke into his house.

"Half-sister," I slurred, pain burrowing into my brow, forcing me to close my eyes. "Oh, Mum... this is so... it's all so..."

"I know," she said, and passed me the bottle. "God must have a sense of humour. Because he's up there laughing at me right now. After all this, I'm still the one who ends up with nothing. No money. Richard goes off and starts seeing some whore. George dies, and my daughter is a complete fucking mess. I just don't know what I could have done to deserve such a shit life."

Any ideas I had about getting away for a breath of fresh air quickly fizzled out. I was numb all the way through to the marrow now. We sat down and watched the broadcast, but I couldn't really hear it or concentrate on the visuals. We passed the bottle back and forth until it was empty. Mum cried, rambled incoherently, and then as time ran away, she grew even nastier, swearing at the TV, spittle flying from her shiny lips. Then that phase passed and she was silent, lighting cigarettes and not smoking them until the ash built up and dropped to the carpet.

All the while, my thoughts become a swirling, nightmarish carnival. George's face stretched and warped, offering an exaggerated laugh for a TV audience, before morphing into pitiful sobs as he lay on the landing of his house. Every time they showed a picture of George on the news, or a still image, I searched his face for any resemblance, but couldn't find it. Probably because all I could think about was what he looked like when Mia was finished with him.

That was when I started to lose my mind.

CHAPTER 26

At some point that night, in the early hours, I think, I had gone to bed, my skull ready to marble from the tension of my thoughts. Lying there in the dark, the room felt as though it were shrinking and expanding in time with my breathing. It was probably dehydration or starvation (I hadn't eaten in over a day), or maybe my conscience was devouring me from the inside out.

I tried to call Mia, but the line wouldn't connect. My guess was that she'd snapped her SIM card in half and had thrown the phone in a river. It was probably for the best; I felt an almost unbearable urge to talk to her.

How could she have known when I didn't?

Lying there, wide awake, I became aware of scratches and knocks coming from the shed again. Something *was* in there; the sounds were too deliberate to be a fox or a cat, the thuds too heavy.

With my mum passed out on the sofa in the living room, the TV throwing a bluish glow against the darkness while taunting me with George's face, I set out to the garden. There was a chill in the summer air as I crept barefoot over the grass, using my phone's dim screen light as a torch.

"Mia," I hissed as I got closer to the shed. "Mia, are you in there?"

The wind sighing through the trees was the only reply I received. I opened the shed door and called her name again. Hugging myself against the cold, I suddenly smelled the passing ghost of her perfume and became sure that she was in there, lurking in the dark, hunkered down where I couldn't see her. Hiding from me.

"If you're there, just say something," I said. "Please, Mia. We need to talk."

Navigating the junk, I swept through the shed, searching for any sign that she had been there. Nothing. Returning to the house, vaguely aware that I had stepped on something sharp, I lingered in the silent kitchen and ran the tap for a glass of water.

Something caught my eye. At first, with the kitchen lights on, I thought it was the ghost of my reflection looking back at me through the window. But it wasn't. Mia was crouched down in the bushes outside, staring directly at me. I opened my mouth to say something, but she quickly darted off like a startled rabbit. I heard the bang and clank as she clambered up and over the fence.

The shock glued my feet to the floor, but when it eventually wore off, I ran to the back door and called her name. Why hadn't she said anything? There was a rustling sound, but I couldn't be sure whether it was the breeze or Mia, scurrying around in the alleyway next to my house. My legs were vibrating madly as I took a single step out of the kitchen, the concrete icy beneath the soles of my feet.

"Mia," I called. "Mia, wait."

And in the wind, I could have sworn, *sworn*, that I heard her return my name.

Ruby.

But she didn't come out to greet me, and after a while, I went back inside.

When the exhaustion finally claimed me that night, I was submerged straight into a nightmare. Mia was standing at the foot of my bed, her black eyes blazing through the crimson red mask of George's blood, her lips pulled back into a ghastly, artificial grin. She was giggling, hands fidgeting about her face.

I wanted to ask what was funny, but the nightmare logic didn't allow me to speak or move, apparently. I just had to lie there while Mia broke into a fit of laughter.

"He wouldn't confess," she said gleefully. "He wouldn't tell me the worst thing he'd ever done. Ruby," she whispered. "He deserved it. You know that."

I shook my head from side to side, trying to scream.

When I managed fight my way out of the nightmare and snap awake, I was lying on the floor. I hadn't even realised that I'd fallen out the bed. My cheeks were wet from crying in my sleep.

There was no escaping it, even in my dreams. I was about to get back on the bed when I heard a thump above me. The loft. A scream coiled in my throat, and I had to clamp both hands over my mouth to keep it from springing out. Something vital inside my head felt as though it were detaching, and I lost my sense of equilibrium. I was on my way to believing that I had imagined the noise in the loft, that my depleted, paranoia-fried mind had invented it, when I heard it again. A thump-thump-thump-thump, directly above me.

Footsteps, but not in the loft.

The roof.

Mia. She was on the roof. Had to be.

Clambering back on the bed, I opened the window and stuck my head out for a better vantage point, squinting against the dark. If she really was up there, then it was only a matter of time before she slipped from the tiles.

But I couldn't see her. A minute went by, then ten.

There were no more thumps or bumps in the night. I managed to convince myself that it had to have been a pigeon, but I couldn't shake the feeling that she was still up there, clutching the chimney.

All you have to do is pick up the phone, make an anonymous call…

"And say what?" I rasped aloud, frightened by the sound of my own voice.

Tell them the truth. Tell them what Mia did. Get her before she gets you.

CHAPTER 27

It didn't take long for the cause of death to be made public and an official murder enquiry to be launched. Mum bought every newspaper and magazine, cross-referencing the articles, probing each column for some new scrap of information regarding the circumstances surrounding George's death. Almost every publication used the photo hanging above George's mantlepiece, depicting him with his ex-wife and daughter, as their front page. There were a lot of cliché headlines, but only one really stood out.

WHO COULD BE SO EVIL?

In the next few days, the media paid tribute to the brilliance of George McDermott. Celebrities gave testimonials about how wonderful he was, while special biography shows were hastily cobbled together to showcase his illustrious career.

The country mourned the loss of one of the most beloved all-round entertainers to grace our screens.

And then, about a week and a half after the discovery of his body, the other stories started to come out.

One morning the newspapers were lamenting the brutal murder of a shining star, and overnight, the media's whole trajectory changed. Allegations of sexual misconduct sprung up after his funeral from women who had worked with him in some capacity over the years. Their identities were withheld for their own safety. Through an inside source (a sergeant in the London Met was suspected, though it was never confirmed), *The Daily Scribe* had obtained evidence that a total of sixteen women had made accusations against George of inappropriate sexual behaviour, while he was still alive. His lawyers and bosses at the television networks had paid to make most of the claims disappear, but weren't able to dissuade a couple of the victims who had been intent on taking the matter to court. There was talk of super injunctions, pay-outs… hush money.

With these new stories unfurling, the country's focus began to sway away from George's death and centre on the misdeeds of his life. A slew of investigative reports arose, ranging from detailed broadsheet articles to controversial documentaries that had the victims offering their story behind the safety of a screen, their voices altered. They painted a very different picture of George McDermott, one closer to the creep I saw in the Polaroids than the humble everyman visiting children's wards.

Then it occurred to me: they might think one of his victims killed him. Someone out for revenge. With all this bad publicity he was receiving posthumously, the police might crack down and centre their efforts on his past victims.

Victims like Mia.

That's what it had really all been about. She didn't give a fuck about running away and starting up a life together. She used me, wrapping me up in her revenge plot so that I became an accomplice to her crime. Maybe she was even trying to frame me for it. I was nothing more than Mia's little toy to be wound up and let loose wherever she wanted.

What I couldn't work out was when, where, or how she had first met George. If I had spent more time flipping through those Polaroids, would I have seen her? Had he really been the source of her misery all along? Were those stories she alluded to about her mum's mistreatment a fabrication, a cover story to get me on her side?

The questions suffocated me.

In those first two weeks since they discovered his body, I had barely slept at all. My head ached constantly, and I whittled away most of my days staring at a wall in a sort of trance state. Eating was out the question, and soon, my clothes began to feel very baggy, my jeans and tracksuit bottoms slipping down my hips where they had been snug before. Acne flared up across my face in an angry red outcrop. I didn't wash or brush my teeth, and whenever I caught my reflection in the mirror on the back of my door, I appeared haggard and oily. I was starting to not recognise myself. My eyes had taken on a sunken quality, sitting deeply in my darkened sockets. The rapid weight loss had altered the shape of my face, and the shelf of my brows seemed to protrude until I looked like a rediscovered neanderthal – a wildling that had wandered back into civilization.

So, I covered the mirror over with a jacket and avoided the one in the bathroom completely.

Every second of every day during those summer holidays, I was tensed in anticipation of that knock at the door. There was no way a crime like that, with as much attention as it had attracted, would remain unsolved. The torment of having to endure these long stretches of silence was almost unbearable. In many ways, I now welcomed the idea of getting caught and arrested so I could finally breathe again and not feel that awful tightness in my chest, or the sickening churn of my guts. At least then I could give them my side of the story, explain that I hadn't meant for any of this to happen. I hadn't done anything.

Mum's mood fluctuated wildly during this time. She shuffled through a complicated range of emotions, from placid indifference to vehement denial. At once, George McDermott was her one true love, the man who could have enriched our lives, and by the end of that glass of gin, he was an egotistical pig; a disgusting whore of a man who only ever cared about himself and the advancement of his career.

It was during one such bout of vitriol, after weeping herself hoarse during a BBC programme called *George McDermott: The Man We Never Knew*, that she turned on me and said, "You *look* like him." The statement was an accusation, as though I'd somehow manipulated my DNA to conspire against her. "It's in your face."

I gave her no argument, planted in the armchair, staring *through* the TV, not really taking in much of what was being shown. That is, until the documentary centred in on George's early career at the Maypole Broadcast Service. A blond, middle-aged woman with a pointy nose came on screen, and a text box popped up to declare her name and relevance: *Shannon Driver, former co-host of Chasing Limelight 1986–1990*.

Before Shannon even began to speak, I felt Mum revving up in her seat, fingers scraping the arm of the sofa.

"He came to the show with the reputation as a ladies' man," Shannon began. "I certainly knew several women who had confessed to one-night stands with him, and I'd witnessed his allure first hand whenever we went out at an award show, or an industry function. Women *threw* themselves at him."

"This ugly fucking bitch," Mum said, white cottonmouth globules dotting the corner of her lips. She sat up so quickly that she spilled her drink on her tatty sundress. At this point, the liquid was thick and dark, and I realised that the gin had finished and so she had been drinking Tia Maria straight. That bottle of Tia Maria had been sitting in the cupboard for years – a gift from one of my dad's friends a few Christmases back, and neither of my parents had touched it due to their dislike of the beverage. "She wanted him herself. You should have seen the way she acted around him. Always peacocking… tits out every chance she could get. But he didn't like her, did he? No! Not with that fucking beak of hers."

Shannon went on: "He was newly married, but he just couldn't adjust to family life. He was young, rich, and famous, and when you have the world eating out the palm of your hand, it's very difficult to abstain from a lot of the vices.

"And soon enough, you'd hear little whispers." Shannon smiled ruefully. "There were rumours that one of his flings fell pregnant."

"Fling? Fling, you fucking hawk-nosed slut!" Mum bellowed, waving an arm until more black liquid fell from the glass. "You wanted him for yourself. Yeah, you wanted him. You fucking fooled no one, love. You fooled no one."

"And buying her silence was extremely costly." Shannon said. When the interviewer asked if she knew who the woman was, Shannon considered, and then said, "Yes. But I wouldn't divulge that. It wouldn't be fair to his ex-wife."

The glass smashed against the TV, but when it failed to silence Shannon Driver, my mum picked up the ashtray and hurled that too. This time, the screen fractured and went black, a thin whisp of smoke escaping from the chasm. The smash and bang of her tantrum frayed my nerves and I covered my ears, curling into the armchair.

"That's it, feel sorry for Kristin sitting in her mansion, with her two Rolls Royces. Why did he marry her in the first place? He didn't love her. He never loved her! He loved me!"

After a while, I said, "I need to go out."

"Then go," she said. She hadn't taken her eyes off the black screen, staring into the cobweb of cracks as though the programme were still playing. "Do whatever you want. What does it matter? What does any of it matter anymore?"

As I turned to leave, she murmured something into her glass before taking a sip. What she said was either "I wish *I* was dead" or "I wish *you* were dead." I just couldn't be sure which.

She was right. What did it matter?

CHAPTER 28

Three weeks crawled by, and I had started to feel very unwell. Noises in the shed almost constantly. I'd go out to check, thinking she'd be there but knowing she wasn't. Once, while my mum sat in the kitchen rifling through her newspapers, scanning the columns for new info about George, I heard a thump and a drag from the shed. I left my room, plodded downstairs, and asked if she'd heard anything.

"Heard what?" she said, without looking up from the newspaper, licking her thumb before flipping through the pages so rapidly that they often tore.

"Noises in the shed. I keep hearing them."

She spared me a glance, her eyes rolling over me, then returned to her newspaper. "It's in your head."

"It *isn't,*" I said, indignantly. I'd grown increasingly irritable in the last few days, the morbid exhaustion fuelling my anger. "I think it's foxes."

"Have you *seen* foxes?" she asked. "You've been in and out of there about a hundred times a day. I thought you were in there tidying, trying to do something useful to fill up your time."

"Like you're filling your time?" I returned fire. "Stacks of newspapers everywhere. His face *everywhere*. It's not bad enough you watch it on the TV constantly."

She had replaced the broken TV with the portable one she kept in her room. It required an indoor ariel that was almost impossible to get a coherent picture out of, no matter how often she fiddled with it.

She made a spitting sound and turned away from me, disgusted. It was eleven in the morning, but she had a carafe of white wine on the table, next to an uneaten omelette. "And when was the last time you took a shower? You stink. You're becoming *offensive*."

Ignoring her, I went out to check the shed, then, finding it undisturbed, returned to my lair.

At some point, I began pulling strands of my hair out.

As the sun slipped away, I made a game of staring up at the ceiling, seeing how long I could concentrate on the hairline crack running across it without getting distracted. What else was I supposed to do? A jigsaw? Watch another breakdown of George McDermott's personal life? Go for a walk? The boredom was excruciating, but it almost helped stave off that insidiously sour brew of guilt and panic until I began hearing more thumps above me: footsteps scuttling across the roof. I couldn't get a good look out my window, but if I went down to the garden, I'd have a better vantage point of the house. I'd be able to see if Mia was up there, walking on the tiles, perched by the chimney.

Rushing out of my room, I almost collided with Mum as she ascended the stairs. Her eyes were bleary, her mouth hanging open like a fish at the market, her tongue almost lolling.

She said some garbled approximation of "Where are you going?"

A patter above us, footsteps carefully navigating the tiles. "Can you hear that?" I asked.

Her face screwed up with revulsion, the alcohol glittering in her eyes. "Hear *what*?"

"Listen," I urged. "There, you hear it?"

Mum steadied herself using the banister and indulged me for a few seconds, her mouth still hanging open.

"You're telling me you can't hear it?"

She cleared her throat, blinked hard, and then swept her messy blond hair away from her face. "Ruby, I want you to come with me for a second."

"No, I can't, I have to check…"

"There's nothing on the roof. And there's nothing in the shed."

"How would you even know?" *You're drunk out of your mind all day,* I wanted to say, but didn't have the nerve or the strength to articulate it. "All you care about are your stupid newspapers."

"Fine. Do what you want. I couldn't care less at this point. Move out my way."

She barged past me, went into her room, and slammed the door so hard I felt the house shudder. I went down to the garden and gazed at the roof, but even with the moonlight it was difficult to see much. Behind me, a sound in the shed made me jump.

"There's nothing in there. And there's nothing on the roof," I said, licking my papery lips with a dry tongue. "She's gone."

It's been three weeks, I thought. *George has been in the news non-stop for three weeks. They have a huge taskforce assigned to finding his killer. And yet the knock hasn't come.*

It might not ever.

And I might not ever see Mia again, and even with everything that she had done to me, this thought brought tremendous sadness, like a heavy black quilt smothering me. She had been my only friend, and now she was gone too. I had nothing, and no one.

Trudging back through the house, I ignored the bumps and thuds that I could still hear, trying to convince myself that it was some acoustic trick of the plumbing, or that maybe our cantankerous boiler was on the blink again.

My mum's snoring was almost inhumanly loud as I made it back to my room, but I was thankful that it drowned everything else out. When I lay down on the bed, fully resigned to my fate, I expected to be staring at the black square of ceiling until the sun rose. Instead, almost miraculously, I fell asleep.

CHAPTER 29

My eyes snapped open, but I was paralysed, unable to move my limbs. It was as though I were strapped to the bed in an asylum, helpless to my surroundings. That slow, almost melancholic whistling began in the garden, floating up to my window. That familiar whine of the kitchen door springs as the man entered the house. The slow, almost shuffling footsteps.

"Mum!" I shouted, but couldn't quite convey the fear I felt to the volume of my voice. The word came out muted, little more than a fragile whisper. I tried to yell "He's coming!" but only squeaked.

The whistling became louder as the man began up the stairs, the wood creaking beneath his weight. I inhaled deeply before forcing the air out of my lungs, and in a frantic rush, I was able to call for my mum, louder this time, but not loud enough. Willing my body to move, I strained with all my might against the invisible bonds that kept me pinned in place.

I'm in hell, my mind told me with absolute certainty. *I must be in hell, because if I were still alive, I would have died of fright by now, and oh my good God, that would be such a relief because I cannot stand this, I cannot stand it! Please, God, help me, help me, help me, help me.*

The veins throbbed in my neck as I strained, finally able to curl my toes. Yet lifting my feet was still impossible. The man was at the top of the stairs, a stride away from my door, when the eerie whistling stopped abruptly.

My doorknob rattled as it was gripped from the other side.

"Please!" I tried to screech. "I'm sorry! I didn't know she was going to do that to you. I swear to God, I didn't!"

The doorknob turned slowly.

"My sweetheart." The mushy words sounded more like gargling than speech. The door opened, and George stepped into my room. The darkness helped conceal the wreckage of his face, though I was still able to make out the unnatural, pulpy shape of his head, where the skull had been shattered and the scalp lifted into flaps. "Oh, look at you. Daddy's little girl. Daddy's angel."

He stepped closer, the phlegmy laughter bubbling away in his throat. The stink of blood filled my room, but there was something else, too. A foul, offensive reek of rot, despicable beyond anything I'd ever smelled before.

"I always knew we'd meet one day," George managed through his mangled mouth. A tinkling sound followed the sentence; the last of his broken teeth dislodging from their swollen housing and falling to the hardwood floor. "Come here and let Daddy kiss you."

I was suddenly awake and on the floor. I hadn't even realised that I'd fallen from the bed. My cheeks were wet from crying in my sleep, and my throat was raw, presumably from screaming myself out of the nightmare.

It had felt so real. The visit was enough of a warning. He wasn't going to let it drop. He wasn't going to allow me the luxury of thinking I'd gotten away with murder, even if it hadn't been me who struck the killing blow. I hadn't struck *any* blow.

I was going to pay for my part in the crime. He was going to make sure of it.

"Ruby, come here," Mum shouted frantically from downstairs the following morning. "They've found them. They've found the one who killed George."

I'd been curled up beneath the duvet, suffocating in my own breath and heat, too scared to poke my head out of the cocoon. If I stayed there, sweating in the duvet's dark, oppressive confines, then the outside world didn't matter; I couldn't see it, and, my deteriorating mind decided, it couldn't see me. But Mum's declaration was like a set of jump leads hooked directly up to my heart, shocking me out of concealment.

Mia. They've caught her.

I staggered out of my bedroom and couldn't seem to control the muscles spasming in my calves, or the clumsy slapping of my feet as I precariously negotiated the stairs.

"What is it?" Panting, I plodded through to the living room, where Mum was pointing her cigarette at the screen. The new hosts of *Wake Up, UK* were breaking the story. Julia Whittaker, George's former co-host, had been too deeply affected by his death to return to the show, which went a long way toward proving – at least in my mum's mind – that they'd been having an affair off-screen. The stand-in presenters, Matt Rose and Nina Casey, who had the combined charismatic appeal of a wet bag of laundry, had worn black armbands in remembrance of George, until the numerous sinister rumours began circulating about his sexual deviancy. Now it was business as usual while they read from the teleprompter, sans armbands.

"... believe that the suspect they have in custody is connected in some way to the murder of George McDermott. For legal reasons, the person cannot be named."

The camera cut to outside Southwark Police Station, where a young female presenter with flowing blond hair and a peach blouse offered her take on the situation as it was developing.

"We're told that in the early hours of this morning, detectives arrested someone in connection with the murder of George McDermott, but it is still unclear what evidence led them to the arrest, or to what extent the suspect's involvement may be."

From the studio, Matt Rose's faux-sombre inflection: "Do we know yet how sure the police are that this suspect is the one that committed this awful crime?"

It was a stupid, cumbersome question, probably designed to stretch out the segment given their limited information. He didn't sound half as intelligent when he went off-script.

"At this time, all we know is that the police have someone in custody who has been arrested on suspicion of murder, but that the person legally cannot be identified," the reporter said, her hair blowing in the breeze as she relayed the information.

"If they can't legally be named, then that must mean they're underage," Nina Casey speculated, doing her best to sound outraged. "Are we talking *teenagers*?"

They continued to babble back and forth, finding new ways of saying the same thing whilst adding their own invaluable nuggets of wisdom to put extra seasoning on the story. "Despite what George has since been accused of–" Matt Rose started to say, before derailing himself completely. They were probably under strict instructions not to mention the sex scandals, for fear it would in some way incriminate the execs at *Wake Up, UK*, who allegedly had prior knowledge of George's crimes. "I mean, there has been some controversy surrounding George McDermott since his death, but regardless – he was still a human being, he was a father, and he didn't deserve to be slaughtered in his own home like that."

"Well, nobody deserves that," Nina Casey supplied, though it came out bland and indifferent, and the complete opposite of how she felt.

"They've got him," Mum croaked, and gave me a grim smile that accentuated the smoker's wrinkles developing around her mouth. "The bastard that killed George. They've finally caught him."

I almost tripped myself up right then by saying "What do you mean *him*?" but caught it at the last instant, offering a non-committal murmur of agreement. Inside, however, I felt all the gnarled knots that had twisted around my muscles like tumours start to loosen – not all the way, but enough so that there was an uncoiling of tension, a distant promise of relief somewhere down the line.

They've got Mia. They know she committed the murder, and she hasn't told them about me, otherwise I'd be in custody too. Wouldn't I?

That optimistic apprehension made me feel like I was recovering from a terrible illness; with each passing hour, I regained strength, managed to eat some food, took a shower, and even went for a walk around the block. Hope had never felt so good. It was as though I were in the middle of shedding a skin, losing the rough edge of this old hide, ready to reset and start afresh.

Two mornings later, the presenters on *Wake Up, UK* announced that the suspect had been released without charge.

CHAPTER 30

Somehow, I made it to the end of the six-week summer holidays. Averaging only about an hour of sleep a night, I was in no shape to return to school, but there was always the chance it might serve as a distraction. Aside from George's nightly visits (always whistling, always *cooing*), and the persistent noises in the shed and roof, I had become physically fragile. I couldn't eat, couldn't seem to carry my own weight more than a few steps without fatigue settling into my bones. And along with my chronic headaches, which would turn the world white for a few blinks at a time like prolonged camera flash, I had begun to vomit a lot. Once, there was blood in my bile. I thought maybe I was dying.

Despite everything, I missed Mia desperately. Gradually, the loneliness had overcome my fear and guilt, but I still held onto a healthy portion of resentment at the predicament she had put us in. It was her wild, unhinged actions that had torn our friendship apart. But had there really ever been a friendship to begin with, or was she just using me this whole time? Even as I walked through the gates on that first day of term, my hair greasy and unwashed, I continued to wonder why I was always being punished. Was I cursed? Things were going wrong for me even before I was born, and I had no idea how to break the cycle. Perhaps I was just destined to live miserably, alone and unloved. God, how dramatic. I hated myself.

While the other students at St Monica's chirped and flapped with their peers at the reunion, I skulked through the courtyard and slunk inside the main building. At registration, we were given our timetables, and when the bell rang to signal first period, I headed over to History.

Miss Milligan welcomed us back enthusiastically, nodding cheerfully as we each entered the room, telling us to sit wherever we felt comfortable. She was like a grandmother receiving a long-overdue visit from her grandkids. Her smile faltered when I passed through her threshold, her eyes scanning me from behind her thick lenses.

"Good morning, Ruby," she said, unable to disguise the distress that my appearance had provoked in her. "Did you have a nice summer holiday?"

"Yes, Miss," I said. "Did you?"

The smile had completely vanished from her face now and was replaced with a scowl of concern. Her nose wrinkled slightly as though she had smelled something spoiled. "I did... thank you." She hesitated a moment, probably assessing my decline, before saying, "Go on, grab a seat now."

I sat by the window, and eventually Miss Milligan began unpacking the Cold War. Becca, who had served me at the petrol station the day that Mia and I had broken into the house on Vincent Street, sat on the opposite side of the room to me. I had seen her in the hallway outside, but apparently her friendliness didn't extend beyond the workplace. She had regarded me with a look of... no, it wasn't disgust, but maybe it was *distrust*. She was wary, as though I might suddenly decide to lunge at her and take a bite out of her face.

About halfway through the lesson, I saw a police car pull up outside the school gates. For a few seconds, the image didn't quite register. Then it was as if a hand had gripped me by the throat and squeezed, cutting off my oxygen. Miss Milligan's voice drowned to a drone as my attention locked to the two police officers who stepped out of the patrol car and began crossing the courtyard. They were coming straight into the main building, where I was having History on the second floor.

The pain in my head was immediate and enormous. There was that white flash, followed by an explosion of black stars. My body jerked and I knocked over my exercise book and textbook, sending them clattering to the floor.

"Oh," Miss Milligan broke off mid-sentence. "Is everything alright, Ruby?"

My answer didn't come right away. Biting the inside of my cheek, waiting for the pain to subside, I slowly said, "Can I go to the... medical... room, please?"

"Is it a headache, dear?" she asked, waddling down the aisle between desks until she was standing next to me, eclipsing the other pupils.

"Yes. I need to go."

"Of course. Let me get you a pass."

Scooping my stationary back into my bag, I rose from the desk, my skin flushing with heat. Something twisted in the emptiness of my stomach, sending a squirt of painful, acidic bile up my throat. Slapping a hand over my mouth, positive that I was about to be sick right there in the class, my body began to gently tremble.

Don't faint, I commanded inwardly. *Please, don't you dare faint.* I was more frightened of passing out than enduring the embarrassment of vomiting, and as soon as Miss Milligan extended the blue cardboard hallway pass, I snatched it and fled. But just before I left the room, I saw Becca, eyeing me closely.

When I was in the hallway, I saw the police officers turn the corner at the west staircase, and I abruptly changed direction. There was another staircase at the other end of the hallway, and if I moved casually enough – which took all the concentration and strength I could summon – then I could avoid the officers completely.

They're here for me. There was no other reason for them to be on this side of the school, in this building. My shoes slapped the stairs as I rushed down them, and I was dripping with sweat by the time I broke out of the building. I was supposed to take the signed hallway pass to the medical room, then get my dismissal to leave. Instead, though, I swerved the reception and continued straight on through the school gate and into the street. The school gates were never locked back then, which was a protocol that changed after my trial. Virtually anyone could come and go into the school premises as they pleased.

My pulse began jackhammering as I half-walked, half-jogged to the bus stop, unable to force my legs to a sprint. Mercifully, a bus arrived a few minutes later and I got on, panting, wincing, my bus pass flapping in my hand as I showed it to the driver.

When I sat down in the chair, I felt as though I'd just finished a triathlon. A stitch stabbed at my side, and the bus's momentum worked against my equilibrium. The lure of oblivion tugged at me, and I fought against it, holding back tears from the stress my body was processing.

Sometime later, feeling marginally better but still a million miles away from anything close to normal, I pressed the bell for my stop. Using the support poles to make my way to the back doors, I waited for the bus to decelerate.

I happened to look over at the space behind the bus driver's booth. Beneath the illuminated sign that would flash the words 'Bus Stopping' once the bell was pressed, was an advertising poster inside a hard plastic window. Except, rather than promoting the latest mobile phone, or local colleges that you could apply to, there was a sign that read: *DO YOU RECOGNISE THIS PERSON?*

There were four grainy, blurred photographs that showed a figure walking down the street. Even with the poor picture quality, I knew it was me. I couldn't be sure, but I thought these were CCTV images capturing me as I made my way back from the hotel in King's Cross, because I was carrying the bag that I had retrieved.

How had they managed to zero in on me? Was it the blood on my clothes that I had tried to hide? It can't have been. There wasn't that much, and by the time I had made it to the hotel it had already darkened. For all anyone knew, I could have spilled hot chocolate or something. It didn't even look like blood. I had washed it.

There wasn't that much blood.

Not that much.

I'd washed my face and hands, too. Hardly any of it got on my clothes. It wasn't even recognisable.

So how had they pieced together these images of me after I left George's house?

Shut up, I instructed my roaring mind. *Just shut up. You can't make anything out in those images. You can't even tell it's a girl, let alone* me. *Just stop wigging out. They don't know anything. If they did, they would have you in the cells already.*

So what were they doing at school?

Christ only knew. But it didn't take long for me to find out.

CHAPTER 31

George was sitting on the end of my bed when the knock came. He had started off in the garden, whistling as he always did, and slowly shambled up to the back door, letting himself in. I just had to lie there and listen to him thudding up the stairs, wheezing and gurgling through his shattered mouth with each step. My body felt like bursting from the anxiety, every muscle clenched to capacity. Occasionally, he would cough wetly, murmur something about me being *Daddy's little angel.* The bedroom door creaked open, and he shuffled across the carpet, finally plonking down on the end of my bed. I couldn't open my mouth to breathe or scream. The stink of his decay was overpowering enough to scatter any rational thought. His clumsy, cold hand fumbled for my foot, stroking it, squeezing reassuringly.

The insistent thumping on the front door shattered the nightmare and dragged me back into the real world, literally kicking and screaming. It was a few minutes after five in the morning, and I had been asleep for less than an hour. I had been off school for the past three days since running out of Miss Milligan's History class. Told Mum I had the flu. She didn't bother to check. Just sat in the living room, swearing at the TV, flipping through her newspapers.

"Open up!" a voice boomed from the doorstep.

I was already on my feet and wandering out into the hallway, where my mum met me, fumbling with the belt of her dressing gown. “Ruby,” she said. “What's happening?”

“Police! Open up!”

From the top of the stairs, I could make out several shapes through the opaque door pane, and strangely, felt an odd sense of relief.

“Police?” Mum said, paling as though the blood were draining from her body.

“It's okay, Mum,” I said, almost completely at ease. “It's okay. I think it's over now.”

When I stepped onto the staircase, she grabbed my arm, fingers embedding in my skin. “What's over now?” she said. “What do you mean by that?” Her breath was warm and bitter. Her eyes wide and bloodshot, began bulging in their sockets. “They might go away. They might–”

A loud bang at the door shook the house. We both yelped in fright.

“They're going to knock the door off,” I said, yanking free of her grasp. To the police I yelled, “Hold on, I'm coming down.”

“OPEN THIS DOOR, NOW!” an insistent, aggressive male voice commanded.

“I will,” I replied, keeping her gaze.

“Ruby,” she said, shaking her head. I could almost see her cogs turning as the realisation dawned on her. “What is this? What's happening? You know something you're not telling me.”

“I didn't do anything,” I said to her. “Just remember that. Please. It wasn't me.”

“What trouble are you in, Ruby? For fuck's sake, what is going on?”

Numbly, I floated down the stairs and pulled the bolt back, before fumbling with the lock. The door swung open, and a sea of bodies flooded into the hallway. There was a blur of confusion. It was like watching a video tape on fast-forward as they crowded the house, and then the jarring, abrupt change in pace as the footage went into slow motion. It took a couple of seconds for me to realise that I couldn't hear them. Their lips were moving but someone had turned the volume dial all the way down. Sweat burst out of my pores. I was nodding. "Yes, yes, yes." I understood why they were there, but I needed them to back up a second, just give me some space to catch my breath. "Yes, fine, just hold on a second. I'll come with you just give me a second."

A hand reached for me. I jerked away, lost my balance, and hit the floor heavily, landing on my side. A nasty jolt of pain in my ribs stole the breath from my lungs. Before I could open my mouth to scream, they were pulling me to my feet, speaking at me, all very calm, almost friendly. It felt like all the air that should have been in my lungs was now locked in my stomach. Then the sound came back on full blast. There was noise all around me: heavy footsteps, jumbled voices over radio, my mum's maniacal screaming, the front door clanging against the wall as more officers huddled in.

They were reading me my rights. They could have been talking to me in Mandarin for all the sense it made.

"You're not taking her anywhere!" Mum was screeching at them, the vehemence coming from some basement level in her that I never knew existed. From behind a wall of bodies, I saw her pick up a glass vase that sat on the hallway table. Before she could even raise it above her head to throw it, she was pinned to the wall and the vase shattered on the hardwood floor. Then she began screaming about our rights, about how they had just assaulted a minor, about how she was going to sue the balls off each and every one of the police officers crowding her house. "You're all going to lose your fucking jobs for this!" She thrashed her head from side to side as it was the only part of her body still unrestrained. "You'll all lose your jobs, and I'll make sure of it! I'll make sure of it! You'll be on the breadline, and I'll fucking laugh and laugh and–"

Before I was ushered out of the house, I heard a sturdy female officer tell my mum that she could come to the station with me to act as my appropriate adult, so long as she calmed down. All she got for her trouble was a mouthful of dehydrated spit, a cavalcade of abuse. And then my mum lunged and bit her face. The officer screamed in shock and pulled back before Mum could really clamp her teeth in, the chaos erupted afresh.

The cuffs were on so tight that I could feel the metal grinding against my wrist bones. The officer who dragged me out kept a hand on the nape of my neck, pushing my head forward, as though they thought I might take inspiration from my mum and try to use it as a weapon.

At least they hadn't made a complete show out of the arrest. There were only four police cars, a van, and about a thousand officers crowding our quiet little street. This armada hadn't gone unnoticed, despite the early hour. Every one of my neighbours was out on their doorstep for the event, heedless of their pyjamas, whispering to one another, pointing. Behind me, I could still hear Mum going berserk, but now her words were muffled.

They bundled me in the back of the van with a female officer who had distinctly ratty features, complete with beady eyes and buck teeth. When the door slammed closed, cutting off the daylight, I became aware of a whistle in my ragged breathing. Beyond the door, garbled chatter, the occasional shout of protest from my mum.

"Are you okay, Ruby?" the female officer asked me. She didn't look old enough to be a policewoman to me. She looked like someone I could have seen at sixth form next year. Although her tone was even, her face was implacable.

"I suppose so." I nodded. The ache in my ribs forced me to lean to the side, and I was having trouble taking a deep breath.

"Are you in pain?" the policewoman asked, frowning. There was no compassion in the question; it was more of a formality, or rather, an annoyance.

"My side," I said, flinching. Just the act of talking teased a complaint from my ribs. "I heard it crack when that man fell on me."

Ignoring my comment, she leaned forward and said, "You don't even know what's coming your way. Take my advice," she warned, levelling her eyes on me. "Just tell the truth. It'll be so much easier if you do."

The van went through the back entrance leading into Ankerly Police Station, a large, grubby building with sooty windows and brickwork the colour of exhaust fumes. I was ushered though the building where, at the front desk, an older sergeant with a weathered face that looked as though the return of Jesus wouldn't have surprised him, gave me a matter-of-fact rundown: I was being charged on suspicion of murder, and if I couldn't afford legal counsel, they would provide it for me.

Bored with the star attraction of the morning, the old sergeant turned his attention to whatever he was writing in a large ledger and grumbled, "Better get her settled in until

Mum gets here then." He sighed and added, "Can't wait to meet her. I hear she's a hoot."

My ratty policewoman friend led me to a claustrophobic cell where the cinderblock had been painted asylum-white. A metal slab attached to the wall with a wipeable plastic mattress served as a bed, atop which was a folded blanket and a single pillow. A dull metal sink and toilet finished the furnishings.

The policewoman ordered me to strip and change into a grey cotton tracksuit that they had provided for me. I did so under her supervision without complaint or a moment's bashfulness. What did it matter? I'd have to get used to it.

"No toilet seat," I murmured.

"What's that?" the policewoman returned.

Pointing to the toilet, I said, "There's no seat."

The icy glint in her eyes, combined with her overlarge teeth, stirred up very faint feelings of unease. "Hover," she said, stretching the word facetiously.

"What happens now?" I asked.

"Now you sit and wait for your brief." She left and slammed the cell door, locking it. Then she closed the wicket, covering up a rectangle of freedom, and I was alone.

The mattress squeaked softly as I lay down on it, dragging the blanket over my body.

When the cell door clanged opened again an hour or so later, I met my solicitor. A stuffy man in his fifties with expensive shoes and punchy exotic cologne entered my cell with his blazer slung over his arm, a briefcase in his other hand.

"Miss Wilcox," he began, extending his free hand for me to shake. He did not smile. "I'm Chris Papadopoulis. Nice to meet you. You're being charged on suspicion of murder.

From what I understand, there's a fair bit to go through and we don't have long. Now, they're going to want to interview you in the next couple of hours, so it's important that you tell me everything ahead of time. Understand?"

"Yes," I said.

"Good. Then, first, let's hear your version of events in as much detail as you can stand." He sat down at the foot of my bed and opened his briefcase, removing a notepad and pen. "And I don't suppose I have to impress upon you how important it is for you to tell me the truth? I'm here to help you, but I can't do that if you leave anything out, or you're not completely honest. Remember, I'm on your side, alright? That means I have to know every detail, no matter how damning. Omit *nothing*. Do you understand? Good. Then let's take it from the top."

The top? What was that, then? The car crash, my mum kicking me out the house, Dad leaving? What?

Meeting Mia?

I told him everything, and he interrupted my flow occasionally to ask questions, making notes, getting it all straight in his own head. When I reached the part about how we broke into George's home, my heart began galloping, my breathing accelerating.

"Do you need some water?" he asked, and I shook my head, knowing that if I put anything in my mouth, I would likely gag and throw it all back up.

I found it easier to tell the story on my feet, pacing the room as I spoke. My voice didn't sound like my own as the details spilled out, my speech so erratic that I began sputtering. It was as though I had suddenly developed a speech impediment that made me mangle words, mispronouncing things or blending certain phrases together.

"So, you see, it's really her fault," I ended, breathlessly, holding my head in my hands.

Chris Papadopoulos removed his glasses and wiped the lenses with his tie, before replacing them. He took a few minutes to digest what I'd just told him while I continued pacing. "Right. And that's everything, is it?"

"Everything," I assured him.

"Fine. Let's get your interview done."

CHAPTER 32

The first interview went well. Too well, in fact. My solicitor accompanied me to the windowless, harshly lit interview room where I was made to sit at a table opposite two detectives – DCI Harper, a matronly woman in her fifties who looked as though she might have trained shotput in her spare time, and DS Corrington, a man with flinty blue eyes that sat in a booze-bloated face. Also in the room was a woman called Lisa Willows, who worked for social services and was assigned as my appropriate adult. She informed me, in a calm and gentle manner, that she was there to explain anything I didn't understand throughout the process.

"This is probably going to be quite overwhelming for you, Ruby," Lisa began, "so if at any point you need to stop, or you don't want to answer something, just say so. Alright?" She smiled, and I immediately had the urge to hug her. Or rather, I wanted her to hug *me*. I didn't need someone to tell me everything would be okay – I knew there was no chance of that. But Lisa had been the first friendly face I'd encountered in so long.

DCI Harper asked me for my version of events, and, without needing to stop and query anything with Lisa or my solicitor, I gave them the full story. They listened to what I had to say with amicable interest, nodding in understanding as I emphasised certain points. When they asked me questions, their voices were soft, sympathetic, as though we were discussing some coursework I'd forgotten to hand in rather than the murder of a celebrity.

At the end, they thanked me for being so honest, expressing how difficult it must have been for me to confess my part in the crime. Then DCI Harper asked if I was hungry and I told her yes, matter of a fact, I was. Now that the weight of that burden had been lifted, I was suddenly aware of the neglect I'd put my body through these past weeks: sleep, food, water, I needed it all now in abundance.

"We've got shepherd's pie in today," DS Corrington told me as they walked me back to my cell. "I recommend it. Oh, and one other thing," he mentioned, clicking his fingers. "We're going to let you have a call with your mum in a little bit."

"How is she?" I asked.

"In shock, as you can imagine. Calmed down a bit now."

When the food arrived ten minutes later, piping hot in a plastic container, I wolfed it down, opening my mouth between bites to let the steam funnel out, sopping up the leftover sauce with the bread roll they'd also generously provided.

Then I went back to sleep. I had a dream that George was standing in the corner of the cell just watching me, his malformed face puffy with decay, but this time I didn't scream myself awake. Maybe now that I was caught and had confessed to my part in his death, George was losing his grip in the tug-o-war for my sanity. I slept soundly until morning. Then, that same afternoon, I was told I was having another interview to clear up a few points. No problem, I said. Happy to help.

This time, when I sat down in the interview room with Lisa Willows and my solicitor, I knew straight away that something was wrong. The façade of friendliness that the detectives had worn was now unmasked. Harper's and Corrington's expressions could have been chipped from a boulder. They watched me expectantly, arms folded across their chests, their hatred for me on full display. When I looked over at my solicitor for some sort of hint as to their shift in demeanour, he was seemingly as ignorant as me. I sought reassurance from Lisa, who could only produce a waning smile, before fixing her focus on the detectives.

Ditching the preamble, DCI Harper went straight in. "I'm told that despite your home situation, you're a very bright girl. Judging by our interview yesterday, I would have fully agreed with that sentiment. That leads me to believe that if I talk to you frankly and fairly, you will do the right thing today and tell us the truth this time."

My solicitor's head turned toward me.

"I did already. What am I supposed to have lied about?"

Corrington's mouth became a tight white line as he studied me. His body language told me that if there were no witnesses, and he could get away with it, he would jump across the table and beat the life out of me.

"I want to give you this opportunity now," Harper began, seeming more of a grumpy old dinner lady than a DCI. "Tell us the truth, tell us what we already know, and I can promise you from this point on, I will do my best to make things as easy as possible for you. You be straight with us, and we can build trust. But without trust, Ruby, we can't help you. And we do want to help you."

"Of course," Corrington cut in, "if you think you're going to get anywhere by lying to us again, then you can do that, too. You should probably be aware, though, that there are about a hundred journalists and paparazzi outside the station itching to get a hold of you since the news broke last night." A cocky half-smile tugged at one side of his mouth. "That's your prerogative. Try and mess us around and treat us like fools, then it only gets worse for you. Are you getting that? Those are your options from here on out. You can cooperate, or you can play the long game. The result is the same, except" – the smile fell away – "if you come clean and work with us, then we can protect you."

"We can do without the threatening implications," Lisa Willows said. "I'll remind you that she is a minor. There's no need for it."

"Threatening?" Corrington feigned innocence. "You think that's threatening? I'd say it was a frank assessment of the circus that's building out there."

"We're very aware," Papadopoulos said dryly, pushing his glasses up the bridge of his nose. "Now perhaps we can discuss what it is you think Ruby has lied about?"

My eyes fell to the light reflecting in the dented metal table. I could see past this tired good cop/bad cop routine. They were trying to trick something out of me, and just on the chance that they didn't have everything tied down the way they said they did, I was happy to keep my mouth shut. I'd played straight with them so far but if they wanted to try and bully me, then good luck; they could talk to the wall.

Sensing that I was going to do the smart thing, or possibly 'no comment' my way out of this little pregame, DCI Harper softly added, "Before you clam up, I think its best you see something. You're a smart girl, Ruby, I know that; your school grades certainly reflect that. You might be thinking that we're full of hot air. But I'd advise you to think again."

Corrington pushed a plastic sleeve toward me. I didn't want to touch it. "Go ahead," he said, leaning back in the chair. "Don't worry, it's not a trick. What's the matter, Ruby? You think we're trying to *coerce* you?" He snorted and laced his fingers behind his head, gloating. "Go on, turn it over. After all, it can't get you in any more trouble, can it?"

For a fleeting moment, my eyes flicked to Papadopoulos, but I could see he was just as puzzled as I was.

"Lisa?" I asked.

"You don't have to look, Ruby," she replied, but I couldn't help but notice a slight frosty edge to her tone now. "You can 'no comment'." Then, to my solicitor, she said, "Mr Papadopoulos, you might want to instruct your client."

"Ruby, you don't have to touch anything, either," he said drolly, his tone almost disinterested, although he continued to stare at the sleeve.

"You can either turn it over, or I will." Corrington shrugged. "You can keep your hands in your lap and 'no comment' all you want. Makes no difference to us."

Hesitantly, my hand touched the plastic sleeve. I heard Corrington's chair creak quietly. When I turned the sleeve over, I saw a grainy black and white image that I couldn't immediately discern.

"What is this?" I asked, timidly. I thought these might have been the blurry images that I had seen on the bus, but apparently not.

"That is you." He leaned forward, and lowering his voice, said, "Caught on CCTV on Monday, July 15, by the Colindale Lane Texaco station. This was the morning you said that you and Mia Swehl walked to George McDermott's house."

"What?" I said, squinting at the image on the blow-up. It was nothing more than a smudged impression of a person, though it did seem like a girl, maybe my height. "That's not me."

"Oh yeah, it is." Corrington stabbed a finger at the sleeve. "We even have a witness who works there who ID'd you. Rebeca Gibson. You know her, obviously; she goes to your school. Says you bought..." Relishing this, he checked his notes. "A bottle of Panda Pops, and ran out of there white as a sheet. And there's more." From his lap, he produced another blow up, though this one was distinctly better quality. It showed three different captions of a girl walking down a street. It was unmistakably me.

"That's you on Gennady Street. Know it?" Harper said.

I looked at Lisa. She said, "You don't have to answer."

"No comment," I replied hesitantly.

"Maybe this will help jog your memory." Corrington produced another blow up, this time showing the still image of me on Gennady Street from a wider angle. "These are still frames taken from the bingo hall opposite the Wimpy. The same Wimpy you told us that you and Mia walked past on your way to Vincent Street, after you went to the petrol station for your drink."

There was something wrong with the image, but I couldn't tell what. I separated the two different blow ups of Gennady Street and studied them.

"Come on. I know you can see it," Corrington said.

"See what?"

"That you're the only one in those photos," Corrington said, leaning back triumphantly.

The interview room slowly began rotating; I felt the shift in balance beneath my feet, a weird dizzying vortex that I couldn't seem to stop. I was on a slow-motion merry-go-round, but at an axis.

What the fuck is going on?

"You've doctored this," I said, as Lisa and Papadopoulos leaned over to inspect the printouts. My head started to hurt. "This isn't the truth," I said, but the frequency of my voice was caught somewhere between manic laughter and horrified screaming. "This isn't the truth at all. You've changed this picture," I said, ripping the printouts from the table. "What is this?"

"Why don't you tell us, Ruby?" Harper said.

I wanted to laugh. I wanted to scream. I wanted someone to stop the room from turning. Stop the ride completely.

"Tell us what *really* happened," Harper said, coaxing me gently, her tone suggesting that I could confide in her unquestionably.

"I already fucking did!" I shrieked at her. "I gave you everything, right down to the last detail."

"Calm down, Ruby," Lisa said soothingly, her hand hovering over my knee as though the proximity of her touch were enough.

"You didn't tell us you stopped at the petrol station. You didn't tell us your school friend worked there," Corrington said. "Actually, she was the one who told us. She put your name forward, said when you came into the petrol station you were nervous, acting strange, skittish. Later she realised that you came in the same day that George McDermott's house was broken into."

"What's the matter with you? Why would I lie? You already have me. It's not like I'm trying to get off, I confessed to everything I did." Papadopoulos placed a finger lightly on my wrist, hoping to settle me.

"But you didn't, did you?" Corrington said, squinting now. That smug meanness was gone and replaced with something else… something simpler.

Caution. He was wary of me.

"I did," I said, calmly as I could manage, flinching from Papadopoulos's touch. "Mia was the one who killed George. I passed out in the bathroom."

Corrington cut in. "No, Ruby."

"Yes. She hit him with the trophy."

"The trophy?" Corrington feigned surprise. "You don't mean…" He licked his thumb and leafed through the printouts before showing me a picture of the British TV Personality of the Year 1993 award, which was now in a zip-locked evidence bag. "This trophy? The same one we found in your garden shed this morning after we raided your house?"

"No." I shook my head so hard that it rattled my brain. "I mean, yes, that's the one, but I didn't… I didn't put it there."

"Yes. You thought that George McDermott was your dad," Corrington said. "You broke in. You hit him with the trophy."

"No!"

"You beat him to a bloody pulp."

"YOU'RE A LIAR!" I exploded, rearing up so quickly that the chair legs screamed against the floor. Lisa clasped my hand and ushered me back down into the chair. Papadopoulos barely reacted at all. "I didn't do any of that! It was Mia. She wanted to break in. She wanted to hurt him. She–"

"There is no Mia, is there, Ruby?" Harper said.

Pain shuttled down the curve of my skull and lanced through my neck. My mouth was so dry that my teeth felt coated in sand.

Corrington cut in. "There's never been any record of a Mia Swehl having ever attended St Monica's. No Mia Swehl in the Bramble Huts programme. We've checked every pupil ever assigned there. No name even remotely similar. No one even fitting the description of her you gave."

"Mia Swehl," Harper cooed, "odd name, that. Took us a moment to get the joke."

"Mia Swehl," Corrington repeated. "*Me-as-well.* I bet you thought that was pretty clever, didn't you? Tell me, Ruby, who exactly did you think you were dealing with yesterday? A pair of idiots?"

"If this is some sort of legal thing that you're getting at, you're going to have to explain it to me," I said, very aware of how eagerly Papadopoulos was studying me. "Lisa, they have to explain it to me because I'm getting really confused."

Lisa opened her mouth, but Harper overrode her. "It's quite simple. You made this mysterious Mia up so you could have someone to pin the crime on. I hate to break it to you, but it's not a new concept, Ruby. You found the letters from your mum's solicitor and thought that George McDermott was your father, and so you broke into his house to confront him."

Corrington added, "You got this little fantasy idea into your head that George was the reason your parents broke up, and so you decided to take all your anger out on him. Why not? He was the reason your whole life was a lie, wasn't it?"

"No… I had no idea he was supposed to be my real dad. My mum… she–"

"We're still yet to substantiate that George was your biological father," Harper said. "But a blood test wouldn't have mattered to you anyway, would it, Ruby? Because you only wanted to release all that rage that you had, didn't you?"

"And let's say, on some wild chance that this little scenario was true, that George really was your dad," Corrington said, "there's no justification for what you did to him. None at all. Nobody deserves what he got, Ruby."

"I… right now I can't even…" I was flabbergasted. I turned to Papadopoulos and said, "Chris, they can't do this, can they?"

"Do what?" he replied, seemingly more confused than I was.

Knowing that he was a waste of time, I appealed to Lisa. "Lisa, they're trying to pin this all on me. They're trying to say I'm lying… that I'm… I'm not going to take the blame for it all. I admitted to my part. Mia did the rest. She did *all* of it. If I'm guilty of anything it's breaking into his stupid fucking house. And I didn't even want to do that."

Lisa's expression was perfectly neutral. There was no offer of sympathy, no hint of understanding. No, what I saw was a woman who had been in her profession for a very long time, had seen all manner of damaged and dangerous children, and I was nothing more than another statistic to her. She was as careful with me as she might have been with a tiger pacing the room.

"You don't have to answer," was all she said.

"Is that it? Is that all you can do for me? They're trying to fit me up for murder and I didn't even do it, and all you can say is I don't have to answer?"

Papadopoulos glanced over at the detectives, eyebrows arched expectantly, prompting them for an answer. "Perhaps you'd like to stop with the mind games and come out with it."

Ignoring him and keeping her attention cemented on me, Harper said, "Those images aren't doctored. And there is no Mia. You did it all. We're quite confident we can prove that."

My brain started stuttering. Papadopoulos's head wagged between them and me, before he leaned in close and whispered, "Don't say another word to them. We need to talk. Right now." Then to the officers, he said, "I'd like a moment alone with my client, please."

Lisa stood up with her notepad, eager to escape the oppressive room.

"Sure thing," Harper replied with a shrug as she and Corrington rose from the table. "I'll bet you have a lot to go over. Take all the time you need. She's going to have a lot of time on her hands from now on."

The detectives got up to leave, but when they were at the door, I yelled at them: "You think I made her up? You really think that?"

"Yes," Corrington said. "We really do."

"Phone records," I blurted desperately. "My mobile. We used to call and text each other all the time. All you have to do is go on my phone. Go through it. You can check."

"We have your phone," Harper said. "We've seen the messages."

"Good. Well, that's good." I turned to Papadopoulos. "See. Mia is on my phone. If you say she didn't go to St Monica's, then I can't explain that; but that's not down to me. That could be an admin error or something, I don't..." The frustration was overriding all my senses, stealing my ability to think and speak straight. "And if you say her name isn't really Mia, then that's something else completely. But the person I used to talk to, my friend, Mia, is a real person, and she is on that phone. Calls, texts – hundreds of text messages."

"We've seen them," Harper said simply. "And we're working on getting the records from the phone company now. We should have the results back by lunchtime, I reckon."

"Then you can trace her, can't you?" I said, feeling as though my lungs were working too hard to push the words out. "You can locate her. Even with the phone off you can locate her." I saw that in a film once.

"Do you know what I think, Ruby? I think that the records are going to show that the messages were passed back and forth from the same location," Harper said. "The same mobile phone mast is going to pinpoint two phones, sending messages and calling from the same place. Your house. Or, as we have found the other phone already, your garden shed."

"You wrote the messages back and forth, Ruby," Corrington added. "We'll be able to prove that, too."

CHAPTER 33

Back in a different interview room, Papadopoulos repeatedly clicked his ballpoint pen as he went through my statement, his furry eyebrows knitting like kissing caterpillars. He looked like Dracula in a subpar, made-for-tv adaptation. He was convinced that I had spun him a tale, that I was trying to outwit him and the London Met by making up some fantastic story to lessen my involvement.

Lisa sat obediently, her only input being to ask whether I'd like a drink or something to eat.

"... Those screenshots they have completely contradicted what you wrote here." Papadopoulos tapped the nib of the pen against the A4. "You've gone on record to say that you and your accomplice..."

"They doctored the photos," I said, rocking gently. "She was with me the whole time. Either that or the cameras just didn't pick her up. That's all I can think."

"Yet they have no record of her." He looked over his glasses at me, a five o'clock shadow already shading his cologne-soaked cheeks. Dark pouches hung beneath his eyes, and I saw a thin, pale band of skin on his hairy finger where a wedding ring had once sat. "This is not a bluff on their part, Ruby, so you need to tell me now, truthfully: was there anyone else with you when you committed this crime?"

Forceps clutched my skull and squeezed, the prongs digging into my temples. The pain that was brewing in my head felt as though it had the potential to be catastrophic, and already my vision began to falter.

"Headache," I hissed. "I have a… really bad headache."

"Ruby." He wrapped his knuckles on the table to get my attention. The sound was jarring and made me close my eyes, clench my jaw. "What you tell me from here on out will determine how well I can represent you. I need to know what you've mislead me on. Now, my original question: was there anyone with you when you broke into the house on Vincent Street?"

"*Mia* was with me." Each word a trial. "It was her idea, the whole thing!"

"How can that be, Ruby? You said she was a pupil at St Monica's in the remedial classes. But she wasn't. You said she was with you when you journeyed to George McDermott's house, but the cameras only show you. Ruby, look at me. It's important that you look at me. Let's start from the top. Who else is involved in this?"

Squinting through my lashes, I said, "Just me and Mia."

"The detectives seem to think you made her up. They are certainly presenting a strong argument to strengthen that point of view. Unless of course, you can prove to me otherwise?"

"P-p-prove? What do you mean? She goes to my school."

"Not according to them, she doesn't. Never has."

"Then they're wrong. They checked the register wrong, or someone… the receptionist didn't do the files right, or messed up in… Why are you looking at me like that?"

"I can't help you if you're not willing to tell me the truth, Ruby. You are in a mountain of trouble, and it won't get any easier at the trial if you stick with this Mia story."

"Mia *story*?" I angled my head to find a comfortable spot for the pain to sit in. "It's the *truth*."

He removed his glasses, ran a thumb and forefinger over his eyelids and exhaled through his nostrils.

"It *is*," I shouted at him, even though it detonated dynamite all across my head. "Why would I tell a lie about her going to my school when it's so easy to disprove?"

"But they *have* proved that this person never attended St Monica's."

"And I don't know why that is. It's not my job to figure that out." When he just looked back at me with a mild stirring of contempt on his face, I added, "Tell them to go to the Barker Lane estate. That's where she lived – that's where her mum still lives. She's a real fucking person, not some fairy tale I just pulled out the air. Why don't they drag her in for questioning and ask why she isn't on the school register?"

There came a slug trail of doubt, then. I spoke to Mia every day at lunch and after school. But had I ever seen her *in* The Bramble Huts. No, I didn't think so. That didn't matter though; I'd seen her enough around school to know she attended St Monica's. There had to have been some sort of administrative mistake because the alternative meant she was just drifting on the grounds, pretending to be a pupil, and that was lunacy, utter demented lunacy.

He continued to stare at me, perhaps analysing my body language, trying to assess the percentage of truth among the intricate web of events.

"Barker Lane," I managed after a moment to breathe. "She lives on Barker Lane. Tell them to go there, talk to her mum."

"Barker Lane," he repeated, writing it down. "Door number?"

"I don't know it," I said.

"Alright. Do you know what floor? What colour door? Anything?"

"I…" A heavy weight pressed down on my chest, compressing my lungs. "I've… never actually been to her flat."

Papadopoulos's expression began to harden. "How can that be, Ruby? You told me yesterday that you had been to her estate."

"She would always meet me at the phone box. I'd never knock her door because she said her mum was a mad drunk, that it was best if we just… and… and… I only went to the abandoned flat that she used to hide out in. And…"

Papadopoulos exhaled and set his pen down. "You invented her, didn't you? Just admit it and we can start again."

"No," I whimpered, still trying to make sense of the mercurial memories, trying to find one cog that might slot into place and get the machine working smoothly again. This was a misunderstanding. "Her name might not be Mia Swehl, but that's what she told me. That's all I knew her as. You can give me a lie detector test, you can… I mean, I don't know why she's not on the camera footage, but maybe they got the dates wrong; and if not, then they did something to the pictures, they airbrushed her out and… Look, she was there the whole time. Her DNA will be all over George because she was the one who killed him. That's all there is to it."

While I set about trying to strengthen my claim, I captured Mia's image in my mind, standing sentry among the swirling chaos. She was always like an older sister. Not like a student at all. Confident, mature… *cunning*.

"What if she didn't go to my school officially?" I said. "What if she was just someone who drifted onto the school grounds and…"

"Every day for two years? Without being detected by a member of staff?"

"It happened before. A few years ago. I think it was in the newspapers. There was this guy, he used to go to the school grounds and pretend to be a teacher. He used to tell kids off, take photos. They caught him and arrested him. The same thing could have happened with Mia. The teachers don't know every single pupil, do they?"

"Listen to what you're saying, Ruby. It's preposterous."

"She's real," I said feebly, beginning to crumble.

"I think before we go any further," Papadopoulos said, "we'll want a psychologist to evaluate you."

"Why? I'm not fucking crazy. Why would you even say that?"

"Because, based on what I've heard from the detectives and everything you've told me, I'm quite confident that there is no Mia Swehl. That leaves two possible explanations." He began counting off on his fingers. "The first, is that you've made the whole thing up in an attempt to lessen your involvement. The second is that you truly believe Mia exists."

"She does," I growled. "Fuck's sake, she does. I spoke to her every day and..."

And you never saw her talk to anyone else at school.

"... and I'd have to be psychotic to have some kind of imaginary friend. What? You think people at school just saw me walking around talking to thin air and didn't bother to tell a teacher? You really think I could function the way I do if I had this invisible person just hanging around, making me do all this terrible shit?"

He regarded me evenly, listening patiently to everything I'd said. "Well, that's what we've got to find out, isn't it?"

CHAPTER 34

They apparently had enough to charge me for the murder of George McDermott, and the next day, I was sent to court for an initial hearing. They drove me in a van that had darkly tinted windows, and despite the additional police presence on the roads, the paparazzi kept pace alongside us, trying to sneak snaps of me.

I'd never been inside a courtroom before. Under any other circumstances I would probably have been very interested in the building, intrigued by the procession of it all. There was nothing special or interesting about the hearing, though. Papadopoulos told me I was going to be presented before a judge, and they would officially charge me and set a date for my next hearing.

My mum did not attend.

The judge, a man with pointy features that reminded me of an illustration from a Roald Dahl book, said that due to the severity and notoriety of the offence, I would be detained on remand at a Youth Offenders Institute. "It is my opinion that Miss Wilcox may pose a significant flight risk," the judge said with his dusty, clipped inflection, "and given the graphic nature of the crime, she also poses an extremely high risk of committing further offences."

He smacked the gavel and I was gone, ushered back into the van. I would not be free again for another ten years.

The visitation room at Earldale Youth Offenders Facility had about as much charm as the claustrophobic shoebox they'd interviewed me in back at the station. The guards gave me a bottle of cola and a chocolate bar that went uneaten as I waited, sat in the corner with my blanket around me, braced against the persistent draught. I hadn't been near a mirror for a while but knew that my body was changing. My skin, which was always oily and breaking out with painful red bumps and boils, had begun to feel loose, somehow, as though it no longer fit the skeleton it was wrapped around. The lack of decent sleep and absence of anything resembling an appetite made me permanently lethargic, and I think it was around that time that my teeth started to loosen. Somewhere in the last few weeks, I'd developed the habit of pulling strands of my hair out – not that the dry, brittle threads took much coaxing from my tender scalp.

And there were the fleas, or at least, that's what I thought they were. I'd be sitting in my cell, reading whatever ragged paperback the guards had chosen to give me, and I'd catch sight of a little black dot on my hand. It always leapt away before I got a chance to slap it, and after a while, I would just observe, trying to get an idea of what I was looking at. The longer I stared, the more of them appeared, until my hands and wrist would be freckled with fleas. When I lay down on my cot at night, I felt certain that they were going in my ears and could feel their miniscule presence in the corners of my mouth.

"Excuse me," I'd said to the guard who brought me breakfast about a week after I'd first encountered the fleas.

"Yeah?" The guard on duty that morning was a gruff, pitiless man who puffed out of his uniform as though he spent his nights pigging down takeaways and beers. A slob of a man without a trace of decency or empathy about him. He wasn't the worst of the guards at Earldale, but he wasn't a sweetheart, either.

"I think my cell has bed bugs," I told him.

"Bed bugs?" He looked past me to the plastic mattress laying atop the cot, and said, "You need a bed before you can have bed bugs, love."

"Okay," I began, exasperated but trying my best to avoid an argument. I'd been nothing but polite since my stay at Earldale, where I'd been bussed off to await sentencing, but all the guards treated me like shit, always eying me expectantly when they brought my meals, as though they'd spat in them. "They're coming from the thing that I sleep on." He was about to dismiss me with a slam of the door wicket, when I urgently added, "Then it's ticks or fleas or something. I keep seeing them."

"All the cells are cleaned and disinfected before a new prisoner moves in," he said, making no effort to give the lie credibility.

That was as far as my complaint went, and sitting there in the visitation room, I noticed that one of the fleas had alighted my knuckle, and I tried to hold as still as I could so that it wouldn't leap away. I knew that very soon, others would join it, and a couple of seconds later I was proved right when I felt the tiniest prickle of something landing on the side of my neck.

There was a rattle of keys at the door and then it opened, as a guard ushered my mum in for our reunion. This was the first I'd seen her since our separation back at the house, where she'd kicked, bitten, and later been cautioned for assaulting several police officers. The woman who entered the visitation room just then was about as far removed from the woman who attacked those officers as a kitten was to a tiger. She shuffled in, wrapped in her tatty, faux fur coat and pulled the chair out across from me without instigating eye contact.

They left the door open with the guard monitoring us in the hallway.

She kept her head bowed as though deep in thought, wondering how she should begin. The flesh around her watery eyes was crinkled and deeply grooved with bags. Her skin was doughy and drained of colour, as though she were afflicted by some terrible sickness. I guess in some ways, she was. She fidgeted with a ragged ball of tissue in her hand before clearing the phlegm from her throat and saying, "They tell me that you've admitted to... doing that bad thing."

Something about the infantile phrasing deeply disturbed me. A second flea landed on the webbing between my thumb and index. Another quickly joined, finding territory on my wrist.

"I wouldn't believe it," she said, slowly and awkwardly, as though reciting a statement from memory, "if I hadn't spoken to your solicitor. And, actually, I don't think I do believe it, even now. At least, not the way they're telling me." Her eyes rolled up in my direction, before rolling back to the floor. "It's a... nightmare." She said this contemplatively as opposed to dramatically, as though that were the simple truth of it. "They say that you're trying to pin the blame on someone else. A friend from school. Except..." She looked up at me again, her mouth slightly agape. Something was off about the cadence and delivery of her speech, and I guessed it was because she was dosed up to the eyeballs on pills.

"Except they think she doesn't exist," I finished.

"Yes, that's right." She said it as though it were a foreign language that needed extra consideration before formulating a response. "The thing is, I can have your solicitor tell me this a hundred times, and then have everyone in this station tell me another hundred, but I won't *accept* it until I hear it from you." She tried to clear the dry, scratchy chimney of her throat, and gave a series of weak coughs. The coughing fit went on uncomfortably long, until I wanted to go around and whack her on the back a few times to clear it.

"What do you want me to–"

"Stop, a minute." She silenced me with a finger, her voice maintaining that dreamy listlessness. "Let me finish before you speak. I know how you can get confused. How you have… got things wrong in the past. But I think I know you well enough to know the truth, even if you don't. I just need you to tell me. And I'm not angry, I'm not sad, I'm not… anything. How can I be? It is, in a horrible sort of way, actually quite funny."

"Funny?" I asked, unsure as to whether I'd heard – or understood her – correctly. "What's funny?"

She reached into her pocket and produced a packet of Silk Cut, tapped a cigarette out, and lit it. After exhaling a plume of smoke to the ceiling, she smiled grimly, pinpricks of light catching in her pupils.

"They were camped outside the house, you know," she said, smiling as though recounting an amusing anecdote. "Dozens of the bastards. They've been knocking the door day and night, shouting things, opening the letterbox, and putting their cameras up to try and get photos of inside. Round the back, too. They broke the garden fence down leaning on it. They wanted pictures of inside the shed." She pointed the cigarette at me and said, "Someone tipped them off. One of the neighbours must have caught wind when you were arrested. We're supposed to have anonymity because you're underage, but one of those bastards has gone and pissed all over that. And the fucking police – they wanted me to leave, said it was for my protection, but I'm not the one who's done anything wrong, am I? I'm not going to be chased away because of what someone else" – she waved a hand limply at me – "has done. The press aren't allowed to trespass on the property; that's the law. I don't give a flying fuck what's in the papers or on the TV, I still have rights. What was I talking about again?"

I shook my head. Didn't have an answer to give her.

"Ah, funny, yes. Well," – she took a long drag from the cigarette, her cheeks sucking in grotesquely – "they camp out there night and day. You'd think they'd get bored and fuck off back to their own houses, but they don't. And I spoke to a solicitor about it, because, well, I can't believe that a circus is just allowed to blow through town and land on my" – she clutched at her chest, and there as something savage about the gesture – "property. But my solicitor said that if I wasn't going to be relocated, then it was best to stay where I was. If I hiked off to a hotel or whatever, they'd follow me and find a way to intrude anyway, so it's all just fucking pointless." She stopped, stubbed the cigarette out angrily, and murmured, "*Intrude*. Yes. So, anyway, I was in the house listening to them shout and leer at me, trying to coax me to the window." Her eyes flashed at me. "They sing songs, you know. It's like chanting. Trying to make me mad."

"What kind of songs?" Four fleas dotted my left hand, and there were at least two on my neck now.

"Songs about you." She nodded. "So, I put the TV up loud, and I put the radio on full blast. And then they make requests. Like I'm a DJ. Fucking useless scumbags. What kind of job is it? But it's funny, the irony of this." She started to chuckle, until the chuckles graduated to great gales of laughter.

I cringed back in my chair, still very much afraid of her. I could almost feel the madness emanating from her like a fever.

"But it isn't irony, is it? I mean, that's the real thing that's troubling me so much about this. Because there is no chance on earth that you just randomly broke into his house, your real dad's house, and killed him by coincidence. You had to have known. And I can only think you did that to hurt me. You knew, didn't you?"

"No," I said. "How could I?"

"Because I left the solicitor's letters out about George's payments, and you read them." She eyed me closely. "I wanted you to read them. I wanted you to find out. Save me a job of having to sit down and spoon feed it all to you."

"I didn't read any of your letters," I said. "I never did anything like that."

"So you're telling me it was your *friend*, then." Her eyes narrowed to glinting slits. "*Is* there a friend, Ruby? Don't you even think about lying to me. Don't you dare. Because I'll know. Even if you don't."

"What do you think?" I asked, throwing it back to her. "You think I'd make something like that up? You think I'd do something like this by myself? That would make me crazy, wouldn't it?"

"Don't try to dance around me. I want to hear it. From your mouth."

I told her the abridged version, giving her all the necessary information without any of the gory details. She did not move while I spoke, her face betraying no hint of shock or disturbance.

"Strange that you say you didn't do anything, and yet, you're the one getting all the blame. Very strange."

"It's more than *strange*." The words came out in a gust. "And nobody believes me. I don't know what else to say. I didn't do any of it."

She turned in her chair then, eyelids drooping. "How can I believe that, Ruby? Have you any idea how fucking insane that sounds? If there really was someone else in that house with you, they'd tear the whole country apart looking for her. There is no way she would be able to get away from it. You know how this sounds, what you're saying?"

"Yes, I do. But they want to pin everything on me because they can't find Mia. It's not even that they can't find her." The frustration was making my temperature rise, and I shifted restlessly in my seat. "They don't even want to *look* for her. They refuse. And why would it be so easy to find her if she was able to go to my school for all that time and nobody picked up on it? They don't know her real name, where she lives. All she'd have to do is cut her hair, dye it..."

"Mia Swehl," she said contemplatively. "Thing is, Ruby, I've never seen her either."

"I know that. Obviously, I know that."

"How can that be? If she was coming by the house, going in our shed, then why haven't I seen her?"

"Because I didn't want you to," I said, and our eyes met then with instant understanding: teenagers – especially teenage girls – were good at keeping things from their parents. Mia was my secret, though she was really no secret at all. I just didn't want mum to spoil her for me. "You heard me talking on the phone to her though."

"I heard *you* taking." She exhaled and seemed to deflate. "But now I think… all that whispering, all those conversations. Maybe you weren't talking to anyone."

"You can't honestly think I would do that, can you?"

She didn't answer immediately. She was somewhere else, somewhere far away.

"Mum? You do believe me?"

Shakily, she rose from the chair and walked around the table that separated us. Then she bent and hugged me. I could smell her shampoo, her moisturizer, hiding behind the cigarette smoke. "Of course, I believe you," she said. "Just like you believe that I didn't crash that car on purpose, don't you?"

"What?" I pulled back, unbalanced by the question.

"We're being honest with each other. I believe you, Ruby. Even if nobody else does. You're my flesh and blood, and you may be a lot of things, but a killer isn't one of them. And you believe me, yes?"

"Yes," I said, forcing the lie to leave my lips.

"Good girl." She patted my shoulder. "So, I believe you, and you believe me, and now we're friends again." Her lips pulled back over her teeth, and she barked with laughter.

The next morning, I was summoned to see the governor at Earldale. As I was escorted through the warren of hallways and valley of staircases, the apprehension began to bloom inside me. The only consolation I had was that whatever new grievance was being brought against me couldn't make my life any worse.

The governor, Mr. Pike, was a tall, bookish man in his fifties with broken blood vessels across his nose and a side parting that seemed too neat to be anything but a hairpiece. He told me to take a seat opposite him in his office, which was about as unremarkable as he was: a few filing cabinets, a computer, a narrow window that looked out onto more grubby brickwork. Framed certificates hung from the grey walls, along with a newspaper article depicting Mr. Pike in front of the facility, smiling goofily at the camera.

He then proceeded to inform me of the bad news with the type of stern sincerity he had developed from years of relaying unfortunate events. He spoke for a few minutes, and when he was finished, he allowed me the opportunity to ask questions. I had none; it was fairly simple to follow, and I didn't doubt the veracity of his words.

In essence, what he told me was this: After visiting me at Earldale, my mum returned home in a taxi to find an ocean of photographers and reporters still foaming at the mouth to get to her. The media and the well-wishing general public that had congregated to hurl obscenities at her were barely contained behind police barricades. My mum was escorted into her house, but not before announcing that she would be back out in an hour or so and would answer any questions that the journalists might have. Word of this impromptu press conference spread with rabid anticipation, and soon, more news station vans arrived on the scene with hopes of getting their cup of blood from my mum.

True to her word, she reappeared within the hour to a rapturous applause from her morbid congregation, dragging a plastic lawn chair behind her, which she plonked down in the pathway of the front garden. She went back into the house, returning with a tall glass of gin and the frenetic camera flash casting her jittery silhouette into the dark porch behind her.

"Ask away," she said, sitting in the lawn chair with her leg crossed, sipping from the gin. By now, two news stations were filming and broadcasting live, interrupting the evening's scheduled programming. If she hadn't unplugged the housephone, she would have heard it ringing incessantly as her legal team tried desperately to dissuade her from this act of self-sabotage.

As per her request, the questions came thick and fast from a chorus of voices, competing to be heard over the clamour. Surprisingly, the civilians in the crowd remained quiet, postponing their pantomime jeers to let the professionals do the digging. Despite their hatred for my mum and me, it was curiosity that quelled any audacious outbursts and kept the football chanting at bay.

The journalists pounced on my mum, covering the ground chronologically from her initial relationship with George McDermott to my troubled past (including the car crash), and soon, the chaotic rhythm of the journalists' competition lost its urgency and became courteous. They all wanted the same thing, and apparently, they were going to get it, and the best way of achieving that was just to play nice.

For her part, my mum answered their questions in excruciating detail, sipping her gin, even smiling. The only time she deviated from the set order of things was to ask, "Is this going out live, right now?" And when she was told it was, she went back inside the house and clicked on the TV to check. "Perfect," she said upon her return, and motioned for more questions.

When challenged by a reporter from her former workplace, Maypole Broadcast Service, about the validity of my defence (which I hadn't even known was public knowledge, considering I'd only told it to detectives and my solicitor), my mum had this to say:

"Ruby has had her problems, like we all have. But George was her father. Nothing you people do or say can change that. It's a fact, and I have the paperwork to prove it." For the first time since the press conference began, my mum was interrupted by an avalanche of boos. She waited for it to subside, even rolling her eyes, before continuing. "You are all so quick to condemn? Well, how's this for a slice of real life: the only reason they are trying to get my daughter put away is because they are under pressure to find the real killer. You are all creating the pressure, and yet, you're happy for this to happen. You're happy for an innocent girl – George's own daughter – to go to prison, maybe for the rest of her life, while the real murderer walks free?"

The tide turned against her, but seeing that my mum wouldn't answer anything unless it was posed in an orderly fashion, the excitement soon dampened.

A few minutes later, some witty soul enquired as to how many drinks my mum had put away. "Only this," she replied, holding up the almost-empty glass.

"Must be a stiff one," someone else said, but it went virtually unheard among the chatter.

They had all noticed the gradual deterioration of her speech and the way she seemed to be almost melting in the lawn chair, sliding down until she was slouched. Her head dipped, and soon her speech was almost unintelligible.

It was only when she fell off the chair that they understood that something was wrong.

And it was only an hour later, when she was pronounced dead at Her Majesty's Royal Hospital, that the country realized they had just watched a woman commit suicide on live TV.

The following excerpt is taken from the unpublished essay, *The Mia Swehl Dilemma* by Dr. Abdul M. I. Shabazz PHD (originally scheduled to appear in issue 156 of *Alternative Psychology*, March 2006)

It was a cold February morning when I first met Ruby Wilcox, a sixteen-year-old girl awaiting trial for her alleged involvement in the murder (or what would later be determined, technically, as patricide) of infamous celebrity George McDermott.

If I had put any stock into the media's portrayal of my subject beforehand, I would have expected to find a demonic beast with horns, cloven hoofs, and a pitchfork waiting for me in Earldale, the children's facility where Wilcox was being housed until the hearing. Instead, what I found was a meek, malnourished, and hollow-eyed girl whose skin had taken an ashen complexion due to her unwillingness to venture beyond her cell. "She doesn't like to leave her room," a warden at Earldale, who has asked to remain anonymous, told me. "She kicks and screams and throws herself on the floor. Most of the girls here are climbing the walls to get out into the courtyard for some fresh air, just to break up the day, but Ruby is the complete opposite."

I had been hired by Judy Dorsey, the third lawyer to helm Wilcox's legal defence, to gather an independent assessment of any suspected mental impairments the child might be suffering. I was not the first child psychologist who had undertaken the task, but the *fifth*, and while I can't speak for the competence of the professionals who assessed Wilcox before me, I can say that I was extremely dubious of their wildly contradictory results.

Wilcox had a complicated medical history stemming from a car accident that left her comatose for a total of ten days. It was reported by her teachers at St Monica's Secondary that Wilcox would often be excused from class for "severe headaches', and in the school year of 00–01, she had racked up nineteen medical absences. It is worth noting, that though much has been made of her "fainting spells', there is no record of any teacher or staff at St Monica's ever reporting an episode. Likewise, Richard Wilcox, Ruby's former step-dad, has gone on record to suggest that Ruby would "... pretend to black out when you told her something she didn't want to hear. If I told her to clean her room, or God forbid, hoover the carpet, her eyes would roll back, and she'd flop... for attention."

I spent a total of six hours speaking with Ruby Wilcox over a period of three days. At first, she remained guarded but impeccably polite, with a continuous edge of cynicism as to my intentions. "What's the point in me telling you anything?" she asked, sitting on her cot with her knees pulled into her chest. "None of you believe a word I say. You think I made Mia up."

Rather than dispute her allegation, or set about antagonizing her further, I allowed her free reign to explain why she believed that Mia Swehl was a real person who had committed the atrocity in Vincent Street, when everybody else believed otherwise. Ruby's evidence, other than her unwavering certainty that she wasn't "... a crazy person who doesn't know what's real from imaginary," crunched down to a series of points that would later be disproven in court. (*It is also worth noting that while only traces of Ruby Wilcox's DNA would be found on George McDermott's body, Wilcox's claim of having an accomplice could not be forensically substantiated. While other DNA was found in the house that couldn't be accounted for, McDermott had thrown a party three days prior to his death, in which approximately thirty people had attended).

After hearing Ruby Wilcox's version of events and reading the copious amount of professional background information available, the first thing that became abundantly clear was that Ruby Wilcox likely suffers from IED (Intermittent Explosive Disorder). This would account for the ferocious attack on George McDermott, which, as the court suggested, may have started as self-defence, and quickly escalated to murder, though premeditation could not be determined.

My professional assessment is that, coupled with IED, Wilcox was clearly showing signs of paranoid schizophrenia, which would account for the intricate daytime hallucinations, manifested namely in the Mia Swehl personality. All other 'professional' assessments that suggested otherwise are not only incompetent, but dangerously negligent.

When asked about her routine in Earldale, Wilcox proclaimed her obvious resentment of the institution, and offered further glimpses into her dwindling psyche. Her paranoia was palpable as she expressed fears that "... the guards are planning to do something to me." She went on further to add "... other girls get annoyed at me because they say I make too much noise at night. But I can't help it if I'm trying to sleep." When I encouraged her to elaborate on this latter comment, Wilcox went on to say "I have these dreams that George is in here with me... that he can walk through the door. Sometimes, when I'm sleeping, I dream that he stands in the corner, right there, and watches me."

"Do you ever see him when you're not sleeping?"

She didn't reply.

"And what about Mia?" I had asked. "Do you see her, too?"

"No. Not in my dreams. And not when I'm awake either. How could I? She's still out there."

It was my conclusion that Ruby Wilcox wholeheartedly believed the delusion that Mia Swehl was a physical, real human being; a friend, surrogate sister, and ultimately, designer of her downfall. For this reason, Ruby Wilcox should not have been made eligible to stand trial.

The reality is that Ruby Wilcox used Mia Swehl as an alter; to be her confidence when she felt cowardly, to be her strength when she was weak, but most significantly, her rage when she felt wrathful. And, with the aid of some mental manoeuvring, Ruby was able to conveniently block out the parts that she didn't want to remember, while simultaneously strengthening the scenes that she did. The Mia Delusion was twofold; at once, Mia was the friend that Ruby needed, someone to converse with and confide in. But Mia would also 'take over' or 'fuse' with Ruby's consciousness during times of extreme stress. It is a case unlike nothing I or any of my peers have ever come across.

The one thing that every professional who has spoken with Ruby Wilcox can agree on, is that Mia Swehl does not exist in any physical sense, outside of Ruby's imagination.

A ***Mia Swehl*** or ***Me-as-Well*** is a term used to describe a type of defence whereby a person assigns the blame of a criminal act upon an imaginary co-conspirator.

Example: He told the court that a man named Victor stole the car, but it was obvious that Victor was a Mia Swehl.

The following is an excerpt from *Dead Behind the Eyes: The Shocking True Story of The Vincent Street Incident* (Ten Year Anniversary Updated Edition) by Simon Ward. Copyright ©2015 Published by Elmwood Press.

After her legal team ordered a battery of psychological tests, looking for anything that might absolve Ruby of responsibility for her actions and get her sent to a psychiatric ward like Broadmoor or Crestwell instead of a wing in Coldham, a group of esteemed experts reached the following conclusions: Ruby suffered from Post-Traumatic Stress Disorder, Borderline Personality Disorder, Manic Depression, and she exhibited traits of extreme narcissism. Confusingly, though, only two of the five experts tasked with diagnosing Ruby concluded that she was showing symptoms of Dissociative Identity Disorder, whereas the other three experts wrote this notion off entirely. Whether Mia Swehl was a hallucination or an intricately manufactured invention, was, remarkably, still up for debate.

This catalogue of complicated mental disorders gave the jury enough to chew on throughout the six-week trial. After all, if a teenage girl who had an alleged history of mental and physical abuse could be impeded by these conditions, then she could not have been in her right mind when deciding to visit George McDermott on that fateful afternoon.

The problem was that throughout the whole ordeal, she had shown enough examples of having been of sound mind and knowing right from wrong. As such, Ruby's legal team then began pushing for her to be assessed using the PCL – Psychopathy Checklist. The judge threw this out as a publicity stunt, as it was the same test that experts had applied to various infamous American serial killers. If Ruby could get anywhere near their scores, then it would strengthen the case of diminished responsibility. When that didn't work, her legal team put forth the compelling argument that as Ruby had (allegedly) been mentally and physically abused by her mother from a young age, she had never learned to cope with her rage. This may have caused some degree of 'fracturing' in her mind, but, as was made clear to the jury, the idea that she could truly conceive a new identity that essentially committed the murders on her behalf, was utterly implausible.

Ruby held on tight to the Mia Swehl defence, always insisting that there had been another person with her in the house: A phantom teenager (or adult, as she had tried to insinuate) of unknown origin who supposedly roamed the halls of St Monica's Catholic School, unnoticed by teachers among the throng of students. Aside from this being one of the leakiest and least-inventive defences brought before a British court, it was also forensically unlikely that another person had committed the atrocities in that house.

It is also important to remember that during her first year of treatment at Crestwell, Dr William Pernell, the clinical psychologist in charge of Ruby's case, reported "... significant improvement after only a few months, through a combination of medication and therapy." Thirty-eight months later, she was handed over to Coldham prison, where she would begin to serve her sentence.

Of the ludicrously lenient sentencing, George's father, Eamon McDermott, said, "This is injustice on an unforgivable scale. I don't care how old the girl was or what they say was wrong with her. Twelve years is an absolute joke. It is spit in our faces." He asserted, as many have since, that the leniency of her sentencing could only be the result of the public's outcry against McDermott's perceived scandalous personal life, and nothing to do with Wilcox's age and questionable mental state. There were even those who have held Wilcox as symbol of retribution, an avenging angel standing for all the victims of her biological father's misogyny.

The Vincent Street Incident will go down as one of the most abhorrent and bizarre cases in British criminal history. Yet, a decade later, the story continues to fascinate as new theories circulate in true crime forums. Most prominent among them, is the impossible yet widely debated idea that "Mia Swehl" was actually a real person and not an invention of Ruby's fevered mind: An adult masquerading as a teenager, who – for reasons unknown – decided to infiltrate a Catholic school, befriend a disturbed pupil, and persuade her to carry out a senseless murder.

How much truth can there be to this narrative? The idea that "Mia Swehl" orchestrated the entire crime through a combination of intimidation and mental manipulation is surely too farfetched to be in any way accurate. And yet, new stories continue to surface from the people who knew Ruby, testifying to her strange and disturbing behaviour from a young age. Even Richard Wilcox, the man who believed he was Ruby's father for thirteen years, has gone on record calling her "... a compulsive liar... a fantasist... you couldn't trust a word that came out of her mouth," someone who would throw violent tantrums for the smallest infringements. "She could stare at a blue sky and spend an hour trying to convince you it was green. She would just lie for no reason, and keep on lying until you started to think, "Well maybe the sky *is* green."

The following is an excerpt from *Mayhem in Mind: The Untold Truth of The Vincent Street Incident* by Floyd Wilkinson (Paanbo Press, 2004)

If we're looking at the whole event from a practical standpoint, then it's obvious Ruby could not have committed the crime all by herself. Ruby was 5′3″ and reported to be 130 pounds at the time of her arrest. She was not a big girl, nor was she athletically outstanding in any department, as illustrated in her last school report (her PE teacher wrote the word "adequate" to describe Ruby's athletic progress).

The counter argument, of course, is that George McDermott was not a big man either. He was only 5′8″ but weighed at least a hundred and sixty pounds (this according to leaked doctor's reports at his last asthma check-up just four months prior to his murder).

Then there's the Mia Swehl defence, which at the time, was obliterated by the press and prosecution alike, and yet, there is enough evidence to suggest that Ruby definitely had an accomplice. What if Mia Swehl was real? What if Mia Swehl was dangerously disturbed enough to break into a house and murder George McDermott, and convince a similarly disturbed and impressionable child like Ruby to take the blame? What if Mia was a stranger off the street, a young adult masquerading as a teen, as Ruby so adamantly suggested?

Most worrying of all, however, is what this theory implies: What if Ruby *was* telling the truth this whole time? What if Mia Swehl managed to slip abroad, disguise her appearance, and avoid the authorities?

What if Mia Swehl… is still out there.

She might live next door to you.

CHAPTER 35

"And that's it." I threw my hands up and let them fall to my lap. "I was charged. Detained. Sentenced. The rest is all documented. There's no controversy or conspiracies there. It's fact from that point on."

Now that my story was told, I didn't feel any tremendous weight lift from my shoulders, but there was some modicum of relief, a slight shift in that perpetual pressure sitting in my chest. Speaking about it, talking through everything that occurred up to, during and after we broke into the house on Vincent Street, was cathartic in a way. It felt like I was relaying a story about a film I'd seen many years before, starring an actress whose name I could no longer remember.

"The judge called me a *damaged and confused young girl,*" I said. A deep sigh travelled up my chest and drifted from my lips. "He believed that there had been emotional neglect and abuse by my mum, but that ultimately, I was responsible for the entire crime. They thought I went in there fuelled by revenge and jealousy. Nothing could be further from the truth. I was just following Mia."

"But they couldn't find Mia," Fidditch said. "No trace of her."

"They didn't look," I countered. "At first, they assumed I was lying. Then they couldn't make up their minds what to do with me. One of the psychologists who interviewed me wanted to test me. He said that he could put these electrodes on my head and scan my brainwaves while he spoke to me about Mia, and it would show whether I was lying or not. He said if Mia was a… a *delusion*, then my brainwaves would show that."

"And did you do it?" Fidditch asked.

"No. I wanted to, just to prove them all wrong, but my legal team blocked it. So, they labelled me crazy, put me in Crestwell for three years. Then, when they felt that they'd pumped me with enough pills, they let me serve my time in Coldham."

"And you still think the police doctored the photos of you on the CCTV."

"Yes," I said. "There is no other explanation."

"Devil's advocate time again," Fidditch said morosely. His tongue flicked out and lapped his lips, his expression becoming hard, purposeful. "So, they never even tried to look for Mia Swehl?"

"No," I said. "To my knowledge, they never did. They never even believed she existed. Nobody did. They thought it was something I invented to try and get off, like an insanity claim. One of my solicitors went down that road, made a push for a stay at Crestwell, part of a diminished responsibility thing. But my lawyers knew nothing was wrong with me. They all knew I was telling the truth. But it was just easier to put me away, out of sight, out of mind. To wrap the whole thing up. Justice served."

He paused, stroked his chin. "What do you think happened to her?"

"Not a clue," I told him, but couldn't seem to shake that feeling of interrogation again, as though I were back in the interview room with Corrington, Harper, and my solicitor. "But that's the scariest thing about all this, isn't it? She could still be out there. She could have changed the way she looks, got married, had kids. She could be living a completely normal life."

"Well, that's just it, isn't it?" he said, and now his questions were firing at me like arrows from a bow: direct, meaningful. Almost as if he'd had them on his mind for some time, storing them in his quiver, waiting for the best opportunity to strike. "If there had been some crazy person coming into your school–"

"Grooming me," I added, feeling it necessary to make the distinction for the sake of this shift in conversation. "That's what it was, *Peter*. I think she was probably older. Eighteen, maybe as old as twenty. I don't know. But she was in control the whole time. She tricked me into this. Groomed me into it."

"Why do you think a person would do that though, Luanne?" Adelpha cut in, her head bobbing up from behind the camera.

"What?" I asked irritably. "What did you say?"

"I asked why you think someone would do that. A complete stranger. Why do you think they would come into your school, posing as a pupil to… groom you, to then ultimately make you take part in such a heinous crime? I mean" – she held out her hands and shrugged – "how would she even know that George was related to you?" She glanced over at Fidditch. "I'm sorry for interrupting. But that part was always unclear to me. How *did* she know?"

"I can only guess," I said, the muscles in my jaw bunching from clenching my teeth.

"Then what's your guess?" Adelpha challenged.

"She had been with George McDermott before," I said. "She met him at a club or a party, maybe. She was obviously unhinged," I said, flashing back to Mia's blank expression staring out through a mask of blood. "George probably used her and discarded her. And she found out that he had a history of this kind of thing – flings, manipulation. She found out that he had paid off other women, like my mum."

"*How*?" Adelpha said forcefully, as though she already knew the answer and was pushing me toward it.

"Mia was a thief." The sentence echoed around the soundstage. "A burglar. She knew how to get into houses. Look at how easily she got into the Vincent Street address. It was like she had been there before. Maybe she... maybe she broke in before, looking for something to blackmail him with and found how he was linked to my mum, a legal letter, a..." My left temple felt as though it were about to cave in. I palmed a hand over my eye, waiting for the pain to pass. "Can we stop now? I mean, that's it." I grimaced as the blunt grinding travelled across to my other temple, and now I was leaning forward, holding my head in my hands like a passenger preparing for a plane crash. "Can we stop?" I seethed. "How much more do you need? Please, let's stop."

"Are you going to pass out?" Fidditch asked, but I could barely hear him through the steadily increasing volume of the pain.

"We need to stop now," Henry's voice, urgent and clear as he swaddled me in a hug.

"We will in a moment," Fidditch said, annoyed. He was saying something else when Henry cut him short.

"No, now. Right this minute." Then to me, "Sweetheart, you're alright. You're okay. Here, squeeze my hand if you need to. There, that's it. Good girl."

There was a streak of light behind my eyes, and I gritted my teeth together. It felt as though I were slipping off the chair and beginning to plummet inward, my heart bumping around. Violent flashes of Mia's blood-streaked face, the black inkwells of her eyes, popping in my mind like fireworks, leaving twitchy, horrific afterimages.

"Control it, Luanne," Henry said, tapping my hand, reassuringly. "Peter, why don't you get her a glass of water, for crying out loud! Give her some help."

A moment later and a glass clinked against my teeth before water slipped into my mouth and pooled down my chin, spilling onto my blouse. The cold shock made me gasp. I made a sound like a snore before my eyes fluttered open. The chair was still on the ground, and the ground was still beneath my feet. Fidditch and Adelpha were watching on, more curious than concerned.

"Time to go, I think," Henry said, helping me up.

"We're not finished," Fidditch said sharply.

"We are," Henry replied, an arm locked around my waist as he practically dragged me through the set. "That's enough. She's given you everything today, what more do you want from her?"

"Henry, she's fine. We have more to discuss!" Fidditch bellowed and his words boomed through the set, bouncing off the plyboard and cavernous soundstage beyond.

"She's falling apart at the seams right in front of you. You've got it on camera, haven't you? Call her a damn Uber."

"*Wait.*" Adelpha's voice slashed across the building, shrill and piercing with its urgency. It brought Henry's feet to a standstill. On rubbery legs, I turned and squinted through teary lashes.

"I don't feel very well," I said. "I think Henry's right. I've done all I can for today. I feel… woozy."

"That's fine, then," Adelpha said. "But there is one more thing that we need to discuss. Peter." She turned to him, handing off the conversation. "Peter, you have to tell her now."

"Tell me what?"

He regarded me for a long time before eventually speaking. "Luanne, I'm afraid we haven't been completely honest with you."

Henry stiffened beside me, hissing in breath.

"What do you mean?" I asked.

"This wasn't the documentary we originally set out to make. Henry, please, just release her a moment, alright? She's not a fawn. You can stand, can't you, Luanne?" When Henry unhanded me without argument, I shuffled from foot to foot, conscious of Henry's position behind me. He was right there, ready to catch me in case I collapsed. He always had been. "What I mean to say is, you weren't the intended subject of this documentary. Mia was."

"You wanted to make a documentary about *her*?" I asked.

"We wanted to find her, and document our journey, yes," Fidditch said. His chest was rising and falling rapidly, his lips shiny with saliva. "You see, we entered into that premise with the belief that the person who groomed you, the one who called herself Mia Swehl, was a living, breathing entity. She wasn't some figment of your imagination."

"We know there were enough holes in the investigation to drive a car through," Adelpha added. "They didn't find Mia's prints in the house because she wiped them all when you left. And you're right: the detectives didn't bother to search her out because they assumed you were lying, or going for the insanity defence. When they checked the abandoned flat on Barker Lane, it was burned down, so no evidence there. But they had you, wrapped up in a neat little bow."

"But what if you were telling the truth, we thought," Fidditch said. "What if Mia Swehl was really still out there. Now, that was something worth pursuing, wasn't it?"

"What're you saying?" I asked.

The momentary silence that followed felt charged with static.

Adelpha got back behind the camera. Aimed it at me.

"We found her," Fidditch replied.

"You..." I started to say, but felt something hot and heavy working its way through my guts. My throat suddenly felt like a matchbox strip. "You found her? Mia?"

"She's a completely different person now," Adelpha confirmed, rising from behind the camera. She looked at me for a very long time, studying, assessing my reaction while remaining completely unreadable herself. "She regrets the whole thing immensely, of course. She feels tremendous remorse."

"Tremendous remorse?" I repeated slowly, the words feeling foreign on my lips. My mind began blanking for seconds at a time – a strobing confusion that I couldn't quite think around.

Adelpha continued, "She's battled some horrific mental health problems, and–"

"Why haven't you called the police?" It was such a simple question, and yet it took all my focus to form the words. I looked from Adelpha to Fidditch through tear-blurred eyes, feeling completely depleted. I couldn't remember ever being so suddenly exhausted in all my life.

"Yes, the ethical thing to do would have been to call the police," Adelpha said. "But..." she exhaled, went for a smile. "But we're trying to make a documentary. A groundbreaking documentary, the likes of which..."

"Fuck your documentary," I said, and even though I wasn't moving, a slow stir of dizziness overtook me. "She's a murderer."

"Yes, well." Fidditch cleared his throat. "As it stands, that hasn't been proven in a court of law. Don't get upset; I'm just stating facts. There are always two sides to a story. But there is another reason that we didn't immediately turn her in. She wants to meet you."

"M... m-meet?"

"To apologise," Fidditch said, almost tranquilly. "Once she goes to the police, that's it, you might lose the opportunity to talk to her like this. You were burned at the stake for her crime, and she understands that. All she would like is the opportunity to apologise. What do you think?"

"I think... I think there's a mistake," I said. "I think you've all gone mad."

"Why?" Adelpha asked quickly.

"Because... because..."

"Isn't this what you wanted?" she said. "This is it. A chance to finally have your vindication, to prove everyone – the whole country, the whole *world* – wrong."

"How do you know it's her?" I blurted.

"She confessed. She told us everything," Fidditch said. "In basically the same way you just told us. The exact same account, just from the other side of the coin."

"Where?" I asked, leaning back, almost toppling. Henry propped me up, steadying me by holding my arms. "Where did you find her?"

"Blackpool," Adelpha said. "She was working in a hot dog stand on the pier by the amusements. So, Luanne, would you like to meet her? To at least hear what she's got to say?"

I'd cycled through this scenario a thousand times over the years. What would I do if I ever saw Mia again? What would I say? Would I scream and shout and try to throttle her maybe? No, maturity had morphed the answer, but the subdued rage, with a throbbing undercurrent of regret, remained. Why did she do this to me? Why did she ruin my entire life? Why? Why *me*?

"This would be the end of the documentary," Fidditch said. "The final scene; a confrontation between you and Mia."

"She can't have agreed to this," I said. "She'll go to prison. And you… you'll go to prison too."

"There will probably be a trial for her, sure." Adelpha said. "But she's willing to face that now. And as for us, well, given the importance of the work we're doing here, the truth we're uncovering, I can't see that we'll face any serious charges. And even if we do, so what? We will have discovered the missing piece of a puzzle that the police and the courts were too negligent to solve themselves. We're dedicated to the truth, and we're willing to accept what that comes with. I'm ready to go to jail for the truth, if that's what it takes. But who would really jail us? Not when we have the media on our side."

I looked up at Henry, but his face was turned away. I didn't need to be a body language expert to understand his extreme discomfort at that moment; I could feel the unease rolling off him in waves. That was understandable; the main thing was that he was there, by my side, the love of my life. He would help me through this as he had the whole shoot.

He was the only person I could count on in the whole world. I loved him and he loved me, and that was all I needed.

But I needed something else, didn't I? I needed people to know the truth.

With that newfound confidence, my legs began to stabilise. "Where is she now?"

"Not far," Adelpha said. "She's been waiting for you."

CHAPTER 36

"Out back," Adelpha said, cocking a thumb over her shoulder. Her face had lost its cartoony cuteness, and her eyes – which had seemed bright and large earlier – were now hard and lifeless. "We wanted to keep her completely separate from you. So, what do you think? Would you like to at least see her, Luanne?"

Adelpha looked at me intensely, as though reading the contours of my face.

"I knew you were all up to something," I said, that ancient apprehension of a confrontation with Mia turning to anger. "You were always going to try and put me in this position. You... you *deceived* me."

"Isn't this what you want, though?" Fidditch asked. "After all, The Vincent Street Incident is as much Mia's story as it yours. Isn't it?"

"You don't *have* to meet her," Adelpha added. "But she won't go on camera otherwise. She's made that quite clear. The only way she will come forward and own up to the crime is if you meet her first."

"Henry," I linked his arm, "I... I don't know. I don't know what to do."

"It's not his decision to make," Adelpha said. "It's yours."

"Shut up," I told her, slashing an arm through the air at her. "It's not your fucking decision either, so just shut up."

"Fine," Adelpha swapped glances with Fidditch and fell silent.

"Henry." I bowed my head into his chest. He was sweating through his shirt. Damp patches ringing his armpits. "What do you think?"

When he looked at me, I saw despair swimming in his eyes, his blotchy red face drooping in an almost puppy-dog imitation of sadness. A single bead of sweat was travelling down the bridge of his nose. "Nobody will believe you otherwise," Henry said. "The story is just so… it's so crazy, Luanne. You can tell it until you're blue in the face, but nobody will believe it. Not unless they see her for themselves."

"But you believe me," I pointed out. "Don't you?"

"Because I know you," he said. "I know you wouldn't lie about this. You've broken it all down for me, explained it. Your average person out there isn't going to be willing to…"

"Suspend disbelief," Fidditch filled in the gap, and although Henry shot him a murderous look of contempt, we all knew it was the right phrasing to use.

"Yes, exactly," Henry said, his hands around the small of my back like a safety harness. "If you don't think you can handle it, then don't do it. But if we leave without you at least talking to her, then she wins. Make no mistake about that, Luanne. You will be allowing her to win."

"She's already won," I moaned. "She's already got away with the murder. What else is there left to take from me?"

"She hasn't won," Henry said, quietly into my ear. "This would be your redemption, your chance to finally point the finger back at everyone and say, 'See! I told you so. I was right and you were all wrong, and what you did to me was wrong, too!'"

"I'm sorry for having... misled you, Luanne," Fidditch said. "But I knew if I'd told you the score from the beginning, then you would've bolted. So, I took a chance. Henry's right. She only wins if you don't face her."

"I don't give a shit what you have to say," I told Fidditch. "You just want your shocking little twist at the end of the documentary. You have no interest in justice, in proving my innocence."

"That's not true, Luanne," Adelpha said. "We do believe in justice. And we don't believe it has been served yet. That's why we're doing this."

I hugged Henry so tightly that my face buried into the soft flesh of his chest. He hugged me back, and I began to cry. "Tell me what you think I should do, Henry, and I'll do it."

Henry stroked my head, running his fingers through my hair. We stood there like that for a little while, gently rocking on the spot, swaying as though we were slow dancing.

"You have to meet her," he said. "But you don't have to do it alone. And you don't have to be scared. I'll be with you."

"We all will," Fidditch added.

Taking a few more minutes to think it over, I eventually said, "Fine. Take me to her."

Adelpha led the way through the back of the soundstage. We walked single file as she opened the fire exit door, provoking a bitter, damp gust of wind to snarl through the corridor.

It was almost pitch-black outside, spitting lightly. The mist-shrouded moon did nothing to brighten the black vista beyond, though there was a single light in the distance, illuminating a door. From it, I could just about make out the shape of a house or barn. Something like that.

"Where are we going?" I asked as I stepped out and into the rain, the grass wetting the cuffs of my jeans.

"Have you seen the other building across the field when you've been driving in? It's mainly used as a warehouse to store old props. There's a big rehearsal space in there too." Adelpha used her phone to light a path ahead of us, her breath fogging the air as she spoke. "She's been waiting in there. I thought it best to let her keep some distance away in case you decided not to talk to her."

"And she's in there by herself?" My shoes squelched in the mud as we walked, sucking at my soles each time I lifted my feet. If I hadn't been clinging to Henry, I would have likely sprawled flat by now.

"Yes," Adelpha said. "All by herself. Like the madwoman in the attic."

"What's that supposed to mean?" I asked, unable to disguise my dislike for Adelpha any longer. She was as slippery as the ground beneath us, and even though I had their assurances, I did not trust her or Fidditch. The only reason I continued to follow her was because I couldn't afford not to. Not anymore.

"It doesn't mean anything," she said, sounding bored, not bothering to compete with the whipping wind. "It's from *Jane Eyre*."

As we neared the warehouse, I was struck by an incredible sense of emptiness in the surroundings. We were trekking through a dark, muddy field, and for all I knew there wasn't another person around for miles.

Sweat pushed through every pore until I was slick inside my clothes. The panic seized me completely, and a series of tremors racked my body, snatching my breath away. Every heartbeat felt like a fist punching into my chest. As I walked, gripping hold of Henry's arm, I felt a terrible, almost ticklish dizziness overtake my senses until my toes curled against the innersoles.

This has to be a mistake. There is no way they have found her. It won't be her. Oh, God, but what if it really is her and she's fooled them the same way she fooled me? This is what you've thought about for all these years, isn't it? You always knew she was still out there, and you always knew this day would come. Either you would find her, or she would find you, but it was inevitable, wasn't it? There is no getting around it. You were always going to see here again...

The toe of my boot clipped a rock and I shunted forward. Fidditch grabbed my other arm to steady me. "Treacherous terrain, isn't it? Don't worry, nearly there now."

My stomach rolled over. Sick hurtled up my throat. I slammed a fist against my mouth and swallowed it down.

"We're all with you, Luanne," Henry said. "We're not going to let anything happen to you."

The warehouse brooded in the darkness, sitting like the only headstone in a cemetery. It conjured to mind a rush of cliché haunted houses, but with a hard undercurrent of real horror; this was a brick-and-mortar building not ten yards in front of me, and it was housing my worst nightmare.

Adelpha pushed open the clunky metal door, which gave an eerie scream at the hinges. "Just through here," she said, waving us in.

We walked directly into another corridor, but it felt as though I'd just entered a mouth and was now being shuttled down a throat.

I was being eaten by a monster.

The peeling walls were perspiring condensation, and the atmospheric, charity-shop smell of old fabric filled the moist air. My muddy shoes slid against the concrete floor as I was marched toward my meeting with fate.

"It's just through here," Adelpha said again, standing in front of a red door at the end of the corridor. "Are you ready?"

Squeezing Henry's hand, I said, "No. But I have to do it."

"That's right," Adelpha said. "I think you do. Well, come on up."

Fidditch stepped to the side to allow me passage. Henry escorted me up to the door. This was beginning to feel ceremonial, as though I were being led to the electric chair.

"Whenever you're ready," Adelpha said. "Open it. She's inside."

My hand touched the cold, slick handle. Looking down at my mud-encased shoes, I saw no light spilling out from beneath the door. Was Mia sitting in the dark? This thought prickled my neck, and a feather lightly tickled the length of my spine. I twisted the handle, opening the door to a wall of darkness. Adelpha placed a hand on my back and persuaded me inside before turning the light on.

"No, wait–" I started to say before Adelpha cut me off.

"Too late for that now, Ruby. Much too late."

CHAPTER 37

I felt as though I'd been standing on a fractured pane of ice that had suddenly broken, submerging me into the freezing water beneath. The lights hummed above as they flickered on, illuminating the room in sections. It was a small, cluttered hall with cloudy mirrors lining the back wall. Bundles of clothes, chairs, and props lay strewn about; the detritus left behind from a rehearsal years or maybe even decades ago.

"Where is she?" I asked, as my eyes adjusted to the light.

Nobody moved or said a word. We all just stood there, deathly still, the tension crackling between us. Pivoting around, I looked back at Henry. "What's happening?" I asked, but he did not answer. Adelpha and Fidditch turned to stone, offering no assistance.

Something is wrong here, my mind screamed at me as all my internal panic sensors began flashing and bleating. *Something is seriously wrong.*

Mia had killed George McDermott, my real dad. I held onto these facts like a dog with a bone, hoping to forge some semblance of courage. Eventually, I swallowed the fear, and said, "What is this? What's going on?" I spun on the spot, hoping to receive an answer, but my questions were met with cold, hard silence.

"Will someone just say something," I snapped, my voice raspy in this antiquated rehearsal room.

Adelpha closed and locked the door we had just come through, sealing us all in.

"Henry? I spun toward him and instinctively reached out for reassurance.

He sucked in his lower lip and looked away from me.

"He… Henry…"

"Are you ready to confess your sins, Ruby?" Adelpha said, and if there had been any lilt to her voice before, it was now replaced with poison. She removed her glasses and threw them aside, where they skidded and clattered across the floor.

"What are you doing?" I asked, backing up, almost tumbling over a small mound of clothes. "Where's Mia? I thought you said Mia was here."

"You just don't give up, do you? My God, I've never met a more stubborn human being in my entire life. I thought you'd start to crack when I mentioned that Mia wanted to meet you. I mean, any other sane person would have given the game up right there and then, but not you. You've really held tight the whole time, haven't you? You are going to try and bluff this to the very end."

"Let me out!" I screamed, scrambling for the door, frantically twisting the handle.

"No!" Adelpha returned fire, sounding furious, animalistic. "Not until you confess *your* sins, Ruby."

"Henry." I lunged to hug him, but he became limp in my arms, recoiling from my touch. "Henry what are you doing? What's going on?"

"I can't," he said, holding his hands up and scampering away. "Luanne, oh, God. I don't know. I'm sorry."

"Henry, please," I begged, my voice taking on a terrible, helpless timbre.

"Ah, that's your first mistake," Adelpha said. "Peter, are you getting this? The lighting's okay?"

From behind a camera that had been set up on the opposite side of the room, Fidditch said, "Yes. Audio and visual all good."

"Splendid. Then we might as well get on with the grand reveals," she said.

This Adelpha woman was insane; I could see it in her face now, which had become so much sterner and malicious without the glasses, her eyes seeming beady and too close together. But I was locked in, at their mercy. My body blazed with heat, a manic bongo percussion starting in my temples.

I desperately searched the maze of mess around the floor for a weapon, something I could use to fend them off should the need arise. The chair was my only option. I picked it up, inhaling a puff of dust, and held it in front of me like a lion tamer, barely able to handle the weight of it.

"Don't any of you come near me. You're all mad. Get that door open now. I want to leave, right this instant!"

"Not a chance," Adelpha said. "Not until you confess your sins, Ruby. That's what this is really all about."

"Confess what? I've told you everything that happened. What *is* this?"

"You've told us the same pack of fucking lies you've been spinning for almost thirty years! The same fucking stupid Mia Swehl routine! Not once have you taken any responsibility for what you did. And you did it alone! Just admit it! I want to hear you admit it!"

"No." I shook my head, and despite the cold, I felt sweat fly from the tips of my hair. "Henry, I don't know why you've done this, but–"

"Oh, God, will you put her out of her misery, Henry?" Adelpha spat.

My heart stopped for a few beats and turned to stone in my chest.

"Wh..."

"*Wh-what? What's going on*?" Adelpha mocked, making a pantomime of pretending to be confused and afraid. "Henry doesn't believe you either. How do you think we found you in the first place, Ruby?" Over her shoulder, she shouted, "Pete, is she in frame? Focus on?"

"Clear as a whistle," he replied, squinting behind the camera.

She clapped her hands enthusiastically; the sound was jarring and intrusive against the tension of the room. "Thank you again for making all this possible, Henry." She was spitting as she spoke and began to giggle at the horror dawning in my face.

"That can't be true," I said, feebly. I closed my eyes, blocking everything out, taking the time to breathe as my heart began pumping double time and the blood rushed through my body. Calmly, and very quietly, I said, "This is a game you're playing. I don't understand it, but I would like it to stop. Henry, if you think this is some way of helping me cope with the past then–"

"He doesn't believe you!" Adelpha repeated belligerently, before bursting into a gale of uncontrollable laughter. "He's known who you are since the day he met you. Is it starting to make sense yet, *Ruby*?"

Slowly opening my eyes, I searched Henry's face for confirmation. This man who I'd been sharing a bed with, who I'd fallen in love with, now seemed completely foreign to me. That meek, wouldn't-hurt-a-fly posture began to dissolve, almost as though he were unzipping out of his Henry suit to reveal the real person inside.

"I'm sorry, Luanne," he said, and now even his voice sounded different; there was more bass in it, more authority. "I didn't think... I didn't mean for this to..." When Adelpha's hideous cackling interrupted him, he snapped. "Will you at least let me explain to her?"

"Explain away," Adelpha said, the contempt dripping from her words like venom from the fangs of a cobra. "Go on. Why don't you tell this... this *butcher* how you've played her like a fucking fiddle. Bravo, Henry." She clapped and cackled.

"You've lied to me this whole time?" I bit down on my tongue, fighting the tears, bottling the scream.

"No, of course not." His cheeks were livid with colour. "Yes, I've always known who you are, but that didn't matter to me. I fell in love with Luanne Anderson, not Ruby Wilcox."

"Then, what is this?" I shrieked, my breath misting the air. I heard Adelpha choke back a giggle.

Henry frowned, fumbling for an explanation. "Gav, at work. He's into all these true crime podcasts, documentaries. He sits there in the staff room reading the books on his Kindle. One day, we're at a pub and he tells me there's rumours they're doing a Netflix show about Vincent Street, and so I thought... well, it's not like we couldn't use the money, Luanne. And it wasn't just about the money, either. It was about closure. I knew McDermott's–"

"Ah, not yet," Adelpha wagged a finger. "Don't give her that part yet."

"*Bastard,*" I growled. "You fucking lying bastard."

"I'm not a liar," he said. "Not intentionally, anyway. Believe it or not, Luanne, I do love you, and I do want to help you. I thought this would help. If there was no Netflix show, I wouldn't have ever mentioned it. But there is. And we have to deal with it. I thought this would help. You even said it yourself. This affects me, too."

"I can't believe you would do this to me. I can't believe you would trick me like this." I dragged my hand roughly down my face, wiping the tears.

"You're not the only one who has secrets, Luanne," Henry said, straightening, wringing his hands together, chewing madly on his lips. Then, with a shrug that erased our entire life together, he said, "I've got debts. I've had some trouble in the past, but–"

"Oh, this is boring me to tears now," Adelpha said. "Henry here made an enquiry about what it might be worth to set up an interview with you. And of course, we had a much better counter proposal. Why not make a documentary? Why not get you to confess on camera? And of course, I can pay you both very well, especially Henry here, if he just goes along with our… method of filming, shall we say." Adelpha's eyes became large and frighteningly intense. She stabbed a finger through the air at me, and I clutched tighter to the chair. "You are not the victim here. George McDermott is." She exhaled, and her breath came out in a shaky crescendo. "*I* am the victim."

"Get back," I jabbed the chair through the air but could feel the strength in my arms waning.

"I will not," she bellowed defiantly, her coarse voice booming. "I will *not* get back. You are going to confess your sins on camera now. You are going to confess that you killed

George McDermott by yourself. Confess that there was no imaginary Mia Swehl, that you made her up!"

"I DIDN'T!" The words tore from my mouth in a violent surge, and I felt something pop in my head, like a lightbulb blowing out.

"You did! You broke into my dad's house and killed him. You did it alone and you are going to take responsibility for it right now!"

"Dad?" I said, but it sounded distant in my ears. The room began to shudder as though we were in the epicentre of an earthquake. The darkness was closing in.

"Dad, that's right. You like to play your stupid little Christmas cracker name jokes, don't you. Mia Swehl, Me-as-well, like you're some kind of criminal mastermind, like nobody would be able to figure it out. To think that I'm related to such a… an idiot, is just incredible." Spit was flying from her mouth as she spoke, saliva dripping from her lips.

More lightbulbs popping in my head, my vision narrowing through a tunnel of darkness. The chair slipped from my hands and clanked to the floor.

"L-le-let me o-ou-out," I stammered, wading through the room as laughter tumbled down around me.

"I thought you might appreciate a good name gag as well, Ruby, seeing as you're so fond of chopping and changing your own name," she said, but I was moving away from the muted sound of her voice, stumbling blindly. My legs abandoned me, and I planked to the floor, barely getting my hands up in time to soften the blow. My ears rang and I tasted blood in my mouth.

"My real name is Lauren McDermott," she said. I tried to roll onto my back but felt as though I were pinned to the ground beneath an enormous weight. "Do you know what Adelpha means, Ruby?"

"Please... leave me alone..." I think I said these words. At least, that was what I wanted to say. Whether my mouth managed them or not, I couldn't be sure.

"Adelpha means *beloved sister*."

CHAPTER 38

It was Henry lifting me from the floor. Even in my compromised state, I still knew his touch, his smell. He sat me down on one of the dusty chairs, and my eyes flickered open as I veered back from the brink of unconsciousness. My head lolled on my neck, and I felt as though I might slide right off the seat and collapse in a heap on the floor again.

"Ah," Adelpha said, strutting in front of me while Henry held my shoulders. His thumb delicately stroked the back of my neck. "The old fainting routine. That's your get-out-of-jail card, isn't it, *beloved* sister? Well, it's not going to work today, unfortunately. No fake fainting anymore."

"Henry, help me," I whispered weakly.

"Help you what?" Adelpha asked. "Nobody's doing anything to you. We're making a documentary."

"... Locked me in," I managed.

"I just want to talk. I haven't hurt you. Nobody has laid a finger on you, have they? Not yet, anyway."

"Henry..." I tried again.

"She really just wants to talk, Luanne," he said, his clammy hands cupping my shoulders now. "Just let her say her piece and it will all be over soon."

My head tipped back, and I released a desperate groan. "Oh God, Henry, why? Why did you have to do this to me?"

"I'm trying to help you, Luanne. I know it doesn't feel like it, but I am. And in a way, so are they. If you keep running, then they'll keep chasing. Don't you see it? They're going to keep chasing you until you stop running, Ruby. You had to stop running sooner or later. Please believe me, Ruby. I love you. I do."

"Yeah, he loves you," Adelpha chimed indifferently. "But we're also paying him. And we're paying you, too. So, let's just get on with it."

"*Please*," I said, my tongue rough as sandpaper, the rims of my lips stinging from the cold. There was more I should have said, more I needed to say, but my brain wasn't quite back online yet. My thoughts were still buffering.

"Did my dad plead when you beat his head in?" Adelpha asked. "I'll bet he probably did." She looked over her shoulder at Fidditch and said, "Peter, bring that camera over here."

"What are you going to do to me?"

Fidditch hurried over like the dutiful dog he was and had the camera aimed directly in my face.

"I'm going to let you go," Adelpha said, with an expression of bemusement as though I'd just asked the stupidest question in the world. "I'm not going to kill you, if that's what you think this is. I'm not a murderer like you, Ruby. This isn't a snuff film. It's a documentary, remember?"

"Kidnap," I croaked. "You've kidnapped me."

"Yeah? Good one. And good luck trying to convince the police that *I* kidnapped *you*. Don't exactly have a stellar reputation for telling the truth with the police, do you?

"All you have to do to get out of here, is confess, on camera, that you were the one who killed my dad. You and you alone. No imaginary friends. No Mia Swehls. You, Ruby

Wilcox. Confess your sins on camera, truthfully, and I will open that door up right now. You can walk out of here the way you walked in, which is more than you deserve. You, Ruby, of sound mind, decided to kill my dad. I just want you to acknowledge it. Take some fucking responsibility for once in your damn life."

"You think I'm crazy..." I said, but before I could finish my sentence, Adelpha slammed in.

"I don't think you're crazy at all. I don't care how many psychologists gave their opinion about you. You're not even a convincing liar. You're nothing more than a narcissist. You made Mia up thinking it would get you off the hook. That's how fucking stupid you are. And everyone bangs on about how clever and calculating you're supposed to be, but you come up with the dumbest fucking defence in the history of dumb defences."

I felt a small fire kindling inside me. "Then what does that make you? You did all this, set this whole thing up to–"

"For the truth, you fucking BUTCHER! I did this for the truth, because I wanted to hear the whole thing, from your mouth – not read it on Wikipedia, or transcripts cobbled together from your court case where it was all fabricated around your little mythical inventions. I don't want the fairy-tale-reimagined version they show on TV. I wanted it from you. And I wanted to film it for my family, who have gone all this time without answers, who have been left with a gaping hole in their lives because of you. So now, right now on this camera, you are going to confess. The truth. That's all this has ever been about." When she finished speaking, her lips were trembling, and her breathing was laboured, as though she'd just stepped off a high-speed treadmill. She flexed and unflexed her fingers, and perhaps it was the pressure of the situation, some trick of the light, but it appeared as though the blood vessels had burst in her eyes, turning the whites red. "You are so locked into this lie that maybe you've actually convinced yourself of it," Adelpha said, her tone losing all its former ferocity. "My God, maybe that's it." Her shoulders slumped, hair falling across her face. "I'm going to get it out of you, Ruby. One way or the other."

"Just do it, Luanne," Henry said behind me, almost pleading, his grip tightening on my shoulders. "Put this whole thing to bed now. You've done the time for it. You don't have a reason to lie any more. Just admit it. You made her up. I've lived with you for two years and I know you're not crazy. You're the sweetest, most thoughtful–"

"*Confess!*" Adelpha boomed, throwing her hands up in the air like a preacher in the pulpit. "Confess that there is no Mia Swehl. Confess to what you did – *alone*. Confess that you went into my dad's house that day knowing exactly what you planned to do. Just tell the truth and that's it."

"Confess, Luanne," Henry chimed. "Please."

"All you have to do is admit what you did, Ruby," Fidditch spoke this time, peeking out from behind the camera. "Then we can all go home and get on with our lives."

Confess. Confess your sins. It rang through the rehearsal room in a monotonous chant, coming from everywhere. Henry's fingers digging into my shoulders to keep me from squirming away. Adelpha's mad unblinking eyes boring into me. Fidditch, bent behind the camera. I wondered what his part in all this was. A decoy? Just another hired hand? Or was he some other relative I didn't know about.

"Confess!" Adelpha slapped me across the face so hard that it twisted my head to the side, stretching the tendons in my neck.

"You can't do it like that," Henry objected. "You can't *hit* her."

Off to the right, on the floor beneath a rickety foldout table, was a toolbox. Next to it was a hammer, the head rusted red from the damp, the handle coated in dust.

"You shut up," Adelpha snarled at him, stabbing a warning finger in his direction. "You're paid to do a job, and that doesn't include telling me how to handle my business, so you just shut it. Don't forget about your bonus clause. If you want me to release the rest of your funds, then you'll just shut your fucking mouth. How you could go to bed every night with this butcher is beyond me. You're nearly as disgusting to me as she is."

"But you can't hit her," Henry insisted weakly. "I won't let you hit her. That's not… That defeats the whole point of what you're trying to do, doesn't it? If you torture her, she'll confess to anything, whether it's the truth or not."

"Torture? You dare use that word with me? You think this is torture? Have you ever seen the crime scene photos, Henry? My dad's house looked like a fucking abattoir when she was finished with it." Adelpha grabbed two handfuls of my short hair and pulled until my scalp seared with pain. "Ruby, you are going to admit it. Those words are going to come from your mouth because I can make things worse for you, do you get it? I can make things so much worse that you will think these last twenty-five years have been a trip to the Maldives." She slapped me again, hitting me in the side of the head.

The hammer, Ruby.

"No fainting. No more bullshit to buy time. You will admit it. Tell me what I already know. There is no Mia Swehl. There never was. It was you alone. You did it. You broke in. You killed my dad. And you made Mia Swehl up to try and get off." Adelpha released my hair, and my head bowed under its own weight. "All I want is for you to own up to what you did. Why is that so fucking hard for you after all these years? Everyone in this room knows the truth. You just have to say it."

Silence, sliced apart by my jagged, breathless weeping.

Get the hammer, Ruby.

"Go on, Luanne," Henry whispered. "You can do it. Come on. Please. It doesn't change anything between us. You just need to do it so we can all move past it."

"Nobody is going anywhere until those words come out of your mouth," Adelpha said. "Confess!"

Her hand cuffed me in the side of the head, making my teeth click together. Everything went black in my vision, and then the room drifted back into focus.

"Even Richard Wilcox knows you're a compulsive liar," she was saying. "He knows you've been fucked in the head long before your mum had the crash. Here." She pulled her phone out and showed me a news article featuring the picture of a dishevelled man walking down the street. He was painfully thin with a candlewax complexion, swamped in tatty clothes. "Here's what you've done to him."

When I tried to turn away, she grabbed me by the cheeks and wrenched my head until I was looking at the screen.

The headline on the article read *INFAMOUS MURDERER RUBY WILCOX'S STEP-FATHER CLOSE TO DEATH.*

"You did this to him," she screamed. "This poor bastard needs a liver transplant because of you. He can't go on living knowing he helped raise a fucking demon. Confess it, Ruby."

Another slap. A prolonged moment of darkness.

Henry's voice, slurred and distant now: "You didn't say anything about hitting her. This is assault! We'll all get arrested."

Despite his words, when I tried to stand, he continued to restrain me.

"You're going nowhere," Adelpha screeched. "Just say it. You made Mia up. You went to my dad's house because you blamed him for Richard abandoning you. It's as simple as that. Just say the words."

"No." the growl came out deep and feral, spittle flying from the gaps in my tightly clamped teeth. Panting, white fireworks exploding before my eyes, I stared at Adelpha, her image shivering in my vision.

"Look at what you did." Adelpha grabbed my hair, forcing me to face her phone again. She was showing me the games room in George McDermott's house, the dry, black blood redecorating the carpet, walls, and sofa. "You fucking animal. You devil. They should never have let you out. You–"

All you have to do is get that hammer, Ruby.

The next time Adelpha hit me, I tasted blood; must've bitten through my tongue.

My mind was roaring, and my ears were ringing. She was showing me something else now, more photos of the house, close-ups of black blood. Then a family picture of Richard, my mum, and me when I was four or five, at a restaurant for my birthday. A balloon. Smiles and cake.

I could see Adelpha's mouth moving but couldn't hear anything now.

Her fist crunched against my nose. Pain shooting up into my eyes. My head crackling. Still no sound. Henry let go of my shoulders and waddled in front of Adelpha trying to form a clumsy protest against her. Fidditch's head floated up from the camera, his face slack with concern.

My eyes began fluttering. The stress was overriding everything, dulling my senses, shutting all systems down. Muscles loosening. I was slipping off the chair, about to plummet, my vision darkening as they continued to argue in front of me.

In the background, I saw someone else come into the room. They were nothing more than a blurry silhouette, drifting, heading straight for us. Was it the police? Some other character in this twisted play? I didn't know, didn't care.

Maybe I wasn't fainting. Maybe I was dying. And maybe that wouldn't be such a bad thing.

I fell off the chair, my head thudding against the floor. Adelpha's face, darkening with rage, swam into view. She was either laughing or screaming, I couldn't be sure which.

That blurry silhouette came closer, approaching behind Adelpha. It was a woman. Someone I knew.

Then the words, very clear in my ear: "Rest. I'll take care of it."

Black.

CHAPTER 39

"Please don't h-h-hurt..."

The confusion engulfed me. I was on the floor, my skull singing so intensely that the fillings in my teeth ached. The driftwood of my memory pulled away from me. It had been a very long time since I went overboard with the booze and got black out drunk – years ago, in fact. But that's what this felt like: the morning after a horrific vodka binge, unable to piece together coherent moments of the night before.

"I-I-I-I didn't... did-did... didn't mean... Oh, my God..."

Something was in my eyes, gunk in my lashes. I sat up. There was a clunk that didn't immediately register, but then I saw what had made the sound. A hammer on the floor next to me.

My fingers seemed to move of their own accord, wrapping around the handle. It was only as I picked the hammer up that I saw my hands were stained red, and now I could smell the blood, high and metallic. There was hair caught in the claw.

"You have to b-b-believe me, L-L-Luanne..."

My nose caught the scent of another smell, too. A dizzying cocktail of perfume and alcohol. I knew that smell.

It was *her* smell.

Adelpha lay on the floor a few feet away from me. What was left of her face was unrecognisable. Light reflected in the red puddle pooling from her head. One of her feet jerked and twitched.

The camera had been knocked over and lay on its side. There had been someone behind that camera, hadn't there? Yes, that's right. Fidditch. Where was he now?

He was over by the entrance, slumped on the floor. His eyes stared lifelessly through the crimson streaks. A smeared, bloody handprint on the wall next to him.

"Honest to God, L-Luanne. I didn't th-th-ink they would h-hit you… I would never have let them…"

The room shivered relentlessly. All this blood and viscera should have terrified me, or made me nauseous at the very least. But there was nothing. No tremble of fear, no squirm in the stomach. I felt completely hollow because none of it was real.

I knew that now.

"I'll do anything, Luanne. Anything you want. I'll tell the police that it was me, that I…"

Who was making all that noise? I scanned the room but couldn't locate the source of the sound. Then I caught him, hunkered down behind a column of chairs, babbling into his hands.

"Hi, Henry," I said, feeling very distant, as though someone else were speaking through my mouth.

"H-h-hi," he replied. His crotch was dark, and he was sitting in a puddle of his own urine. His complexion had completely curdled.

"What happened here?" I asked, stepping over Adelpha, my foot almost sliding in her blood. His eyes locked onto the hammer in my fist.

"I was trying to help you, I swear on the Bible. I swear on anything. Please don't h-hurt me."

"I'm not going to hurt you, Henry," I said, now feeling oddly serene. None of this really mattered. "But I've got one of my headaches. I fainted."

"Y-yeah, I saw."

"So, it looks like I'm missing some time." I walked toward him, and he yelled in fright, kicking his legs and scooting further behind the chairs. "Mia was here, wasn't she?"

His face shuffled through expressions before his features slackened, his eyes widening. He licked his lips, opened his mouth to speak, but settled for a nod instead.

"Thought so." I sighed, surveying the carnage. "I always knew she'd be back. Yeah, this looks like her work." The hammer slid from my hand and clanged on the floor. Henry cried out again, his mouth hanging open, his breath ragged and uneven. It was strange. I'd lived with him for two years, spent so much time in his company, but I had never seen that look on his face before. Funny how fear can do that.

I went over to the camera. It had been recording their whole sordid interrogation. This was all the evidence I needed. I wasn't going to take the blame for any of this. They held me against my will. They attacked me. And then Mia came. She was here after all.

"You saw her, then?" I asked over my shoulder, fiddling to free the camera from the tripod. It was heavy and cumbersome. "You believe me now, don't you, Henry? You believe that she's real."

"I… I want to go home," he said in a warbling falsetto.

"Yeah," I said quietly. "I suppose it has been a long night, hasn't it? Go on, then. Hurry along."

He remained rooted for a moment, blinking stupidly, before slowly clambering to his feet, knocking over chairs in the process. He looked past me at Adelpha's body and a fresh wave of terror crested in him. Backing away, almost toppling over more chairs, he skirted the room until he came to the entrance.

Thumbing blood out of my eye, I watched as he walked past Fidditch. A short, thin cry yipped from Henry's lips, and he began to hyperventilate loudly. Henry was at the door, twisting and rattling the handle, but it wouldn't open.

"Locked," I called. "Remember?"

How did Mia get in? Don't know. Don't care.

He pawed at the lock, whimpering and muttering, praying to God. Finally, he unbolted it and pushed the door open. Then he ran without looking back. I had never seen Henry run before. It was ungainly and awkward, and his footsteps slapped and echoed in the corridor. He fell in a heap, scrambled back to his feet, and burst out into the field beyond.

"Goodbye, Henry," I whispered, and stood there for a very long time. Not moving. Just… waiting.

Eventually, I heard the soft tread of footsteps behind me. The fine hairs on my neck sprung up, my cheeks breaking out in gooseflesh. The smell of perfume and alcohol. Footsteps getting closer.

I could feel her *breathing* on my hair.

"Mia?" I said, her name flat in the silence.

She didn't say anything. Just breathed. I could sense her body close to mine.

I hated her. I was terrified of her. But in the end, I said the only thing I could. The truth: "Mia… I've… I've missed you."

A feathery whisper, though I wasn't sure if it was only in my mind: "I've always been with you, Ruby. We're two sides of–"

"The same coin," I finished.

She giggled the way she did back in school when we were shoplifting. She stroked my hair lightly with her fingers. A smile tugged at my lips.

"Mia." I turned, tears sparkling in my eyes.

But she was gone.

EPILOGUE

FROM: Hello@FloydWilkinsonWrites.com
TO: OmarK@PaanboPress.com
SUBJECT: CONFIDENTIAL: R. Wilcox Visit / Official Offer etc

Hey Omar,

I've literally just got back from visiting our friend at Gladstone and wanted to get everything down while it's still fresh (I didn't get to record the conversation while in there as previously agreed, but will get into that). This is going to be a long one (strap in), but I can clarify anything that's unclear when I see you on Thursday. Also, goes without saying, but please do not circulate this email ANYWHERE, not even internally.

A bit of background: I was told by an administrator at the prison that I'd be able to visit with Ruby, providing she agreed – which she did via her solicitor, and I was added to her visitation list. When I got to Gladstone though, I was told that she wouldn't leave her cell. I did explain that she had agreed, and that I had done all my due diligence ahead of time. (For what it's worth, I also explained to the admin guy that I was the one who had written the *GOOD* book about Ruby and the Vincent Street Incident, but it didn't make any difference). I asked if there was anything I could do to get her to come down and talk, and said that I had even brought a selection of pastries for her etc. The admin guy said no, and he couldn't pass the message back to her. BUT (!) he said if I waited until 6, he could have a coffee with me at the Krispy Kreme in town.

The admin guy (let's call him "Nathan") meets me after 6, and he's with a guard from Gladstone (let's call her "Sarah") who just finished her shift. I offered to buy coffee and donuts, but Nathan said if I wanted to know what was happening with Ruby, then I'd need to pay Sarah £300 (an ATM conveniently outside the Krispy Kreme). "Trust me, it's worth the money," Nathan says, and it saves this whole thing being a wasted journey (PS I'm invoicing you for the £300 as a business expense). This is what Sarah told me.

To start off with, Ruby's shaved all her hair and eyebrows off. Nobody's quite sure why. She doesn't leave her cell and hardly talks to anyone. The prisoners in the neighbouring cells have made at least two complaints about Ruby making noise at night though. What kind of noises? (Wait for it) She's held in a place they call 'The Bowery', which is a wing on a sublevel of the prison for some of the more notorious Cat-A prisoners. On that wing, the cells are all single occupancy, with air vents, and the other prisoners are saying that Ruby sits up all night talking as though she has a cell mate (which of course she doesn't). But get this – she is talking in two different voices (!!!), like having a conversation… Now it should be stressed that this is hearsay and sounds a bit too *Norman Bates* to be true, but given who we are talking about it's worth looking into further.

There are a few other bits she mentioned (she keeps complaining about fleas in the cells, thinking the food is poisoned etc.), and that she requested a visit to the Healthcare Unit to speak with one of the mental health specialists. This was apparently very unlike her. This next part is EXTREMELY confidential (even though I'm almost certain it's largely embellished). Allegedly, Ruby made a complaint about people entering her cell at night and hiding under her bed. She is convinced that someone – not a guard – has access to her cell. Now, this Sarah woman tells me that Ruby keeps pulling this routine, saying that strange people are in the canteen watching her, and she is implying that they're ghosts. What she is trying to do (according to Sarah) is get transferred to a mental hospital like Broadmoor or somewhere like that. Again, could all be bullshit, but if there's any truth in that, it's good intel to have.

Now the kicker. Hope you're still strapped in. Nathan says that for £500 he can show me the full hammer attack footage from the rehearsal room murders on his phone (affectionately titled *One Girl, One Hammer*). This footage, as far as I know, hasn't even been distributed to the press although I'm sure that charging people to watch it is their whole racket.

Well, I watched it, and it is beyond disturbing (I'm too paranoid to invoice you for this – you're welcome). Obviously not the most ethical thing I've ever done, but at least I now understand why the judge gave her a whole life tariff. Omar, she *changes*. I wish I was exaggerating. It's like watching a wild animal attack. The noises she was making are *insane*. It is extremely hard to watch.

Sarah tells me that she's sure she can convince Ruby to speak to me for the book, but it's going to take some time. I'll start with more written correspondence with Ruby, and send her some cakes, fizzy drinks things like that. But we'll have to pay Sarah (yes, WE) for her efforts, as she's going to work on getting Ruby on our side. I don't mind handling that but let's discuss the particulars on Thursday. Omar, we have to move fast on this though, because Simon Ward has also been in contact with Gladstone Prison wanting to interview Ruby for *his* fucking book (told you he would), though, given his stance on her overall, I don't think he has a leg to stand on. I am also sure that Nathan and Sarah pulled the same routine with Ward, and that he has already seen the *One Girl, One Hammer* video.

One last thing to mention. Sarah claims she has seen Ruby turn into Mia. ALLEGEDLY, one of the other guards (though I'm sure it was Sarah herself), began showing Ruby footage of Richard Wilcox and the Vincent Street crime scene photos, and this triggered Ruby to adopt the Mia persona. They allegedly have a video of her turning into Mia but want 1k for a viewing. Sarah says, and I quote: "It's like talking to a completely different person."

That is the hook for this next book: A conversation with Mia Swehl. So, we were wrong with the first book – we gave Ruby the benefit of the doubt. This time, we get Mia's side of the story. Then it's a *Sunday Times* Bestseller, promotional tour, film rights etc., etc.

Anyway, I'm going to try and sleep now but I'm almost positive I'm going to have nightmares.

Maybe in the morning I'll go to church and confess my sins.

ACKNOWLEDGEMENTS

Huge thank you to the entire Datura Team for all the hard work that went into this book.

A massive thank you to my agent, Laura Williams, for all the encouragement, support and advice.